MW00469916

DARK DAYS
&
MUCH DARKER DAYS

'THE DETECTIVE STORY CLUB is a clearing house for the best detective and mystery stories chosen for you by a select committee of experts. Only the most ingenious crime stories will be published under the THE DETECTIVE STORY CLUB imprint. A special distinguishing stamp appears on the wrapper and title page of every THE DETECTIVE STORY CLUB book—the Man with the Gun. Always look for the Man with the Gun when buying a Crime book.'

Wm. Collins Sons & Co. Ltd., 1929

Now the Man with the Gun is back in this series of COLLINS CRIME CLUB reprints, and with him the chance to experience the classic books that influenced the Golden Age of crime fiction.

THE
DETECTIVE STORY
CLUB

LIST OF TITLES

THE MAYFAIR MYSTERY • FRANK RICHARDSON

THE PERFECT CRIME • ISRAEL ZANGWILL

CALLED BACK • HUGH CONWAY

THE MYSTERY OF THE SKELETON KEY • BERNARD CAPES

THE GRELL MYSTERY • FRANK FROËST

DR JEKYLL AND MR HYDE • R. L. STEVENSON

THE RASP • PHILIP MACDONALD

THE HOUSE OPPOSITE • J. JEFFERSON FARJEON

THE PONSON CASE • FREEMAN WILLS CROFTS

THE TERROR • EDGAR WALLACE

THE MYSTERY AT STOWE • VERNON LODER

THE BLACKMAILERS • ÉMILE GABORIAU

THE MURDER OF ROGER ACKROYD • AGATHA CHRISTIE

THE CRIME CLUB • FRANK FROËST & GEORGE DILNOT

THE NOOSE • PHILIP MACDONALD

THE LEAVENWORTH CASE • ANNA K. GREEN

THE CASK • FREEMAN WILLS CROFTS

THE BIG FOUR • AGATHA CHRISTIE

FURTHER TITLES IN PREPARATION

DARK DAYS

A STORY OF CRIME BY
HUGH CONWAY

&

**MUCH DARKER DAYS
BY ANDREW LANG**

WITH AN INTRODUCTION BY
DAVID BRAWN

COLLINS
CRIME
CLUB

COLLINS CRIME CLUB

An imprint of HarperCollins*Publishers*

1 London Bridge Street

London SE1 9GF

www.harpercollins.co.uk

This edition 2016

Dark Days first published in J. W. Arrowsmith's Christmas Annual 1884
Published by The Detective Story Club Ltd
for Wm Collins Sons & Co. Ltd 1930
Much Darker Days first published by Longmans, Green & Co. 1884

Introduction © David Brawn 2016

A catalogue record for this book is available from the British Library

ISBN 978-0-00813-774-8

Typeset in Bulmer MT Std by
Palimpsest Book Production Ltd, Falkirk, Stirlingshire

Printed and bound in Great Britain by Clays Ltd, St Ives plc

INTRODUCTION

'HUGH CONWAY has that first essential of the popular novelist—strong narrative power. His story is the first consideration always. Not that he does not possess other attributes to success: graphic description, which carries with it—not necessarily, but certainly in the case of Hugh Conway—atmosphere. He can, too, draw a most convincing character, as the present book will show. We look to *Dark Days* for a story that will hold our mature minds just as the fireside tales of our grandfathers held us as children—and we get it!'

So began the Editor's introduction to Collins' Detective Story Club edition of *Dark Days*, republished in May 1930 almost 50 years after the story had been devoured by a reading public in love with the work of Hugh Conway. With respect to the Editor, however, 'narrative power', 'graphic description' and 'atmosphere' might have been key for the popular novelist, but they were not by 1930 the most essential ingredients of a successful detective novel. This was the era in which readers craved cerebral ingenuity over dramatic characterisation and saw the emergence of what has since been described (perhaps unfairly) as the 'humdrum' school of crime writers. *Dark Days* was a late Victorian detective story, a novelette with its roots in early Gothic tales and the sensation novels of the 1860s, and was published in a format that owed its existence to the early work of Charles Dickens: the Christmas Annual.

Cheap reading matter had been around for decades in the form of 'chap books', unbound leaflets sold by street vendors, usually only eight pages in length, which were so short they led to stories being serialised over multiple issues. By the 1840s, with more widespread literacy and the invention of rotary printing presses which allowed for fast production, the mass distribution of these stories among the working classes took off with the 'penny bloods', weekly publications churned out by versatile writers catering for every taste. Illustrated with a black-and-white engraving on the first page, these serialised adventures rapidly turned from swashbuckling tales of pirates and highwaymen to more outlandish and thrilling themes—and increasingly towards stories of crime and murder. One of the most notorious and most popular run of 'bloods' narrated the exploits of the murderous Sweeney Todd, the demon barber of Fleet Street, whose victims ended up in meat-pies: *The String of Pearls* began publication in 1846 and ran for 18 weeks, inspiring many similar sensationalised crime stories that unashamedly blurred the boundaries of true crime and heady fiction, some of which ran for months on end.

One of the finer Victorian traditions that grew out of this appetite for serial fiction was the Annual, in which publishers of serials and periodicals would release special Christmas editions outside their normal run, enticing new readers with one-off short stories, cartoons and festive humour. Seasonal ghost stories were especially popular, as were mysteries, and standalone short stories began to flourish as a result. Major book publishers such as Routledge's also issued special Christmas Annuals, with more sophisticated novella-length content, although price was critical. The real foundation of the Annual as a British publishing phenomenon can be traced back to Charles Dickens' *A Christmas Carol*, surely the most enduring Christmas story of modern times.

Dickens began writing his 'little carol' in October 1843, finishing it by the end of November, in time to be published for Christmas with hand-coloured illustrations by John Leech. Financing the printing of 10,000 copies himself after a disagreement with his publishers, the book was nevertheless far from the success its author had hoped for. 'The first 6,000 copies show a profit of £230 and the last four will yield as much more. I had set my heart and soul on a thousand clear,' Dickens wrote. The price of five shillings, even for a lavishly bound book as this was, was too expensive for most pockets, but the story grew in popularity and did not deter him from writing more Christmas novellas: *The Chimes*, *The Cricket on the Hearth*, *The Battle of Life* and *The Haunted Man and the Ghost's Bargain* followed over the next five years, and as the prices were dropped from shillings to just pence, sales grew from ten thousand to hundreds of thousands.

With the Christmas Annual having established itself as a regular fixture of the publishing calendar, an unlikely benefactor was 33-year-old Bristol auctioneer Frederick John Fargus. Under the pseudonym 'Hugh Conway', his first published story, 'The Daughter of the Stars', appeared in *Thirteen at Dinner and What Came of It*, the first Christmas Annual from local publisher J.W. Arrowsmith in 1881. A rapid succession of songs, poems and stories by Conway followed in various publications over the next two years, culminating in the short novel *Called Back*, which formed the basis of Arrowsmith's third Christmas Annual in 1883. Having sold an unremarkable 3,000 copies by Christmas—barely half its initial print run—no one can have predicted that by 1887 it would have gone on to sell a staggering 350,000 copies and been translated into all the major European languages. As Graham Law observes in his excellent article 'Poor Fargus' for *The Wilkie Collins Journal* in 2000, this sudden turn of events seems to have been precipitated by an enthusiastic review on 3 January 1884 in Henry Labouchère's widely-read society weekly, *Truth*:

'Who Arrowsmith is and who Hugh Conway is I do not know, nor had I ever heard of the Christmas Annual of the former, or of the latter as a writer of fiction; but, a week or two ago, a friend of mine said to me, "Buy

Arrowsmith's Christmas Annual, if you want to read one
of the best stories that have appeared for many a year." A
few days ago, I happened to be at the Waterloo Station
waiting for a train. I remembered the advice, and asked
the clerk at the bookstall for the Annual. He handed it to
me, and remarked, "They say the story is very good,
but this is only the third copy I have sold." It was so foggy
that I could not read it in the train as I had intended, so
I put the book into my pocket. About 2 that night, it
occurred to me that it was nearing the hour when decent,
quiet people go to bed. I saw the Annual staring me in
the face, and took it up. Well, not until 4.30 did I get to
bed. By that time I had finished the story. Had I not, I
should have gone on reading. I agree with my friend—nay,
I go farther than him, and say that Wilkie Collins never
penned a more enthralling story.'

Spurred on by his new-found fame, Hugh Conway wrote a
vast amount of new fiction in 1884, including a highly regarded
full-length novel, *A Family Affair*. But it was his two subsequent
Annuals for Arrowsmith that cemented his reputation as a
bestseller: *Dark Days* in 1884 and *Slings and Arrows*, published
posthumously in 1885. For, as detailed in Martin Edwards'
informative introduction to *Called Back*, also in this series, the
author died in Monte Carlo on 15 May 1885, aged only 37. He
had been writing for only four years.

Dark Days was particularly successful: it was widely translated and like *Called Back* there was a stage play to help
increase its longevity. It also attracted an unlikely champion.
Within weeks of its appearance, a parody entitled *Much
Darker Days* by the noted Scottish author, literary critic and
folklorist Andrew Lang was published by Longmans, Green
& Co. under the pseudonym 'A. Huge Longway'. Lang was
active as a journalist and was the literary editor of *Longman's
Magazine*, and clearly saw an opportunity to capitalise on

Conway's success by publishing his biting satire. Interestingly, a second edition published the following April contained what was tantamount to an apology, seemingly for causing offence:

'Parody is a parasitical, but should not be a poisonous, plant. The Author of this unassuming jape has learned, with surprise and regret, that some sentences which it contains are thought even more vexatious than frivolous. To frivol, not to vex, was his aim, and he has corrected this edition accordingly.'

The revision contained numerous minor changes: names were altered to create greater distance from the original (Basil became Babil, Sphynx was changed to Labbywrinth, and Roding became Noding), and a few sentences were removed and in one instance changed altogether (from 'a public which devoured *Scrawled Black* will stand almost anything' to the more facetious 'And *this* Christmas, I fancy, no narrative is likely to be found more beguiling').

The version in this new volume is based on the unexpurgated first printing, although occasional extra lines added in the revised edition have been inserted to give the fullest version of the story and of Lang's wit. So as not to spoil the drama of *Dark Days*, and to fully appreciate the satire of *Much Darker Days*, it is recommended that the reader resists the temptation to read the parody first!

With Hugh Conway having been compared favourably to the author of *The Woman in White* (1860) and *The Moonstone* (1868), books that had defined the emerging British detective novel, it was not without irony that Wilkie Collins himself was approached by J.W. Arrowsmith to fill Conway's shoes and write their 1886 Christmas Annual. This he did with *The Guilty River*, although when it failed to sell as well as any of Conway's

Annuals, Collins turned down the offer to write any more and passed the baton to Walter Besant.

The following year, however, it was Beeton's Christmas Annual that was to be the game-changer of the season, introducing a character who would become as famous as Ebenezer Scrooge from that Dickens tale 44 years earlier. With two shorter stories by R. André and C.J. Hamilton, Beeton's 1887 Annual contained *A Study in Scarlet* by Arthur Conan Doyle—the debut of Sherlock Holmes. The sensational and dramatic 'shilling shockers' epitomised by Hugh Conway were about to be superseded by a new kind of detective fiction.

DAVID BRAWN
May 2016

DARK DAYS

BY
HUGH CONWAY
[FREDERICK JOHN FARGUS]

TO MY FRIEND
J. COMYNS CARR

CONTENTS

I	A PRAYER AND A VOW	1
II	A VILLAIN'S BLOW	12
III	'THE WAGES OF SIN'	27
IV	AT ALL COST, SLEEP!	38
V	A WHITE TOMB	47
VI	THE SECRET KEPT	56
VII	THE MELTING OF THE SNOW	65
VIII	FLIGHT	76
IX	SAFE—AND LOVED!	84
X	THE SWORD FALLS	93
XI	SPECIAL PLEADING	103
XII	TEMPTED TO DISHONOUR	111
XIII	THE LAST HOPE	119
XIV	THE CRIMINAL COURT	128
XV	THE BLACK CAP	137
XVI	'WHERE ARE THE SNOWS THAT FELL LAST YEAR?'	146
XVII	CLEAR SKIES	155

EDITOR'S PREFACE

HUGH CONWAY has that first essential of the popular novelist—strong narrative power. His story is the first consideration always. Not that he does not possess other attributes to success: graphic description, which carries with it—not necessarily, but certainly in the case of Hugh Conway—atmosphere. He can, too, draw a most convincing character, as the present book will show. We look to *Dark Days* for a story that will hold our mature minds just as the fireside tales of our grandfathers held us as children—and we get it!

Dark Days is a novel of a love that won through the intricacies and horrors of a most uncanny crime. It is told in the first person by Doctor North, the central figure in the plot, a fact which largely explains the poignancy of the book. The autobiographical form always gives the reader a direct contact with the situations in which the main character finds himself. He therefore goes through *his* experiences and finds himself swayed by the very emotions that move his 'hero'.

Philippa is surely the most beautiful murderess that ever crossed the pages of fiction. Her crime is horrifying, but is it not justified? Was the world not better rid of a man of Sir Mervyn Ferrand's type—an idler, an 'adventurer', in the degraded sense of the word? Perhaps . . . but murder is murder in the eyes of the law. Doctor North was convinced of the moral innocence of his beloved as will the reader be, no doubt, but he has to go through dark days indeed before the whole of the mystery is cleared up.

The novel is arresting on not a few points, but most intriguing of all is the fact that *the criminal* of the novel is the *victim* of the crime!

THE EDITOR
FROM THE ORIGINAL DETECTIVE STORY CLUB EDITION
May 1930

CHAPTER I

A PRAYER AND A VOW

WHEN this story of my life, or of such portions of my life as present any out-of-the-common features, is read, it will be found that I have committed errors of judgment—that I have sinned not only socially, but also against the law of the land. In excuse I can plead but two things—the strength of love; the weakness of human nature.

If these carry no weight with you, throw the book aside. You are too good for me; I am too human for you. We cannot be friends. Read no further.

I need say nothing about my childhood; nothing about my boyhood. Let me hurry on to early manhood; to that time when the wonderful dreams of youth begin to leave one; when the impulse which can drive sober reason aside must be, indeed, a strong one; when one has learnt to count the cost of every rash step; when the transient and fitful flames of the boy have settled down to a steady, glowing fire which will burn until only ashes are left; when the strength, the nerve, the intellect, is or should be at its height; when, in short, one's years number thirty.

Yet, what was I then? A soured, morose, disappointed man; without ambition, without care for the morrow; without a goal or object in life. Breathing, eating, drinking, as by instinct. Rising in the morning, and wishing the day was over; lying down at night, and caring little whether the listless eyes I closed might open again or not.

And why? Ah! To know why you must sit with me as I sit lonely over my glowing fire one winter night. You must read

1

my thoughts; the pictures of my past must rise before you as
they rise before me. My sorrow, my hate, my love must be yours.
You must, indeed, be my very self.

You may begin this retrospect with triumph. You may go
back to the day when, after having passed my examination with
high honours, I, Basil North, was duly entitled to write M.D.
after my name, and to set to work to win fame and fortune by
doing my best towards relieving the sufferings of my fellow-
creatures. You may say as I said then, as I say now, 'A noble
career; a life full of interest and usefulness.'

You may see me full of hope and courage, and ready for any
amount of hard work; settling down in a large provincial town,
resolved to beat out a practice for myself. You may see how,
after the usual initiatory struggles, my footing gradually grew
firmer; how my name became familiar; how, at last, I seemed
to be in a fair way of winning success.

You may see how for a while a dream brightened my life;
how that dream faded, and left gloom in its place. You may see
the woman I loved.

No, I am wrong. Her you cannot see. Only I myself can see
Philippa as I saw her then—as I see her now.

Heavens! How fair she was! How glorious her rich dark
beauty! How different from the pink-white and yellow dolls
whom I have seen exalted as the types of perfection! Warm
Southern blood ran through her veins and tinged her clear
brown cheek with colour. Her mother was an Englishwoman;
but it was Spain that gave her daughter that exquisite grace,
those wondrous dark eyes and long curled lashes, that mass of
soft black hair, that passionate impulsive nature, and, perhaps,
that queen-like carriage and dignity. The English mother may
have given the girl many good gifts, but her beauty came from
the father, whom she had never known; the Andalusian, who
died while she was but a child in arms.

Yet, in spite of her foreign grace, Philippa was English. Her
Spanish origin was to her but a tradition. Her foot had never

touched her father's native land. Its language was strange to her. She was born in England, and her father, the nature of whose occupation I have not been able to ascertain, seems to have spent most of his time in this country.

When did I learn to love her? Ask me rather, when did we first meet? Even then as my eyes fell upon the girl, I knew, as by revelation, that for me life and her love meant one and the same thing. Till that moment there was no woman in the world the sight of whom would have quickened my pulse by a beat. I had read and heard of such love as this. I had laughed at it. There seemed no room for such an engrossing passion in my busy life. Yet all at once I loved as man has never loved before; and as I sit tonight and gaze into the fire I tell myself that the objectless life I am leading is the only one possible for the man who loved but failed to win Philippa.

Our first meeting was brought about in a most prosaic way. Her mother, who suffered from a chronic disease, consulted me professionally. My visits, at first those of a doctor, soon became those of a friend, and I was free to woo the girl to the best of my ability.

Philippa and her mother lived in a small house on the outskirts of the town. They were not rich people, but had enough to keep the pinch of poverty from their lives. The mother was a sweet, quiet, lady-like woman, who bore her sufferings with resignation. Her health was, indeed, wretched. The only thing which seemed likely to benefit her was continual change of air and scene. After attending her for about six months, I was in conscience bound to endorse the opinion of her former medical advisers, and tell her it would be well for her to try another change.

My heart was heavy as I gave this advice. If adopted, it meant that Philippa and I must part.

But why, during those six months, had I not, passionately in love as I was, won the girl's heart? Why did she not leave me as my affianced bride? Why did I let her leave me at all?

The answer is short. She loved me not.

Not that she had ever told me so in words. I had never asked her in words for her love. But she must have known—she must have known! When I was with her, every look, every action of mine must have told her the truth. Women are not fools or blind. A man who, loving as I did, can conceal the true state of his feelings must be more than mortal.

I had not spoken; I dared not speak. Better uncertainty with hope than certainty with despair. The day on which Philippa refused my love would be as the day of death to me.

Besides, what had I to offer her? Although succeeding fairly well for a beginner, at present I could only ask the woman I made my wife to share comparative poverty. And Philippa! Ah! I would have wrapped Philippa in luxury! All that wealth could buy ought to be hers. Had you seen her in the glory of her fresh young beauty, you would have smiled at the presumption of the man who could expect such a being to become the wife of a hard-working and as yet ill-paid doctor. You would have felt that she should have had the world at her feet.

Had I thought that she loved me, I might perhaps have dared to hope she would even then have been happy as my wife. But she did not love me. Moreover, she was ambitious.

She knew—small blame to her—how beautiful she was. Do I wrong her when I say that in those days she looked for the gifts of rank and riches from the man who loved her? She knew that she was a queen among women, and expected a queen's dues.

(Sweetest, are my words cruel? They are the cruellest I have spoken, or shall speak, against you. Forgive them!)

We were friends—great friends. Such friendship is love's bane. It buoys false hopes; it lulls to security; it leads astray; it is a staff which breaks suddenly, and wounds the hand which leans upon it. So little it seems to need to make friendship grow into love; and yet how seldom that little is added!

The love which begins with hate or dislike is often luckier than that which begins with friendship. Lovers cannot be friends.

Philippa and her mother left my neighbourhood. Then went to London for a while. I heard from them occasionally, and once or twice, when in town, called upon them. Time went by. I worked hard at my profession the while, striving, by sheer toil, to drive the dream from my life. Alas! I strove in vain. To love Philippa was to love her for ever!

One morning a letter came from her. I tore it open. The news it contained was grievous. Her mother had died suddenly. Philippa was alone in the world. So far as I knew, she had not a relation left; and I believed, perhaps hoped, that, save myself, she had no friend.

I needed no time for consideration. That afternoon I was in London. If I could not comfort her in her great sorrow, I could at least sympathise with her; could undertake the management of the many business details which are attendant upon a death.

Poor Philippa! She was glad to see me. Through her tears she flashed me a look of gratitude. I did all I could for her, and stayed in town until the funeral was over. Then I was obliged to think of going home. What was to become of the girl?

Kith or kin she had none, nor did she mention the name of any friend who would be willing to receive her. As I suspected, she was absolutely alone in the world. As soon as my back was turned she would have no one on whom she could count for sympathy or help.

It must have been her utter loneliness which urged me, in spite of my better judgment, in spite of the grief which still oppressed her, to throw myself at her feet and declare the desire of my heart. My words I cannot recall, but I think—I know I pleaded eloquently. Such passion as mine gives power and intensity to the most unpractised speaker. Yet long before my appeal was ended I knew that I pleaded in vain. Her eyes, her manner, told me she loved me not.

Then, remembering her present helpless condition, I checked myself. I begged her to forget the words I had spoken; not to answer them now; to let me say them again in some months' time. Let me still be her friend, and render her such service as I could.

She shook her head; she held out her hand. The first action meant the refusal of my love; the second, the acceptance of my friendship. I schooled myself to calmness, and we discussed her plans for the future.

She was lodging in a house in a quiet, respectable street near Regent's Park. She expressed her intention of staying on here for a while.

'But alone!' I exclaimed.

'Why not? What have I to fear? Still, I am open to reason, if you can suggest a better plan.'

I could suggest no other. Philippa was past twenty-one, and would at once succeed to whatever money had been her mother's. This was enough to live upon. She had no friends, and must live somewhere. Why should she not stay on at her present lodgings? Nevertheless, I trembled as I thought of this beautiful girl all alone in London. Why could she not love me? Why could she not be my wife? It needed all my self-restraint to keep me from breaking afresh into passionate appeals.

As she would not give me the right to dispose of her future, I could do nothing more. I bade her a sad farewell, then went back to my home to conquer my unhappy love, or to suffer from its fresh inroads.

Conquer it! Such love as mine is never conquered. It is a man's life. Philippa was never absent from my thoughts. Let my frame of mind be gay or grave Philippa was always present.

Now and then she wrote to me, but her letters told me little as to her mode of life; they were short friendly epistles, and gave me little hope.

Yet I was not quite hopeless. I felt that I had been too hasty in asking for her love so soon after her mother's death. Let her recover from the shock, then I will try again. Three months was the time which in my own mind I resolved should elapse before I again approached her with words of love. Three months! How wearily they dragged themselves away!

Towards the end of my self-imposed term of probation I fancied that a brighter, gayer tone manifested itself in Philippa's letters. Fool that I was! I augured well from this.

Telling myself that such love as mine must win in the end, I went to London, and once more saw Philippa. She received me kindly. Although her garb was still that of deep mourning, never, I thought, had she looked more beautiful. Not long after our first greeting did I wait before I began to plead again. She stopped me at the outset.

'Hush,' she said; 'I have forgotten your former words; let us still be friends.'

'Never!' I cried passionately. 'Philippa, answer me once for all, tell me you can love me!'

She looked at me compassionately. 'How can I best answer you?' she said, musingly. 'The sharpest remedy is perhaps the kindest. Basil, will you understand me when I say it is too late?'

'Too late! What can you mean? Has another—?'

The words died on my lips as Philippa, drawing a ring from the fourth finger of her left hand, showed me that it concealed a plain gold circlet. Her eyes met mine imploringly.

'I should have told you before,' she said softly, and bending her proud head; 'but there were reasons—even now I am pledged to tell no one. Basil, I only show you this, because I know you will take no other answer.'

I rose without a word. The room seemed whirling around me. The only thing which was clear to my sight was that cursed gold band on the fair white hand—that symbol of possession by another! In that moment hope and all the sweetness of life seemed swept away from me.

Something in my face must have told her how her news affected me. She came to me and laid her hand upon my arm. I trembled like a leaf beneath her touch. She looked beseechingly into my face.

'Oh, not like that!' she cried. 'Basil, I am not worth it. I should not have made you happy. You will forget—you will find another. If I have wronged or misled you, say you forgive me. Let me hear you, my true friend, wish me happiness.'

I strove to force my dry lips to frame some conventional phrase. In vain! Words would not come. I sank into a chair and covered my face with my hands.

The door opened suddenly, and a man entered. He may have been about forty years of age. He was tall and remarkably handsome. He was dressed with scrupulous care; but there was something written on his face which told me it was not the face of a good man. As I rose from my chair he glanced from me to Philippa with an air of suspicious enquiry.

'Doctor North, an old friend of my mother's and mine,' she said with composure. 'Mr Farmer,' she added; and a rosy blush crept round her neck as she indicated the newcomer by the name which I felt sure was now also her own.

I bowed mechanically. I made a few disjointed remarks about the weather and kindred topics; then I shook hands with Philippa and left the house, the most miserable man in England.

Philippa married, and married secretly! How could her pride have stooped to a clandestine union? What manner of man was he who had won her? Heavens! He must be hard to please if he cared not to show his conquest to the light of day. Cur! Sneak! Coward! Villain! Stay; he may have his own reasons for concealment—reasons known to Philippa and approved of by her. Not a word against her. She is still my queen; the one woman in the world to me. What she has done is right!

I passed a sleepless night. In the morning I wrote to Philippa. I wished her all happiness—I could command my pen, if not my tongue. I said no word about the secrecy of the wedding, or the evils so often consequent to such concealment. But, with a foreboding of evil to come, I begged her to remember that we were friends; that, although I could see her no more, whenever she wanted a friend's aid, a word would bring me to her side. I used no word of blame. I risked no expression of love or regret. No thought of my grief should jar upon the happiness which she doubtless expected to find. Farewell the one dream of my life! Farewell Philippa!

Such a passion as mine may, in these matter-of-fact, unromantic days, seem an anachronism. No matter, whether to sympathy or ridicule, I am but laying bare my true thoughts and feelings.

I would not return to my home at once. I shrank from going back to my lonely hearth and beginning to eat my heart out. I had made arrangements to stay in town for some days; so I stayed, trying by a course of what is termed gaiety to drive remembrance away. Futile effort! How many have tried the same reputed remedy without success!

Four days after my interview with Philippa, I was walking with a friend who knew everyone in town. As we passed the door of one of the most exclusive of the clubs, I saw, standing on the steps talking to other men, the man whom I knew was Philippa's husband. His face was turned from me, so I was able to direct my friend's attention to him.

'Who is that man? 'I asked.

'That man with the gardenia in his coat is Sir Mervyn Ferrand.'

'Who is he? What is he? What kind of a man is he?'

'A baronet. Not very rich. Just about the usual kind of man you see on those steps. Very popular with the ladies, they tell me.'

'Is he married?'

'Heaven knows! I don't. I never heard of a Lady Ferrand, although there must be several who are morally entitled to use the designation.'

And this was her husband—Philippa's husband!

I clenched my teeth. Why had he married under a false name? Or if she knew that name by which she introduced him to me was false, why was it assumed? Why had the marriage been clandestine? Not only Sir Mervyn Ferrand, but the noblest in the land should be proud of winning Philippa! The more I thought of the matter, the more wretched I grew. The dread that she had been in some way deceived almost drove me mad. The thought of my proud, beautiful queen some day finding herself humbled to the dust by a scoundrel's deceit was anguish. What could I do?

My first impulse was to demand an explanation, then and there, from Sir Mervyn Ferrand. Yet I had no right or authority so to do. What was I to Philippa save an unsuccessful suitor? Moreover, I felt that she had revealed her secret to me in confidence. If there were good reasons for the concealment, I might do her irretrievable harm by letting this man know that I was aware of his true position in society. No, I could not call him to account. But I must do something, or in time to come my grief may be rendered doubly deep by self-reproach.

The next day I called upon Philippa. She would at least tell me if the name under which the man married her was the true or the false one. Alas! I found she had left her home the day before—left it to return no more! The landlady had no idea whither she was gone, but believed it was her intention to leave England.

After this I threw prudence to the winds. With some trouble I found Sir Mervyn Ferrand's town address. The next day I called on him. He also, I was informed, had just left England. His destination was also unknown.

I turned away moodily. All chance of doing good was at
an end. Let the marriage be true or false, Philippa had
departed, accompanied by the man who, for purposes of his
own, passed under the name of Farmer, but who was really
Sir Mervyn Ferrand.

I went back to my home, and amid the wreck of my life's
happiness murmured a prayer and registered an oath. I prayed
that honour and happiness might be the lot of her I loved; I
swore that were she wronged I would with my own hand take
vengeance on the man who wronged her.

For myself I prayed nothing—not even forgetfulness. I
loved Philippa: I had lost her for ever! The past, the present,
the future were all summed up in these words!

CHAPTER II

A VILLAIN'S BLOW

THEY tell me there are natures stern enough to be able to crush love out of their lives. Ah! Not such love as mine! Time, they say, can heal every wound. Not such a wound as mine! My whole existence underwent a change when Philippa showed me the wedding-ring on her finger. No wonder it did. Hope was eliminated from it. From that moment I was a changed man.

Life was no longer worth living. The spur of ambition was blunted; the desire for fame gone; the interest which I had hitherto felt in my profession vanished. All the spring, the elasticity, seemed taken out of my being. For months and months I did my work in a perfunctory manner. It gave me no satisfaction that my practice grew larger. I worked, but I cared nothing for my work. Success gave me no pleasure. An increase to the number of my patients was positively unwelcome to me. So long as I made money enough to supply my daily needs, what did it matter? Of what use was wealth to me? It could not buy me the one thing for which I craved. Of what use was life? No wonder that such friends as I had once possessed all but forsook me. My mood at that time was none of the sweetest. I wanted no friends. I was alone in the world; I should be always alone.

So things went on for more than a year. I grew worse instead of better. My gloom deepened; my cynicism grew more confirmed; my life became more and more aimless.

These are not lovers' rhapsodies. I would spare you them if I could; but it is necessary that you should know the exact state of my mind in order to understand my subsequent conduct.

Even now it seems to me that I am writing this description with my heart's blood.

Not a word came from Philippa. I made no enquiries about her, took no steps to trace her. I dared not. Not for one moment did I forget her, and through all those weary months tried to think of her as happy and to be envied; yet, in spite of myself, I shuddered as I pictured her lot as it might really be.

But all the while I knew that the day would come when I should learn whether I was to be thankful that my prayer had been answered, or to be prepared to keep my vow.

In my misanthropical state of mind I heard without the slightest feeling of joy or elation that a distant relative of mine, a man from whom I expected nothing, had died and left me the bulk of his large property. I cared nothing for this unexpected wealth, except for the fact that it enabled me to free myself from a round of toil in which by now I took not the slightest interest. Had it but come two or three years before! Alas! All things in this life come too late.

Now that I was no longer forced to mingle with men in order to gain the means of living, I absolutely shunned my kind. The wish of my youth, to travel in far countries, no longer existed with me. I disposed of my practice—or rather I simply handed it over to the first comer. I left the town of my adoption, and bought a small house—it was little more than a cottage—some five miles away from the tiny town of Roding. Here I was utterly unknown, and could live exactly as I chose; and for months it was my choice to live almost like a hermit.

My needs were ministered to by a man who had been for some years in my employment. He was a handy, faithful fellow; honest as the day, stolid as the Sphynx; and, for some reason or other, so much attached to me that he was willing to perform on my behalf the duties of housekeeping which are usually relegated to female servants.

Looking back upon that time of seclusion, as a medical man, I wonder what would eventually have been my fate if events had not occurred which once more forced me into the world of men? I firmly believe that brooding in solitude over my grief would at last have affected my brain; that sooner or later I must have developed symptoms of melancholia; Professionally speaking, the probabilities are I should have committed suicide.

Even in the depth of my degradation I must have known the dangers of the path which I was treading; for, after having passed six dreary months in my lonely cottage, I was trying to brace myself to seek a change of scene. I shrank from leaving my quiet abode; but every day formed afresh the resolve to do so.

Yet the days, each the same as its forerunner, went by, and I was still there. I had books, of course. I read for days together; then I would throw the volumes aside, and, with a bitter smile, ask myself to what end was I directing my studies. The accumulation of knowledge? Tush! I would give all the learning I had acquired, all that a lifetime of research could acquire, to hold Philippa for one brief moment to my heart, and hear her say she loved me! If in the whirl of men, in the midst of hard work, I found it impossible to conquer my hopeless passion, how could I expect to do so living as I at present lived?

There! My egotistical descriptions are almost over. Now you know why I said that you must sit by the fire and think with me; must enter, as it were, into my inner self before you can understand my mental state. Whether you sympathise with me or not depends entirely upon your own organisation. If you are so constructed that the love of one woman, and one only, can pervade your very being, fill your every thought, direct your every action, make life to you a blessing or a curse—if love comes to you in this guise, you will be able to understand me.

That night, when I first presented myself to you, my wounds seemed less likely than ever to heal; forgetfulness seemed farther and farther away. Somehow, as my thoughts took the well-worn road to the past, every event seemed recent as yesterday, every scene vivid as if I had just left it. Hour after hour I sat gazing at the glowing embers, but seeing only Philippa's beloved face. How had life fared with her? Where was she at this moment? The resolve to quit my seclusion was made anew by me. I would go into the world and find her—not for any selfish motive. I would learn from her own lips that she was happy. If unhappy, she should have from me such comfort as the love of a true friend can give. Yes, I would leave this wretched life tomorrow. My cheek flushed as I contrasted what I was with what I ought to be. No man has a right to ruin his life or hide his talents for the sake of a woman.

I had another inducement which urged me to make a change in my mode of life. I am ashamed that I have not spoken of it. That morning I had received a letter from my mother. I had not seen her for six years. Just as I entered man's estate she married for the second time. My step-father was an American, and with many tears my mother left me for her new home. Some months ago her husband died. I should have gone to her, but she forbade me. She had no children by her second husband; and now that his affairs were practically wound up she purposed returning to England. Her letter told me that she would be in London in three days' time, and suggested that I should meet her there.

Although of late years we had drifted apart, she was dear, very dear to me. I hated the thought of her seeing me, her only child, reduced to such a wreck of my former self; yet for her sake I again renewed my resolve of leaving my seclusion.

Yet I knew that tomorrow I should forswear myself, and sink back into my apathy and aimless existence. Ah! I knew not what events were to crowd into the morrow!

But now back to the night. It was midwinter, and bitterly cold out of doors. My lamp was not yet lighted; the glow of my fire alone broke the darkness of the room. I had not even drawn the curtains or shut the shutters. At times I liked to look out and see the stars. They shone so peacefully, so calmly, so coldly; they seemed so unlike the world, with its strife and fierce passions and disappointments.

I rose languidly from my chair and walked to the window, to see what sort of a night it was. As I approached the casement I could see that the skies had darkened; moreover, I noticed that feathery flakes of snow were accumulating in the corner of each pane. I went close to the window and peered out into the night.

Standing within a yard of me, gazing into my dimly-lit room— her face stern and pale as death, her dark eyes now riveted on my own—was a woman; and that woman was Philippa, my love!

For several seconds I stood, spellbound, gazing at her. That I saw more than a phantom of my imagination did not at once enter into my head. In dreams I had seen the one I loved again and again, but this was the first time my waking thoughts had conjured up such a vision. Vision, dream, reality! I trembled as I looked; for the form was that of Philippa in dire distress.

It was seeing the hood which covered her head grow whiter and whiter with the fast-falling snow which aroused me to my senses, and made every fibre thrill with the thought that Philippa, in flesh and blood, stood before me. With a low cry of rapture I tore asunder the fastening of the French casement, threw the sashes apart, and without a word my love passed from the cold, bleak night into my room.

She was wrapped from head to foot in a rich dark fur-trimmed cloak. As she swept by me I felt she was damp with partially-thawed snow. I closed the window; then, with a throbbing heart, turned to greet my visitor. She stood in the centre of the room. Her mantle had fallen to the ground, and through the dusk I could see her white face, hands, and neck. I took her hands in mine; they were cold as icicles.

'Philippa! Philippa! Why are you here?' I whispered. 'Welcome, thrice welcome, whether you bring me joy or sorrow.'

A trembling ran through her. She said nothing, but her

cold hands clasped mine closer. I led her to the fire, which I stirred until it blazed brightly. She knelt before it and stretched out her hands for warmth. How pale she looked; how unlike the Philippa of old! But to my eyes how lovely!

As I looked down at the fair woman kneeling at my feet, with her proud head bent as in shame, I knew intuitively that I should be called upon to keep my oath; and knowing this, I re-registered it in all its entirety.

At last she raised her face to mine. In her eyes was a sombre fire, which until now I had never seen there. 'Philippa! Philippa!' I cried again.

'Fetch a light,' she whispered. 'Let me see a friend's face once more—if you are still my friend.'

'Your friend, your true friend for ever,' I said, as I hastened to obey her.

As I placed the lamp on the table Philippa rose from her knees. I could now see that she was in deep mourning. Was the thought that flashed through me, that it might be she was a widow, one of joy or sorrow? I hope—I try to believe it was the latter.

We stood for some moments in silence. My agitation, my rapture at seeing her once more seemed to have deprived me of speech. I could do little more than gaze at her and tell myself that I was not dreaming; that Philippa was really here; that it was her voice I had heard, her hands I clasped. Philippa it was, but not the Philippa of old!

The rich warm glowing beauty seemed toned down. Her face had lost its exquisite colour. Moreover, it was as the face of one who has suffered—one who is suffering. To me it looked as if illness had refined it, as it sometimes will refine a face. Yet, if she had been ill, her illness could not have been of long duration. Her figure was as superb, her arms as finely rounded, as ever. She stood firm and erect. Yet I trembled as I gazed at that pale proud face and those dark solemn eyes. I dared not for the while ask her why she sought me.

She was the first to break silence. 'You are changed, Basil,' she said.

'Time changes everyone,' I answered, forcing a smile.

'Will you believe me,' she continued, 'when I say that the memory of your face as I saw it last has haunted even my most joyful moments? Ah me, Basil, had I been true to myself I think I might have learned to love you.'

She spoke regretfully, and as one who has finished with life and its love. My heart beat rapidly; yet I knew her words were not spoken in order to hear me tell her that I loved her passionately as ever.

'I have heard of you once or twice,' she said softly. 'You are rich now, they tell me, but unhappy.'

'I loved you and lost you,' I answered. 'How could I be happy?'

'And men can love like this?' she said sadly. 'All men are not alike then?'

'Enough of me,' I said. 'Tell me of yourself. Tell me how I can aid you. Your husband—'

She drew a sharp quick breath. The colour rushed back to her cheek. Her eyes glittered strangely. Nevertheless, she spoke calmly and distinctly.

'Husband! I have none,' she said.

'Is he dead?'

'No'—she spoke with surpassing bitterness—'No; I should rather say I never was a wife. Tell me, Basil,' she continued fiercely, 'did you ever hate a man?'

'Yes,' I answered emphatically and truly. Hate a man! From the moment I saw the wretch with whom Philippa fled I hated him. Now that my worst suspicions were true, what were my feelings?

I felt that my lips compressed themselves. I knew that when I spoke my voice was as stern and bitter as Philippa's. 'Sit down,' I said, 'and tell me all. Tell me how you knew I was here—where you have come from.'

Let me but learn whence she came, and I felt sure the

knowledge would enable me to lay my hand on the man I wanted. Ah! Life now held something worth living for!

'I have been here some months,' said Philippa.

'Here! In this neighbourhood?'

'Yes. I have seen you several times. I have been living at a house about three miles away. I felt happier in knowing that in case of need I had one friend near me.'

I pressed her hands. 'Go on,' I said, hoarsely.

'He sent me here. He had grown weary of me. I was about to have a child. I was in his way—a trouble to him.'

Her scornful accent as she spoke was indescribable.

'Philippa! Philippa!' I groaned. 'Had you sunk so low as to do his bidding?'

She laid her hand on my arm. 'More,' she said. 'Listen! Before we parted he struck me. Struck—me! He cursed me and struck me! Basil, did you ever hate a man?'

I threw out my arms. My heart was full of rage and bitterness. 'And you became this man's mistress rather than my wife!' I gasped. Neither my love nor her sorrow could stop this one reproach from passing my lips.

She sprang to her feet. 'You!' she cried. 'Do you—think—do you imagine—? Read! Only this morning I learnt it.'

She threw a letter towards me—threw it with a gesture of loathing, as one throws a nauseous reptile from one's hand. I opened it mechanically.

'Yes,' she said, 'you were right in thinking I had fallen low. So low that I went where he chose to send me. So low that I would have forgiven the ill treatment of months—the blow, even. Why? Because until this morning he was my husband. Read the letter. Basil, did you ever hate a man?'

Before I read I glanced at her in alarm. She spoke with almost feverish excitement. Her words followed one another with headlong rapidity. But who could wonder at this mood with a woman who had such a wrong to declare? She grew calm beneath my glance.

'Read,' she said, beseechingly. 'Ah, God! I have fallen low; but not so low as you thought.'

She buried her face in her hands whilst I opened and read the letter. It was dated from Paris, and ran so:

'As it seems to me that we can't exactly hit it off together, I think the farce had better end. The simplest way to make my meaning clear is to tell you that when I married you I had a wife alive. She has died since then; and I dare say, had we managed to get on better together, I should have asked you to go through the marriage ceremony once more. However, as things are now, so they had better stop. You have the satisfaction of knowing that morally you are blameless.

'If, like a sensible girl, you are ready to accept the situation, I am prepared to act generously, and do the right thing in money matters. As I hate to have anything hanging over me unsettled, and do not care to trust delicate negotiations to a third party, I shall run across to England and see you. I shall reach Roding on Wednesday evening. Do not send to the station to meet me; I would rather walk.'

The letter was unsigned. My blood boiled as I read it; yet, in spite of my rage, I felt a grim humour as I realised the exquisite cynicism possessed by the writer. Here was a man striking a foul and recreant blow at a woman whom he once loved—a blow that must crush her to the earth. His own words confess him a rogue, a bigamist; and yet he can speak coolly about money arrangements; can even enter into petty details concerning his approaching visit! He must be without shame, without remorse; a villain, absolutely heartless!

I folded the letter and placed it in my breast. I wished to keep it, that I might read it again and again during the next twenty-four hours. Long hours they would be. This letter would aid me to make them pass. Philippa made no objection to my keeping it. She sat motionless, gazing gloomily into the fire.

'You knew the man's right name and title?' I asked.

'Yes, from the first. Ah! There I wronged myself, Basil! The rank, the riches perhaps, tempted me; and—Basil, I loved him then.'

Oh, the piteous regret breathed in that last sentence! I ground my teeth, and felt that there was a stronger passion than even love. 'That man and I meet tomorrow,' I told myself softly.

'But you spoke of a child?' I said, turning to Philippa.

'It is dead—dead—dead!' she cried, with a wild laugh. 'A fortnight ago it died. Dead! My grief then; my joy today! See! I am in mourning; tomorrow I shall put that mourning off. Why mourn for what is a happy event? No black after tomorrow.'

Her mood had once more become excited. As before, her words came with feverish rapidity. I took her hands in mine; they were now burning.

'Philippa, dearest, be calm. You will see that man no more?'

'I will see him no more. It is to save myself from seeing him that I come to you. Little right have I to ask aid from you; but your words came back to me in my need. There was one friend to turn to. Help me, Basil! I come to you as a sister may come to a brother.'

'As a sister to a brother,' I echoed. 'I accept the trust,' I added, laying my lips reverentially on her white forehead, and vowing mentally to devote my life to her.

'You will stay here now?' I asked.

'No, I must go back. Tomorrow I will come—tomorrow. Basil, my brother, you will take me far away—far away?'

'Where you wish. Every land is as one to me now.'

She had given me the right, a brother's right, to stand between her and the villain who had wronged her. Tomorrow that man would be here! How I longed for the moment which would bring us face to face!

Philippa rose. 'I must go,' she said.

I pressed food and wine upon her: she would take nothing. She made, however, no objection to my accompanying her to her home. We left the house by the casement by which she entered. Together we stepped out on the snow-whitened road. She took my arm, and we walked towards her home.

I asked her with whom she was staying. She told me with a widow-lady and two children, named Wilson. She went to them at Sir Mervyn Ferrand's command. Mrs Wilson, he told her, was a distant connection of his own, and he had made arrangements for her to look after Philippa during her illness.

It was but another proof of the man's revolting cynicism. To send the woman who falsely believed herself to be his wife to one of his own relations! Oh, I would have a full reckoning with him!

'What name do they know you by?' I asked.

'He said I was to call myself by the false name, which, for purposes of his own, he chose to pass under. But I felt myself absolved from my promise of secrecy. Why should I stay in a strange house with strange people by Sir Mervyn Ferrand's request, unless I could show good cause for doing so? So I told Mrs Wilson everything.'

'She believed you?'

'She was bound to believe me. I would have no doubt cast upon my word. I showed her the certificate of my marriage. Whatever she may have thought at first, she saw then that I was his wife. No one else knows it except her. To her I am Lady Ferrand. Like me, she never dreamed to what man's villainy can reach. Oh, Basil, Basil! Why are such men allowed to live?'

For the first time Philippa seemed to break down. Till now the chief characteristics of her mood had been scorn and anger. Now, sheer grief for the time appeared to sweep away every other emotion. Sob after sob broke from her. I endeavoured to calm her—to comfort her. Alas! How little I could say or do to these ends! She leaned heavily and despondingly on my arm, and for a long while we walked in silence. At last she told me her home was close at hand.

'Listen, Philippa,' I said; 'I shall come in with you and see this lady with whom you are staying. I shall tell her I am your brother; that for some time I have known how shamefully your husband has neglected you; and that now, with your full consent, I mean to take you away. Whether this woman believes in our relationship or not, matters nothing. I suppose she knows that man is coming tomorrow. After his heartless desertion, she cannot be surprised at your wish to avoid meeting him.'

I paused. Philippa bent her head as if assenting to my plan.

'Tomorrow,' I continued, 'long before that wretch comes here to poison the very air we breathe, I shall come and fetch you. Early in the morning I will send my servant for your luggage. Mrs Wilson may know me and my man by sight. That makes no difference. There need be no concealment. You are free to come and go. You have no one to fear. On Thursday morning we will leave this place.'

'Yes,' said Philippa, dreamily, 'tomorrow I will leave—I will come to you. But I will come alone. In the evening most likely, when no one will know where I have gone.'

'But how much better that I should take you away openly and in broad daylight, as a brother would take a sister!'

'No; I will come to you. You will not mind waiting, Basil. There is something I must do first. Something to be done tomorrow. Something to be said; someone to be seen. What is it? Who is it? I cannot recollect.'

She placed her disengaged hand on her brow. She pushed back her hood a little, and gave a sigh of relief as she felt the keen air on her temples. Poor girl! After what she had that day gone through, no wonder her mind refused to recall trivial details and petty arrangements to be made before she joined me. Sleep and the certainty of my sympathy and protection would no doubt restore her wandering memory.

However, although I again and again urged her to change her mind, she was firm in her resolve to come to me alone. At last, very reluctantly, I was obliged to give way on this point; but I was determined to see this Mrs Wilson tonight; so when we reached the house I entered with Philippa.

I told her there was no occasion for her to be present at my interview with her hostess. She looked frightfully weary, and at my suggestion went straight to her room to retire for the night. I sat down and awaited the advent of Mrs Wilson. She soon appeared.

A woman of about five and thirty; well but plainly dressed. As I glanced at her with some curiosity, I decided that when young she must, after a certain type of beauty, have been extremely good-looking. Unfortunately hers was one of those faces cast in an aquiline mould—faces which, as soon as the bloom of youth is lost or the owners thereof turn to thinness, become, as a rule, sharp, strained, hungry and severe-looking. Whatever the woman's charms might once have been, she could now boast of very few.

There were lines round her mouth and on her brow which told of suffering; and, as I judged it, not the calm, resigned suffering, which often leaves a sweet if sad expression on the face; but fierce, rebellious, constrained suffering, such as turns a young heart into an old one long before its time.

As she entered the room and bowed to me her face expressed undisguised surprise at seeing a visitor who was a stranger to her. I apologised for the lateness of my call; then hastened to tell her its object. She listened with polite impassability. She made no comment when I repeatedly spoke of my so-styled sister as Lady Ferrand. It was clear that, as Philippa had said, Mrs Wilson was convinced as to the valid nature of the marriage. I inveighed roundly against Sir Mervyn Ferrand's heartless conduct and scandalous neglect of his wife. My hearer shrugged her shoulders, and the meaning conveyed by the action was that, although she regretted family jars, they were no concern of hers. She seemed quite without interest in the matter; yet a suspicion that she was acting, indeed rather over-acting, a part, crossed my mind once or twice.

When I told her it was Lady Ferrand's intention to place herself tomorrow under my protection, she simply bowed. When I said that most likely we should leave England, and for a while travel on the continent, she said that my sister's health would no doubt be much benefited by the change.

'I may mention,' she added, for the first time taking any real part in the talk, 'that your sister's state is not quite all it should be. For the last day or two I have been thinking of sending for the medical man who attended her during her unfortunate confinement. He has not seen her for quite a week. I mentioned it to her this afternoon; but she appears to have taken an unaccountable dislike to him, and utterly refused to see him. I do not wish to alarm you—I merely mention this; no doubt you, her brother, will see to it.'

The peculiar stress she laid on the word 'brother' told me that I was right in thinking the woman was acting, and that not for one moment did my assumed fraternity deceive her. This was of no consequence.

'I am myself a doctor. Her health will be my care,' I said. Then I rose.

'You are related to Sir Mervyn Ferrand, I believe, Mrs Wilson?' I asked.

She gave me a quick look which might mean anything. 'We are connections,' she said carelessly.

'You must have been surprised at his sending his wife away at such a time?'

'I am not in the habit of feeling surprise at Sir Mervyn's actions. He wrote to me and told me that, knowing my circumstances were straitened, he had recommended a lady to come and live with me for a few months. When I found this lady was his wife, I own I was, for once, surprised.'

From the emphasis which she laid on certain words, I knew

it was but the fact of Philippa's being married to the scoundrel that surprised her, nothing else. I could see that Mrs Wilson knew Sir Mervyn Ferrand thoroughly, and something told me that her relations with him were of a nature which might not bear investigation.

I bade her good-night, and walked back to my cottage with a heart in which sorrow, pity, love, hatred, exultation, and, it may be, hope, were strangely and inextricably mingled.

CHAPTER III

'THE WAGES OF SIN'

MORNING! No books; no idle listless hours for me today. Plenty to do, plenty to think about; all sorts of arrangements to make. Farewell to my moody, sullen life. Farewell to my aimless, selfish existence. Henceforward I should have something worth living for—worth dying for, if needs be! Philippa was coming to me today; coming in grief, it is true; coming as a sister comes to a brother. Ah! After all the weary, weary waiting, I shall see her today—tomorrow—every day! If a man's devotion, homage, worship, and respect can in her own eyes reinstate my queen, I shall someday see the bloom come back to her cheek, the bright smile play once more round her mouth, the dark eyes again eloquent with happy thoughts. And then—and then! What should I care for the world or its sneers? To whom, save myself, should I be answerable? Then I might whisper in her ear, 'Sweet, let the past vanish from our lives as a dream. Let happiness date from today.'

Although Philippa would grace my poor cottage for one night only, I had a thousand preparations to make for her comfort. Fortunately I had a spare room, and, moreover, a furnished one. Not that I should have troubled, when I went into my seclusion, about such a superfluity as a guest-chamber; but as it happened I had bought the house and the furniture complete; so could offer my welcome guest fair accommodation for the night.

I summoned my stolid man. I told him that my sister was coming on a visit to me; that she would sleep here tonight, but that most likely we should go away tomorrow. He could stay and look after the house until I returned or sent him instructions what to do with it. William manifested no surprise. Had I told him to make preparations for the coming of my wife and five children, he would have considered it all a part of the day's work, and would have done his best to meet my requirements.

He set to work in his imperturbable, methodical, but handy way to get Philippa's room in trim. As soon as this was done, and the neglected chamber made cosy and warm-looking, I told him to borrow a horse and cart from somewhere, and fetch the luggage from Mrs Wilson's. He was to mention no names; simply to say he had come for the luggage, and to ask if the lady had any message to send.

Then I sat down in the room which my love would occupy, and mused upon the strange but unhappy chance which was bringing her beneath my roof. I wished that I had an enchanter's wand to turn the humble garniture of the chamber into surroundings meet for my queenly Philippa. I wished that I had, at least, flowers with which I could deck her resting-place; for I remembered how passionately she loved flowers. Alas! I had not seen a flower for months.

Then I drew out Sir Mervyn Ferrand's letter, read it again and again, and cursed the writer in my heart.

William was away about two hours; then he made his appearance with some boxes. I was delighted to see these tangible signs that Philippa meant to keep her promise. Till that moment I had been troubled by something like the doubt, that after all she might, upon calm reflection, rescind the resolution formed in her excitement. Now her coming seemed to be a certainty.

Nevertheless, William brought no message; so there was nothing for me to do but wait patiently until she chose to cross my threshold.

Although my pleasing labours of love were ended, I was not left idle. There was another task to be done today. I set my teeth and sat down, thinking quietly as to the way in which it might be best performed. Tonight I meant to stand face to face with that black-hearted scoundrel known as Sir Mervyn Ferrand!

I consulted the time-table. His letter named no particular hour; but I saw that if he carried out his expressed intention of being here tonight, there was but one train by which he could come; there was but one way from Roding to the house at which Philippa had been staying. He meant to walk, his letter said; this might be in order to escape observation. The train was due at Roding at seven o'clock. The weather was cold; a man would naturally walk fast. Mrs Wilson's house must be four miles from the station. Let me start from there just before the train arrives, and I should probably meet him about half-way on his journey. It would be dark, but I should know him. I should know him among a thousand. There on the open lonely road Sir Mervyn Ferrand, coming gaily, and in his worldly cynicism certain of cajoling, buying off, or in some other way silencing the woman who had in an evil day trusted to his honour and love, would meet, not her, but the man who from the first had sworn that a wrong to Philippa should be more than a wrong to himself! He would meet this man, and be called to account.

Stern and sinister as were my thoughts—freely and unreservedly as I record them: as indeed I endeavour in this tale to record everything—I do not wish to be misjudged. It is true that in my present mood I was bent upon avenging Philippa with my own hand; true that I meant, if possible, to take at some time or another this man's life; but at least no thought of taking any advantage of an unarmed or unsuspecting man entered into my scheme of vengeance. I designed no murderous attack. But it was my intention to stop the man on his path; to confront him and tell him that his villainy was known to me; that Philippa had fled to me for aid; that she was now in my custody; and that I, who stood in the position of her brother, demanded the so-called satisfaction which, by the old-fashioned code of honour, was due from the man who had ruthlessly betrayed a woman. Well I knew that it was probable he would laugh at me—tell me that the days of duelling were over, and refuse to grant my request. Then I meant to see if insults could warm his noble blood; if my hand on his cheek could bring about the result which I desired. If this failed, I would follow him abroad, cane him and spit upon him in public places.

A wild scheme for these prosaic law-abiding days; yet the only one that was feasible. It may be said that I should have taken steps to have caused the miscreant to be arrested for bigamy. But what proof of his crime had we as yet, save his own unsigned confession? Who was to move in the matter— Philippa—myself? We did not even know where this wife of whom he had spoken lived, or where she died. There were a hundred ways in which he might escape from justice, but whether he was punished for his sin or allowed to go scot-free, Philippa's name and wrongs must be bruited about, her shame made public. No; there was but one course to take, and but one person to take it. It rested with me to avenge the wrongs of the woman I loved by the good old-fashioned way of a life against a life.

Truly, as I said, I had now plenty to live for!

The hours went by, yet Philippa came not. I grew restless and uneasy as the dusk began to make the road, up which I gazed almost continually, dim and indistinct. When the short winter's day was over, and the long dark night had fairly begun, my restlessness turned into fear. I walked out of my house and paced my garden to and fro. I blamed myself for having yielded so lightly to Philippa's wish—her command rather—that I should on no account fetch her. But then, whenever did I resist a wish, much less a command, of hers? Oh, that I had been firm this once!

The snow-storm of the previous evening had not lasted long—not long enough to thoroughly whiten the world. The day had been fine and frosty, but I knew that the wind had changed since the sun went down. It was warmer, a change which I felt sure presaged a heavy downfall of snow or rain.

There was a moon, a fitful moon; for clouds were flying across it, dark clouds, which I guessed would soon gather coherence and volume, and veil entirely that bright face, which now only showed itself at irregular intervals.

The minutes were passing away. I grew nervous and excited. Why does she not come? My hope had been to see my poor girl safely housed before I started to execute my other task. Why does she not come? Time, precious time, is slipping by! In the hope of meeting her, I walked for some distance up the road. 'Why does she delay?' I groaned. Even now I should be on my way to Roding, or I may miss my prey. Heavens! Can it be that she is waiting to see this man once more? Never! Never! Perish the thought!

But, all the same, every fibre in my body quivered at the bare supposition of such a thing,

I could bear the suspense no longer. For the hundredth time I glanced at my watch. It wanted but ten minutes to seven o'clock, and at that hour I had resolved to start from Mrs Wilson's, on my way to Roding. Yet now I dared not leave my own house. Any moment might bring Philippa. What would she think if I was not there to receive and welcome her?

Five more precious moments gone! I stamped in my rage. After all, I can only do one half of my task; the sweet, but not the stern half. Shall I, indeed, do either? The train must now be close to Roding. In an hour everything may be lost. The man will see her before she leaves the house. He will persuade her. She will listen to his words; for did he not once love her? He must have loved her! After all, he broke the laws for the sake of possessing her, and—cursed thought!—she loved him then; and she is but a woman!

So I tortured myself until my state of mind grew unbearable. At all hazard I must prevent Ferrand from meeting Philippa. Oh, why had she not come as she promised? Could it be she was detained against her will? In spite of her uninterested manner, I distrusted the woman I had seen last night. It is now past seven o'clock. Philippa's house, from which I had reckoned my time, was nearly three miles away. I must give up my scheme of vengeance. I must go in search of Philippa. If I do not meet her I must call at Mrs Wilson's, find out what detains her, and if needful bear her away by force.

By this time my steps had brought me back to my own house. I called William, and told him I was going to walk up the road and meet my expected guest. If by any chance I should miss her, he was to welcome her on my behalf, and tell her the reason for my absence.

'Best take a lantern, sir,' said William; 'moon'll soon be hidden, and them roads is precious rough.'

'I can't be bothered with that great horn affair,' I said, rather testily.

'Take the little one—the bull's-eye—that's better than nothing,' said William. To humour him I put it into my pocket.

I ran at the top of my speed to the house at which I had last night left Philippa. It took me nearly half an hour getting there. I rang the bell impetuously. The door was opened by a maid-servant. I enquired for Mrs Farmer, knowing that Philippa had passed under this name to all except her hostess. To my surprise I was told that she had left the house, on foot and alone, some little while ago. The maid believed she was not going to return, as her luggage had that morning been sent for.

The first effect of this intelligence was to cause me to blame my haste. I must have missed her; no doubt passed her on the road. No; such a thing was impossible. The way was a narrow one. The moon still gave some light. If I had met Philippa, I must have seen her. She must have seen me, and would then have stopped me. She could not have gone the way I came.

But where was she? In what direction was I to seek her? Argue the matter as I would—loath as I was to allow myself to be convinced, I was bound to decide that she must have taken the path to Roding. There was no other. She had gone, even as I was going, to meet Ferrand. She may have started, intending to come to me; but at the last moment a desire to see the man once more—I fondly hoped for the purpose of heaping reproaches on his head—had mastered her. Yes, whatever her object might be, she had gone to meet him. And my heart sank as conviction was carried to it by the remembrance that coupled with her refusal to permit me to fetch her was an assertion that she had something to do before she came to me. That, as I now read it, could be but one thing—to meet this man!

Never again, if I can help it, shall his voice strike on her ear! Never again shall their eyes meet! Never again shall the touch of even his finger contaminate her! Let me follow, and stand between her and the scoundrel. If they meet he will wound her to the heart. Her pride will rise; she will threaten. Then the coward will try another line. He will plead for mercy; he will swear he still loves her; he will bait his hook with promises. She will listen; hesitate; perhaps yield, and find herself once more deceived. Then she will be lost to me for ever. Now she is, in my eyes, pure as when first we met. Let me haste on, overtake, pass her; meet her betrayer, and, if needful, strike him to the ground.

As I turned from the house I became aware that a great and sudden change had come over the night. It seemed to me that, even in the few minutes which I had spent in considering what to do, the heavy clouds had banked and massed together. It was all but pitch-dark; so dark that I paused, and drawing from my pocket the lantern with which William's foresight had provided me, managed after several trials to light it. Then, impatient at the delay, I sped up the road.

I was now almost facing the wind. All at once, sharp and quick, I felt the blinding snow on my face. The wind moaned through the leafless branches on either side of the road. The snowflakes whirled madly here and there. Even in my excitement I was able to realise the fact that never before had I seen in England so fierce a snow-storm, or one which came on so suddenly. And, like myself, Philippa was abroad, and exposed to its full fury. Heavens! She might lose her way, and wander about all night.

This fear quickened my steps. I forced my way on through the mad storm. For the time all thought of Sir Mervyn Ferrand and vengeance left my heart. All I now wanted was to find Philippa; to lead her home, and see her safe beneath my roof. 'Surely,' I said, as I battled along, 'she cannot have gone much further.'

I kept a sharp look-out—if, indeed, it can be called a look-out; for the whirling snow made everything, save what was within a few feet of me, invisible. I strained my ears to catch the faintest cry or other sound. I went on, flashing my lantern first on one and then on the other side of the road. My dread was, that Philippa, utterly unable to fight against the white tempest, might be crouching under one of the banks, and if so I might pass without seeing her or even attracting her attention. My doing so on such a night as this might mean her death.

Oh, why had she not come as promised? Why had she gone to meet the man who had so foully wronged her? After what had happened, she could not, dared not love him. And for a dreary comfort I recalled the utter bitterness of her accent last night when she turned to me and said, 'Basil, did you ever hate a man?' No, she could not love him!

These thoughts brought my craving for vengeance back to my mind. Where was Ferrand? By all my calculations, taking into account the time wasted at starting, I should by now have met him. Perhaps he had not come, after all. Perhaps the look of the weather had frightened him, and he had decided to stay at Roding for the night. I raged at the thought! If only I knew that Philippa was safely housed, nothing, in my present frame of mind, would have suited me better than to have met him on this lonely road, in the midst of this wild storm. If Philippa were only safe!

Still no sign of her. I began to waver in my mind. What if my first supposition, that I had passed her on the road, was correct? She might be now at my cottage, wondering what had become of me. Should I go further or turn back? But what would be my feelings if I did the latter, and found when I arrived home that she had not made her appearance?

I halted, irresolute, in the centre of the road. Instinctively I beat my hands together to promote circulation. I had left my home hurriedly, and had made no provision for the undergoing of such an ordeal as this terrible, unprecedented snow-storm inflicted. In spite of the speed at which I had travelled, my hands and feet were growing numbed, my face smarted with the cold. Heaven help me to decide aright, whether to go on or turn back!

The decision was not left to me. Suddenly, close at hand, I heard a wild peal, a scream of laughter which made my blood run cold. Swift from the whirling, tossing, drifting snow emerged a tall grey figure. It swept past me like the wind; but as it passed me I knew that my quest was ended—that Philippa was found!

She vanished in a second, before the terror which rooted me to the spot had passed away. Then I turned and, fast as I could run, followed her, crying as I went, 'Philippa! Philippa!'

I soon overtook her; but so dark was the night that I was almost touching her before I saw her shadowy, ghost-like form. I threw my arms round her and held her. She struggled violently in my grasp.

'Philippa, dearest! It is I, Basil,' I said, bending close to her ear.

The sound of my voice seemed to calm her, or I should rather say she ceased to struggle.

'Thank heaven, I have found you!' I said. 'Let us get back as soon as possible.'

'Back! No! Go on! Go on!' she exclaimed. 'On, on, on, up the road yet awhile—on through the storm, through the snow—on till you see what I have left behind me! On till you see the wages of sin—the wages of sin!'

Her words came like bullets from a mitrailleuse. Through the night I could see her face gleaming whiter than the snow on her hood. I could see her great, fixed, dark eyes full of nameless horror.

'Dearest, be calm,' I said, and strove to take her hands in mine.

As I tried to gain possession of her right hand something fell from it, and, although the road was now coated with snow, a metallic sound rang out as it touched the ground. Mechanically I stooped and picked up the fallen object.

As I did so Philippa with a wild cry wrested herself from the one hand whose numbed grasp still sought to retain her, and, with a frenzied reiteration of the words 'The wages of sin!' fled from me, and was lost in the night.

Even as I rushed in pursuit I shuddered as the sense of feeling told me what thing it was I had picked up from the snowy ground. It was a small pistol! Cold as the touch of the metal must have been, it seemed to burn me like a coal of fire. Impulsively, thoughtlessly, as I ran I hurled the weapon from me, far, far away. Why should it have been in Philippa's hand this night?

I ran madly on, but not for long. My foot caught in a stone, and I fell, half stunned and quite breathless, to the ground. It was some minutes before I recovered myself sufficiently to once more stand erect. Philippa must now have obtained a start which, coupled with her frenzied speed, almost precluded the possibility of my overtaking her.

Moreover, a strange, uncontrollable impulse swayed me. The touch of that deadly weapon still burnt my hand. Philippa's words still rang in my ears. 'On, on, on, up the road yet awhile!' she had cried. What did she mean? What had been done tonight?

I must retrace my steps. I must see! I must know! Philippa is flying through the cold, dark, deadly night; but her frame is but the frame of a woman. She must soon grow exhausted, perhaps sink senseless on the road. Nevertheless, the dreadful fears which are growing in my mind must be set at rest; then I can resume the pursuit. At all cost I must know what has happened!

Once more I turned and faced the storm. Heavens! Anything might happen on such a night as this! I went on and on, flashing my lantern as I went on the centre and on each side of the road. I went some distance past that spot where I judged that Philippa had swept by me. Then suddenly, with a cry of horror, I stopped short. At my very feet, in the middle of the highway, illumined by the disc of light cast by my lantern, lay a whitened mass, and as my eye fell upon it I knew only too well the meaning of Philippa's wild exclamation—'The wages of sin! The wages of sin!'

CHAPTER IV

AT ALL COST, SLEEP!

DEAD! Before I knelt beside him and, after unbuttoning his coat, laid my hand on his breast, I knew the man was dead. Before I turned the lantern on his white face I knew who the man was. Sir Mervyn Ferrand had paid for his sin with his life! It needed little professional skill to determine the cause of his death. A bullet fired, it seemed to me, at close quarters had passed absolutely through the heart. He must have fallen without a moan. Killed, I knew, by the hand of the woman he had wronged.

A sneering smile yet lingered on his set features. I could even imagine the words which had accompanied it, when swift and sudden, without one moment's grace for repentance or confession, death had been meted out to him. At one moment he stood erect and full of life, mocking, it may be, her who had trusted him and had been betrayed; at the next, before the sentence he was speaking was completed, he lay lifeless at her feet, with the snowflakes beginning to form his winding-sheet!

Oh, it was vengeance! Swift, deadly vengeance! But why, oh why had she wreaked it? Philippa, my peerless Philippa, a murderess! Oh, it was too fearful, too horrible! I must be dreaming. All my own thoughts of revenge left me. It was for the time pity, sheer pity, I felt for the man, cut off in the prime of his life. Whilst I knew he was alive I could look forward to and picture that minute when we should stand coolly seeking to kill one another; but now that he was dead, I hated him no longer. Ah! Death is a sacred thing. Dead! Sir Mervyn Ferrand dead, and slain by Philippa!

It could not be true! It should not be true! Yet I shuddered as I remembered the passion she had thrown into those words, 'Basil, did you ever hate a man?' I gave a low cry of anguish as I remembered how I had hurled from me the pistol she had let fall—the very weapon which had done the dreadful deed.

Killed by Philippa! Not in a sudden burst of uncontrollable passion, but with deliberate intent. She must have gone armed to meet him. She must have shot him through the heart; must have seen him fall. Then, only then, the horrible deed which she had wrought must have been fully realised! Then she had turned and fled from the spot in a frenzy. Oh, my poor girl! My poor girl!

Utterly bewildered by my anguish, I rose from my knees and stood for a while beside the corpse. It was in that moment I learnt how much I really loved the woman who had done this thing. Over all my grief and horror this love rose paramount. At all cost I must save her—save her from the hands of justice; save her from the fierce elements which her tender frame was even at this moment braving. And as I recalled how she had sought me yesterday with the tale of her wrong— how she had wildly fled from me, a few minutes ago, madly, blindly into the night; as I thought of the injuries she had suffered, and which had led her to shed this man's blood; as I contrasted her in her present position with what she was when first I knew her and loved her, the pity began to fade from my heart; my thoughts towards the lifeless form at my feet grew stern and sombre, and I found myself beginning, by the old code of an eye for an eye, to justify, although I regretted, Philippa's fearful act. Right or wrong, she was the woman I loved; and I swore I would save her from the consequences of her crime, even—heaven help me!—if the accusation, when made, must fall upon my shoulders.

Yet it was not the beginning of any scheme to evade justice which induced me to raise the dead body and bear it to the side of the road, where I placed it under the low bank on which the hedge grew. It was the reverence which one pays to death made me do this. I could not leave the poor wretch bang in the very middle of the highway, for the first passer-by to stumble against. Tomorrow he would, of course, be found. Tomorrow the hue and cry would be out! Tomorrow Philippa, my Philippa, would—Oh, heavens! Never, never, never!

So I laid what was left of Sir Mervyn Ferrand reverentially by the side of the lonely road. I even tried to close his glassy eyes, and I covered his face with his own handkerchief. Then, with heart holding fear and anguish enough for a lifetime, I turned and went in search of the poor unhappy girl.

Where should I seek her? Who knew what her remorse may have urged her to do? Who knew whither her horror may have driven her? It needs but to find Philippa lifeless on the road to complete the heaviest tale of grief which can be exacted from one man in one short night! I clenched my teeth and rushed on.

I had the road all to myself. No one was abroad in such weather. Indeed, few persons were seen at night in any weather in this lonely part of the country. I made straight for my own house. The dismal thought came to me, that unless Philippa kept to the road she was lost to me for ever. If she strayed to the right or to the left, how on such a night could I possibly find her? My one hope was that she would go straight to my cottage; so thither I made the best of my way. If she had not arrived, I must get what assistance I could, and seek for her in the fields to the right and left of the road. It was a dreary comfort to remember that all the ponds and spaces of water were frozen six inches thick!

I hesitated a moment when I reached her late residence. Should I enquire if she had returned thither? No; when morning revealed the ghastly event of the night, my having done so would awake suspicion. Let me just go home.

Home at last! In a moment I shall know the worst. I opened the slide of my lantern, which was still alight, and threw the

rays on the path which led to my door. My heart gave a great
bound of thankfulness. There on the snow, not yet obliterated
by more recent flakes, were the prints of a small foot. Philippa,
as I prayed but scarcely dared to hope she might, had come
straight to my house.

My man opened the door to me. It was well I had seen
those footprints, as my knowledge of Philippa's arrival enabled
me to assume a natural air.

'My sister has come?' I asked.

'Yes, sir; about a quarter of an hour ago.'

'We missed each other on the road. What a night!' I said,
throwing off my snow-covered coat.

'Where is she now?' I asked.

'In the sitting-room, sir.' Then, lowering his voice, William
added, 'She seemed just about in a tantrum when she found
you weren't at home. I expect we shall find her a hard lady
to please.'

William, in spite of his stolidity, occasionally ventured upon
some liberty when addressing me.

His words greatly surprised me. I forced myself to make
some laughing rejoinder; then I turned the handle of the door
and entered the room in which Philippa had taken refuge.

Oh, how my heart throbbed! What would she say to me?
What could I, fresh from that dreadful scene, say to her? Would
she excuse or palliate, would she simply confess or boldly justify,
her crime? Would she plead her wrongs in extenuation? Would
she assert that in a moment of ungovernable rage she had done
the deed? No matter what she said, she was still Philippa, and
even at the cost of my own life and honour I would save her.

Yet as I advanced into the room a shudder ran through me.
Fresh to my mind came the remembrance of that white face,
that still form, lying as I had left it, with the pure white snow
falling thickly around it.

Philippa was sitting in front of the fire. Her hat was removed;
her dark hair dishevelled and gleaming wet with the snow

which had melted in it. She must have heard me enter and close the door, but she took no notice. As I approached her she turned her shoulder upon me in a pettish way, and as one who by the action means to signify displeasure. I came to her side and stood over her, waiting for her to look up and speak first. She must speak first! What can I say, after all that has happened tonight?

But she kept a stony silence—kept her eyes still turned from mine. At last I called her by her name, and, bending down, looked into her face.

Its expression was one of sullen anger, and, moreover, anger which seemed to deepen as she heard my voice. She made a kind of contemptuous gesture, as if waving me aside.

'Philippa,' I said, as sternly as I could, 'speak to me!'

I laid my hand upon her arm. She shook it off fiercely, and then started to her feet.

'You ask me to speak to you,' she said; 'you, who have treated me like this! Oh, it is shameful! Shameful! Shameful! I come through storm and snow—come to you, who were to welcome me as a brother! Where are you? Away, your wretched servant tells me. Why are you away? I trusted you! Oh, you are a pretty brother! If you had cared for me or respected me, you would have been here to greet me. No! You are all in a league—all in a league to ruin me! Now I am here, what will you do? Poison me, of course! Kill me, and make away with me, even as that other doctor killed and made away with my poor child! He did! I say he did! I saw him do it! "A child of shame," he said; so he killed it! All, all, all—even you—you, whom I trusted—leagued against me!'

She was trembling with excitement. Her words ran one into the other. It was as much as I could do to follow them; yet the above is but a brief condensation of what she said. With unchecked volubility she continued to heap reproaches and accusations, many of which were of the most extravagant and frivolous nature, on my head. At last she was silent, and re-seated herself in her former attitude; and the sullen, discontented, ill-used look again settled on her face.

And yet, although I, who loved her above all the world, was the object of her fierce reproaches, no words I had as yet listened to came more sweetly to my ear than these. A great joy swept through me; a tide of relief bore me to comparative happiness. Whatever dreadful deed the poor girl had that night accomplished, she was morally innocent. Philippa was not accountable for her actions!

As a doctor, I read the truth at once. The rapid flow of words, the changing moods, the vehement excitement, the sullen air, the groundless suspicions—one and all carried conviction, and told me what was wrong. Mrs Wilson's words of yesterday, which warned me that Philippa's health should be enquired into, added absolute certainty.

My professional brethren who may happen to read this will understand me when I say that, although it is long since I have practised as a doctor, I am sorely tempted, as I reach this stage of my story, to give in detail the particulars which induced me to arrive at such a belief. No physician, no surgeon, lives who does not feel it his duty as well as his pleasure to give an accurate account of any out-of-the-common case which has come under his notice. But I am not writing these pages for the benefit of science; and having no wish to make my tale assume the authority of a hospital report, shall restrain myself, and on technical points be as brief as possible.

In short, then, Philippa had fallen a victim to that mania which not uncommonly shows itself after the birth of a child—that dread, mysterious disease which may, at the moment when everything seems going well, turn a house of joy into a house of mourning; a disease the source of which I have no hesitation in saying has not yet been properly traced and investigated. So far as I know, there is no monograph on the subject, or certainly there was none at that time.

Still, it is admitted by all the authorities that this species of insanity is not unfrequently produced by a severe mental shock, especially when that shock is accompanied by an overwhelming sense of shame. Statistics show us that unmarried women who are mothers, and feel the degradation of such a position acutely, are peculiarly liable to be attacked by the mysterious malady. Esquirol was, I believe, the first to notice this fact, and the correctness of his view has subsequently been confirmed by many others.

Such being the case, it is small wonder that Philippa, waking yesterday morning to receive the intelligence that her marriage with Sir Mervyn Ferrand had been a farce, should have been thrown into a state extremely susceptible to the attack of the disease. Her careless exposure of herself to the wintry air, when last night she sought me and claimed my aid, most probably hastened the attack of the foe. Mrs Wilson had noticed her strange manner. I myself have remarked upon her rapid changes from calmness to excitability. It was clear to me that even when she visited me last night the mischief had begun to develop itself. I blamed my blindness bitterly. I ought to have seen what was wrong. Considering her agitated state, I ought to have been warned, and have taken precautions; but I had attributed those fitful changes, the meaning of which was now only too plain to me, to the natural agitation experienced by a passionate yet pure-minded woman, who found herself betrayed and brought to shame. Oh, had I but guessed the real cause, or rather the way in which her grief had affected her, all the dark work of that night might have been left undone!

Although in many ways it added to the difficulties and dangers which surrounded us, the discovery of the truth was an unspeakable relief to me. No right-minded man could now call the poor girl guilty of crime. The man's blood was indeed on her hands; yet she had shed it, not knowing what she did. Her frenzy must then have been at its height. The idea of his coming that night must in some way have occurred to her. The desire to see him must have driven her to go and meet him.

Her wrongs—perhaps the dread she now felt of him may have induced her to arm herself; perhaps she carried the weapon for self-protection. Anyway, she was mad when she started; she was mad when she drew the trigger; she was mad when she broke from my grasp; she was mad now as she sat by my fire, eyeing me with morose, suspicious glances. She was mad—and innocent!

Her manner towards me troubled me but little. It is a well-known peculiarity of the disease that the patient turns with hatred from those who were the nearest and dearest to her. Fits of sullen, stubborn silence, alternating with fierce outbursts of vituperation, are the most common characteristics of the mania. Piteous, startling as it is to see the change wrought in the sufferer, the malady is by no means of such an alarming nature as it seems. In fact the majority of cases are treated with perfect success.

But all this is professional talk. Again I say that the discovery of Philippa's state of mind was an immense relief to me. My conscience was cleared of a weight which was pressing upon it. I felt braced up to use every effort, and thoroughly justified in following whatever course I thought best. Moreover, a new relationship was now established between Philippa and myself. For a while every feeling save one must be banished. We were now doctor and patient.

After much persuasion, I induced her to let me feel her pulse. As I expected, I found it up nearly to 120. This did not alarm me much, as in the course of my practice I had seen several of these cases. The preliminary treatment was simple as A B C; at all cost sleep must be obtained.

Fortunately, I had a well-stocked medicine-chest. In a few minutes I had prepared the strongest dose of opium which I dared to administer. In such a case as the present I knew that no driblets would avail; so I measured out no less than sixty drops of laudanum.

Sleep the girl must have. That poor seething, boiling brain must by artificial means be forced to rest for hours. After that rest I should be able to say what chance there was of saving life and reason.

But preparing a dose of medicine, and making a patient like this take it, are two different things. I tried every art, every persuasion. I implored and commanded. I threatened and insisted. Philippa was obdurate. Poor soul! She knew I meant to poison her. On my part, I knew that unless she swallowed that narcotic tonight, her case was all but hopeless.

I rested for a while; then I sent for lukewarm water. After some resistance she suffered me to bathe her throbbing temples. The refreshing coolness which followed the operation was so grateful to her that she let me repeat the action again and again. A softer and more contented look settled on her beautiful face.

I seized the moment. Once more I pressed the potion upon her. This time successfully. My heart trembled with joy as I saw her swallow the drug. Now she might be saved!

I still continued the comforting laving of her temples, and waited until the drug took its due effect. By-and-by that moment came. The large dark eyes closed, the weary head sank heavily on my shoulder, and I knew that Philippa had entered upon a term of merciful oblivion.

I waited until her sleep was sound as the sleep of death; then I summoned my man. I had already told him that my sister was very ill. Between us we bore her to her room and laid her on the bed. I loosened her dress, cut the wet boots from her cold feet; did all I could to promote warmth and such comfort as was possible under the circumstances. Then I left her, sleeping that heavy sleep which I prayed might last unbroken for hours, and hours, and hours.

CHAPTER V

A WHITE TOMB

FROM the moment when the true state of Philippa's mind flashed upon me, to the moment when I left her sleeping that heavy sleep, I had little time to think of anything else than the best means of saving her life, and, if possible, her reason. True, throughout the whole of my operations to effect this end, a dim sort of horror pervaded me—a recollection of the ghastly object which lay on the roadside, some three miles from us; but it was not until I turned from my patient's door that the terrible situation in which she was placed presented itself to me in all its dread entirety. Half broken-hearted, I threw myself wearily into my chair, and covered my face with my hands.

What was to be done? What was to be done? Tomorrow morning the body would be found. I felt certain that when enquiry was made suspicion would at once point towards Philippa. Mrs Wilson knew of her starting from home in the evening, alone and on foot. She knew, moreover, that Sir Mervyn Ferrand was her husband; that he had ill-used her. She would most certainly know to whom Philippa had fled. It did not follow that because I was ignorant as to who were my neighbours they knew nothing about me. At any rate, William, my man, would know the truth. So far as I could see, tomorrow or, by the latest, the next day Philippa would be arrested for the crime. Most probably, I also should be included in the arrest. For that I seemed to care nothing; except that it might hinder me from helping my poor girl.

Any hope of removing Philippa—there, put it in plain words—any hope of flight, for days, even weeks, was vain. Let everything go as well as can be in such cases, the girl must

47

be kept in seclusion and quiet for at least a fortnight or three weeks. I groaned as I thought of what would happen if Philippa was arrested and carried before the magistrates, accused of the awful crime. From that moment until the day of her death she would be insane.

Yet, what help was there for it? The moment the deed is known—the moment Mrs Wilson learns that Sir Mervyn Ferrand has been found shot through the heart, she will let it be known that Lady Ferrand is at hand; and Lady Ferrand, who has been passing under the name of Mrs Farmer, will be sought, and found. And then—and then!

Even if she did not die at once—even if she recovered—oh, the shame of the trial! No jury could or would convict her; but for Philippa, my queen, to stand in the dock, to plead for her life. To know that, whether convicted or acquitted, the deed was done by her. To know that all England is talking of her wrongs and her vengeance. Horrible! Horrible! It shall never be. Rather will I give her a draught of opium heavy enough to close her eyes for ever. There will be plenty more of the drug left for me!

Fool that I was! Why did I do things by halves? Why, for her sake, did I not hide the dead man where none would find him? Why did I not rifle his pockets, so that suspicion should have pointed to a vulgar murderer; someone who had killed him for mere plunder? Why did I not, at least, destroy any letters or papers which were about him? Identification might then have been rendered difficult, and perhaps been delayed for weeks. In that time I might have saved her.

Why do I not do this now? I started to my feet; then sank back into my chair. No; not even for Philippa's sake could I go again to that spot. If I did so, I should return as mad as she is now.

Not being able to bring myself to adopt the gruesome alternative, I could do nothing, save wait events—nothing, at least, to avert the consequences of her delirious act.

But for her something must be done. How could she, in her frenzied state, be left here—her only companions two men? Nurses must be at once procured. I summoned William, and told him he must go to London by the first train in the morning.

William would have received my instructions to go to the Antipodes with imperturbability. He merely expressed a doubt as to whether anyone would be able to get to London tomorrow on account of the snow. I walked to the window and looked out.

The night was still one mad whirl of snowflakes. The window-panes were half-covered by such as managed to find a resting-place there. As I watched what I could see of the wild white dance, I found myself thinking that by now that dead man on the road must be covered an inch deep—must have lost shape and outline. I shivered as I turned away.

'They are sure to keep the line to town open,' I said. 'If you can get to Roding, you can get to London.'

'Oh, I can get to Roding right enough!' said William.

Then I told him what he was to do. He was to take a letter to one of the Nursing Institutions, and bring back two nurses with him. No matter what the weather was when they reached Roding, they were to come to my house at once, even if they had to hire twenty horses to drag them there. He was also to get me a few drugs which I might want.

William said no more. He nodded, to show that he understood me; and I knew that if it were possible to do my bidding it would be done.

Of his own accord he then brought me food. I ate, for I knew that I should want all my strength to support the anxieties of the next day or two.

I stayed up the whole night. Oh, that awful night! Shall I ever forget it? The solitude—the raging snow-storm outside—the poor creature, to whose side I crept noiselessly every half an hour. She lay there with a face like marble, calm and beautiful. The long, dark lashes swept her pale cheek. The only movement was the regular rise and fall of the bosom. Oh, happy oblivion! Oh, dreaded wakening! As I looked at her, in spite of the love I bore her, I believe that, had I thought such a prayer would be answered, I should for her sake have prayed that those lashes might never again be lifted.

Morning at last broke on my dreary vigil. Philippa still slept. I returned to the sitting-room and drew back the curtains from the window. Yes; it was morning—such morning as leaden, wintry skies can give. It was still snowing as heavily, if not more heavily, than it had snowed last night. For twelve hours the flakes had fallen without intermission.

There was little wind now; it had dropped, I knew, about an hour ago. The world, so far as I could see, was clad in white; but the snow lay unevenly. The wind had blown it into drifts. On my garden path its depth might be counted by inches; against my garden wall, by feet.

William now made his appearance. He prepared some breakfast for himself, and then, having done justice to it, started for Roding. It occurred to me that he might be the first to find the object which lay on the roadside.

Except that so doing might delay him and cause him to miss his train, this mattered little. I was now calmly awaiting the inevitable. Someone must make the discovery. However, as I wanted the nurses, I said to him:

'Remember, this is life and death. Nothing must stop you.' He touched his hat in a reassuring manner, and tramped off through the snow.

I returned to my patient's bedside, and sat watching her, and waiting for her to awake. She had now slept for nearly eleven hours, and I knew that return to life might take place at any moment. I longed for, and yet I dreaded, her awakening. When the effects of the opiate were gone, how should I find her? Alas! I knew that the chances were a thousand to one that her brain would still be full of strange delusions; that she would turn from me, as she turned last night, with loathing and anger. But my greatest fear was that she would, upon coming to herself, or rather to her poor insane self, be conscious of the act she had accomplished. It was the fear of this which made me wish that the opium would hold her in its drowsy grasp for hours longer.

This wish was granted. Hour after hour I sat by her motionless form. Now and again I glanced from the beautiful, senseless face, and looking out of the window saw the snow still falling. Would my messenger ever be able to reach town; if he did so, would he be able to return? I was bound to have a woman's aid. The presence of the roughest daughter of the plough would be welcome to me when Philippa awoke. And it was now time she did so.

Although I felt her pulse almost every other minute, and could find no reason for alarm, I am bound to say that her long sleep, protracted far beyond any I had in my experience seen produced by the exhibition of narcotics, rendered me very uneasy. I shall, I am sure, scarcely be credited when I say that Philippa's unconsciousness lasted for sixteen hours—from half-past nine at night to half-past one on the following afternoon. I began then to think the duration abnormal, and determined to take some steps towards arousing her.

But I was spared the responsibility. She stirred on the couch. Her head turned languidly on the pillow. Her dark eyes opened, closed, and opened again. She looked at me in a dazed manner, not at first seeming to know me, or to understand why I was near her, or where she was. A prey to the wildest anxiety, I leaned over her, and waited until she spoke.

Little by little her bewilderment seemed to leave her. Her eyes rested with curious enquiry upon mine. 'Basil,' she said, faintly, but in a tone of surprise, 'you here! Where am I?'

'Under my roof—your brother's roof,' I said.

'Ah! I remember,' she said, with a deep sigh. Then she closed her eyes, and once more seemed to sleep.

What did she remember? It seemed to me too great a mercy to expect that those hours of oblivion had effected a cure, but my hope was that she did not remember what had happened when she met Sir Mervyn Ferrand on the road. I was almost trembling with excitement. I was longing to really know in what state her mind was. Besides, I thought she had slept as long as was good for her. I took her hands and called her by name.

Once more she opened her eyes. They expressed no fear of me, no dislike to me. They conveyed no reproach. They were calm, sad, weary, but gave no evidence of any mental disorder.

'Have I been ill long, Basil?' she asked.

'Not very long. You are going to get better soon.'

'I came to your house, did I not?'

'Yes; and here I mean to keep you. Do you feel weak?'

'Very weak. Basil, I have dreamt such horrible things.'

'You have been feverish and delirious. People like that always fancy strange things.'

She was indeed as weak as a child; but for the time, at least, she was perfectly sane. I could have cried for joy as I heard her faint but collected words. I ventured to hope that I had before me one of those very rare cases—such as I had seen described, but had not as yet met with—where the patient awakes from the long, artificially produced sleep perfectly free from all maniacal symptoms. If this were so with Philippa, if the return of reason were to be permanent, I knew that a few weeks' careful nursing and judicious treatment might quite restore her to health. Even as this comforting thought came to me, I remembered the peril in which she stood. Tomorrow—aye, even today—the thing which I dreaded might happen, and sweep away all the good the narcotic had done her.

She was now fully awake, and perfectly quiet. I gave her some refreshment; then, seeing she was lying in peaceful silence, I thought it better to leave her. As I quitted her room I drew down the blind, fearing that the whirling snow might bring recollections which it was my one wish to keep from invading her mind.

The long dreary day wore away. The light faded, and another night began. Philippa still lay calm, silent, and almost apathetic. I did nothing to rouse her. I went to her side as seldom as possible. I feared that her seeing me might recall the events of the last night, and that recollections so awakened might destroy all the good which I felt sure had been accomplished by the long hours of oblivion and quiet. Could I have deputed the task to another, I would not have even shown myself to my patient. Most anxiously, as evening came, I awaited the appearance of my faithful William and the nurses.

Would they be able to reach us in such weather? It was still snowing fiercely. For more than twenty-four hours the mad white revel had continued without intermission. Indeed, that storm which burst upon the world as I turned from Philippa's house on the preceding night is now historical; it was the beginning of the heaviest and longest fall which the record of fifty years can show. For two nights and a day the snow came down in what may almost be called drifting masses. During that dismal day I saw from my window the heaps against the wall grow deeper and deeper, and even in my preoccupied state of mind found myself marvelling at the sustained fury of the storm.

At eleven o'clock at night I sadly gave up all hope of the much-needed assistance arriving. After all, it seemed that William had found it impossible to fight against the weather; so I made my preparations for another night of solitary watchfulness. I was all but worn out with fatigue; yet I dared not sleep. If the mania returned, what might happen, were I not at hand to restrain Philippa's actions? My hope that the madness had really left my patient, not, if she were properly treated, to return, was a growing one, but not yet strong enough to allow me to leave her for any length of time.

My delight then may be imagined when, looking for the hundredth time up the road, I saw close at hand two flashing lights, and knew that William, the faithful, had done my bidding.

In a few minutes two respectable women from one of the best of the London Nursing Institutions were within my walls.

The train had, of course, been late, very late. At one or two places on the line it had almost given up the battle, and settled down quietly until dug out; but steam and iron had conquered, and at last it did get to Roding. There William, knowing my dire necessity, offered such a magnificent bribe that he soon found an enterprising carriage proprietor who was willing to make the attempt to force two horses and a carriage over the six miles of road between Roding and my house. The attempt was successful, although the rate of progression was slow; and William triumphantly ushered his charges into my presence.

After giving them time for rest and refreshment, I explained the nature of the case, set out the treatment I wished to be adopted, and then led them to Philippa. I left the poor girl in their charge for the night, then went to take the sleep of which I stood so much in need.

But before going to bed I saw William. I dreaded to hear him say what gruesome sight he had seen that morning; yet I was bound to learn if the deed had yet been made public.

'Did you manage to get to Roding all right this morning?' I asked with assumed carelessness.

'I managed all right, sir,' said William, cheerfully.

'Snow deep on the road?'

'Not so deep as I fancied 'twould be. All drifted and blown up to one side, like. I never seen such a thing. Drift must have been feet deep this morning. What must it be now, I wonder? Something like the Arctic regions, I should think, sir!'

For the first time for hours and hours, a ray of hope flashed across me. William had walked that lonely road this morning, and noticed nothing except the drifted snow! I remembered how I had placed the dead man in the little hollow at the bottom of the bank. Could it be that the kindly, merciful snow, which I have already described as beginning to form his winding-sheet, had hidden and buried him? That a pure white shapeless heap, which told no tales, concealed for a while the dark deed from the world? Oh that Philippa were well enough to leave this place tomorrow! We might fly, and leave no trace behind us. She might never know what she had done in her madness. The fearful secret would be mine alone. A burden it would be, but one which I might easily find strength enough to bear. Bear it! I could bear it, and be happy; for something told me that, could I but save her from the peril which menaced her, Philippa and I would part no more in this world until death, the only conqueror of such love as mine, swept us asunder.

Once more I looked out into the night. Still the snowflakes whirled down. Oh, brave, kind snow! Fall, fall, fall! Pile the masses on the dead wretch. Hide him deep in your bosom. Fall for weeks, for months, for ever! Save my love and me!

CHAPTER VI

THE SECRET KEPT

IT is needless to say that when I awoke the next morning my first thought was of Philippa: but my first action was to go to my window and look at the skies. My heart sank within me as I saw that the snow had ceased falling, and the wintry sun was shining. I threw up the sash; the cold air cut me like a knife. I gathered up a handful of snow from the window-sill. It crumbled in my fingers like tooth-powder. I guessed at once that a hard black frost had succeeded the snow. I ran downstairs and glanced at the thermometer outside my sitting-room window. It registered twelve degrees of frost. My spirits rose; I felt that Philippa would be saved. The wind was due east: so long as it stayed there the frost would last, and that white tomb on the roadside hide the secret of the dreadful night.

I found, moreover, that Philippa's condition was all that could, under the circumstances, be hoped for. Since she had awakened from that long sleep into which the opiate had plunged her there had been no recurrence of the delusions; no symptoms which gave me any alarm. She was, of course, weak in body, but quite quiet and collected. She spoke but little, and the few words which she did speak had no bearing on forbidden or disturbing subjects.

Day after day went by, and still the brave black frost held the world in its iron grip, and kept the secret of the night. Morning after morning I woke to find the wind still blowing from the east, the skies clear and showing every evidence of a long spell of hard weather. A presentiment that we should be saved was now firmly established in my mind. The heavens themselves seemed to be shielding us and working for us.

I have not given the year in which these things occurred; but many who can remember that mighty fall of snow, and the time which the frost kept it on the earth, will be able to fix the date. Since that year there has been no weather like it.

Day by day Philippa grew better and stronger. I spare you, as I promised to, all description which is not absolutely necessary of my treatment of my patient, and all technical summary of the case; but before many days had gone by I knew that, as I hoped, I had to deal with one of those rare instances in which the balance of the mind is restored by forced sleep, and the complete restoration of health is but a matter of time and care.

As soon as it became a certainty that all danger to life or reason was at an end, I began to consider what course to adopt. The moment she was well enough to risk the journey, or even, if a thaw set in, before then, Philippa must fly from the scene of the tragedy in which she had played so terrible, yet morally irresponsible, a part. We must put lands and seas between ourselves and the fatal spot. But how to persuade her that such flight was absolutely necessary? Brother and sister as we now termed ourselves, would she ever consent to accompany me abroad? Had I the right to put the woman I loved in such an equivocal position? No! A thousand times no! And yet I knew there was no safety for her in England; and with whom could she leave England save with me?

I dared not urge upon her my true reason for flight. It was my greatest hope that the events of that night had left her mind when the madness left her, never to be recalled. And now time was pressing; ten days had passed by. The glorious frost still kept our counsel, but it could not last for ever. 'The time must come when the white heaps of snow would melt and vanish away, and then Sir Mervyn Ferrand's cold dead face would appear, and tell the tale of his death to the first passer-by.

I had scarcely quitted the house since that night. Yet one day a kind of morbid fascination had led me to walk along the road towards Roding, and to halt at what I judged to be

the spot where I laid the dead man by the side of the road. I
fancied I could single out the very drift under which that
awful thing lay, and a dreary temptation to probe the white
heap with my stick, and make sure, assailed me. I resisted it,
and turned away from the spot.

There was a certain amount of traffic on the road. By now
the snow had been beaten down by cart-wheels and people's
feet, so that it was quite possible to walk from one place
to another. As I reached the house from which Philippa fled to
seek refuge with me, I encountered Mrs Wilson. I was going
to pass without any sign of recognition, but she stopped me.

'I thought you were going to take your sister away?' she said.

'Lady Ferrand was unfortunately taken very ill when she left
you. She is now hardly well enough to be moved.'

'Has she heard from Sir Mervyn?' asked Mrs Wilson,
abruptly.

'Not to my knowledge,' I replied.

'It is strange. You know, I suppose, that he was expected at
my house that night?'

'Certainly I do. It was for that reason my sister left you.'

Mrs Wilson looked at me thoughtfully. 'She will not meet
him again?'

'Never,' I said, thinking as I spoke that my words bore a
meaning only known to myself.

'Does she hate him?' she asked, suddenly.

'She has been cruelly wronged,' I said, evasively.

She laid her hand on my arm. 'Listen,' she said. 'If I thought
she hated him, I would see her before she leaves, and tell her
something. If I thought he hated her, I would tell him. I will
wait and see.'

She turned away and walked on, leaving me to make the best
of her enigmatical words. She was evidently a strange woman,
and I felt more sure than ever was in some way mixed up with
Sir Mervyn Ferrand's early life. I had a great mind to follow
her and demand an explanation, but caution told me that the

less I said to her the better. It was from this woman's knowledge of the relationship between Philippa and the dead man that, when the secret of the night was laid bare, the greatest danger must arise.

After walking a few paces, Mrs Wilson turned and came back to me. 'Give me an address,' she said; 'I may want to write to you.'

I hesitated; then I told her that any letters sent to my bankers in London would reach me sooner or later. It was too soon to excite suspicion by concealment of one's movements.

It was after I had gazed at that white tomb by the roadside that my impatience to remove Philippa grew fiercer and fiercer. Moreover, I had at last made up my mind what to do with my precious charge. As soon as she was well enough to bear the journey, I resolved to take her to London, and place her in the hands of one of the truest, noblest, tenderest women in the world, my mother.

She was in London, waiting for me to join her. I had written, telling her that the serious illness of a friend prevented me from leaving my home for some days. Now I resolved to go to her, and tell her all Philippa's sad tale—all save the one dark chapter of which she herself, I hoped, knew nothing. I would take her to my mother. I would tell my mother how I loved her; I would appeal to her love for me, and ask her to take my poor stricken girl to her heart, even as she would take a daughter; and I dared to hope that, if only for my sake, my prayer would be granted.

Philippa was by now thoroughly convalescent. As I lay down my pen for a moment and think of that time, with its fears and troubles, it is a marvel to me that I could have dared to wait so long before moving her from the neighbourhood. I can only attribute my lingering to the sense of fatality that all would go right, or to the professional instinct which forbade me urging a patient to do anything which might retard recovery; but the time had at last come.

Save for her quiet and subdued manner, my love was almost her old self again. Her words and manner to me were tender, affectionate and sisterly. I need hardly say that during that time no word crossed my lips which I would have recalled. Love, if not the thought of it, I had laid aside until happier days dawned; for—I say it advisedly, and at risk of censure—Philippa was to me pure and innocent as on the day when first we met. If her hands were stained with the blood of Sir Mervyn Ferrand, she knew it not. Her wrongs had goaded her to madness, and her madness was responsible for the act, not she herself.

The man's name never crossed her lips. For all she spoke of him he might never have existed, or, at the most, been but a part of a forgotten dream. As soon as she was well enough to rise from her bed, and I could for hours enjoy her society, we talked of many things; but never of Sir Mervyn Ferrand and the immediate past.

But, nevertheless, there were times when her look distressed me. Now and again I found her gazing at me with anxious, troubled eyes, as if trying to read something which I was hiding from her. Once she asked me how she came to my house that night.

'Out of the whirling snow,' I said as lightly as I could. 'You came in a high state of fever and delirium.'

'Where had I been? What had I been doing?'

'You came straight from Mrs Wilson's, I suppose. I know no more.'

Then she sighed, and turned her head away; but I soon found her troubled dark eyes again fixed on my own. I could do nothing but meet their gaze bravely, and pray that my poor love might never, never be able to fill those hours which were at present a blank to her.

At last, exactly a fortnight from the fatal day, we left my home. I was now what is legally termed an accessory after the act, and was making every effort to save the poor girl from justice. In order to avert suspicion, I decided it was better not to shut up my house; so I left the faithful William to take care of it, and await my instructions. At present it was advisable that any enquirers should learn that I had gone to London with my sister, and that the time of our return was uncertain. By-and-by, if all went well, I could get rid of my cottage in an ordinary way. I, for one, should never wish to visit the place again.

Philippa acquiesced in all my arrangements. She was quite willing to accompany me to town. She trusted me with childish simplicity. 'But, Basil, afterwards—what afterwards?' she asked.

Even in the midst of the menacing peril it was all I could do to refrain from kneeling at her feet and telling her that my love would solve the question of the future.

'I have a surprise for you in London,' I said, as cheerfully as I could. 'Trust yourself to me; you will not regret it.'

She took my hand. 'Whom else have I to trust?' she said simply. 'Basil, you have been very good to me. I have made your life miserable; it is too late to atone; but I shall never forget these days.'

Her eyes were full of tears. I kissed her hand reverently, and told her that when I saw the old smile back upon her lips, all I had done would be a thousand times repaid; but as I spoke I trembled at the thought of what might be in store for both of us.

We drove to Roding, and were perforce obliged to take the road which passed by Mrs Wilson's house. Philippa half rose from her seat, and seemed to be on the point of asking me some question; but she changed her mind, and relapsed into silence. I felt a horrible dread lest the roadside objects and landmarks should awaken recollection, and my heart beat violently as we neared the white heap by the hedge, that heap which I believed held our secret. I felt that I grew deadly pale. I was forced to turn my head away and look out of the opposite window. My state of mind was not made easier by knowing that Philippa was gazing at me with that troubled look in her eyes. Altogether I felt that the strain was becoming too much for me, and I began to wonder if my life would ever again know a happy or secure moment.

After a long silence Philippa spoke. 'Tell me, Basil; have you heard from that man?'

I shook my head.

'Where is he? He was coming that night. Did he come?'

'I suppose not. Why do you ask?'

'Basil, a kind of horrible dream haunts me. There was something I dreamed of that fearful night, something I dream of now. Tell me what it was.'

The perspiration rose to my brow. 'Dearest,' I said, 'no wonder you dream. You are well now, but that night you were quite out of your senses. Your fancies are but the remains of that delirium. Think no more of that wretch; he is probably living in Paris, after the manner of his kind. Think only that life is going to be calm and happy.'

Anything to keep the knowledge of her fatal act from her! I forced myself to talk in a light, cheerful manner. I jested at the appearance of the few muffled-up country people whom we passed on the road. I pointed out the beauty of the trees on the wayside, each branch of which bore foliage of glistening snow. I did all I could to turn her thoughts into other channels—to drive that strange questioning look from her eyes. Right glad I felt when we were at last in the train, and the first stage of our flight an accomplished fact.

Upon reaching London, I drove straight to the hotel at which my mother was staying. It was one of those high-priced respectable private hotels in Jermyn Street. I engaged rooms for my sister and myself. I sent Philippa to her room to rest, and then went to find my mother. In another minute I was in her arms, and ere half an hour was over I had told her Philippa's story, and my love for the woman on whose behalf I besought her protection.

Yes, I had done right to trust to her. I knew her noble nature; her utter freedom from the petty trammels of society. I knew the love she bore her son. Let me here thank her once more for what she did for me that day.

She heard all my outpourings in silence. I told her all, save two things—the name of the man who had wronged my love, and the fate which had overtaken him. I told her, as I have told you, how I had loved—how I loved Philippa; how I now dared to hope that in time to come my love would be rewarded. I prayed her to take my poor girl to her heart, and by treating her as a daughter restore, if it were possible, her self-respect.

My mother heard me. Her sweet face grew a shade paler. Her lips quivered, and the tears stood in her eyes. I knew all that was passing through her mind. I knew how proud she was of me, and what great things she had hoped I should do in the world. She was a woman, and, woman-like, had counted upon her son's bettering himself by marriage; but, in spite of all this, I knew I was right in counting upon her aid. Once again, my sweet mother, I thank you.

She rose. 'Let me see the woman you love. Where is she? I will go to her.'

'She is here, in this house. Ah, mother, I knew you would do this for me.'

She kissed my forehead. 'Bring her to me,' she said.

I went out, and sent word to Philippa that I wanted her. She soon came to me. She had removed the stains of travel, and, although pale, looked the perfection of graceful beauty. I led her to my mother's room. She stopped short as she saw it was tenanted by a lady. A quick blush crossed her cheek.

'Philippa, dearest,' I said, 'this is my mother. I have told her all, and she is waiting to welcome you.'

Still she stood motionless, save that her head bent down and her bosom heaved. My mother came to her side, and, placing her kind arms round her, whispered some words which I neither heard nor tried to hear. Philippa broke into a storm of sobs, and for some moments wept on my mother's shoulder.

Then she raised her head and looked at me, and my heart

leapt at the expression in her tearful eyes. 'Basil, my brother, you are too good to me!' she ejaculated.

My mother led her to the sofa, and, with her arms still round her, sat down by her side. I left them, knowing that my love had now the truest, noblest heart to sob against; the quickest, most sympathetic ear to listen to the tale of her wrongs; and the softest, kindest voice to soothe and console her.

Ah! How happy I should have felt, could that one night's dark work have been undone—could that white tomb for ever hold its ghastly secret!

CHAPTER VII

THE MELTING OF THE SNOW

THE first stage of our flight towards safety accomplished, I sat down to once more review the situation, and to take such counsel as I could give myself. I endeavoured to foreshadow the consequences of the inevitable discovery of Sir Mervyn Ferrand's death. I tried calmly to ascertain in what quarter the danger of discovery was situated, and how best to guard against or turn aside the peril.

Undoubtedly the chief person to fear was Mrs Wilson. She alone knew that the man intended to reach Roding that night. She alone knew in what relation, or supposed relation, he stood to Philippa. The very night of his death would be fixed by the snow-storm; and I felt sure that as soon as the dead man was identified Mrs Wilson could not fail to associate her quest's sudden departure and subsequent illness with the terrible event. The moment she revealed what she knew or suspected, suspicion must point to the right person, and pursuit must at once follow. My heart grew sick, as, think how I would, I could see no loop-hole by which to escape from this danger.

About secondary things I troubled but little. Upon calm reconsideration, I did not believe that my stolid William would for a moment jump at the right conclusion. If he were led to suspect either of us, it would be me, not Philippa; and I well knew that he was so much attached to me that, although he felt certain I had done the deed, he would feel equally certain that I had good and proper reasons for doing it, and no word to my detriment would pass his reticent lips. No, there was little to fear from William.

I blamed myself deeply for the impulse which had urged me to hurl the fatal weapon away. Why did I not keep it and bury it fathoms deep? If that pistol were found, it would possibly furnish a clue which might be followed up, and undo everything. My only hope was that I had thrown it to some spot where it might lie for years undiscovered, until all association between it and the murder had disappeared.

To sum up briefly, I was bound to decide that the damning circumstantial evidence which could be furnished by Mrs Wilson drove me back to my original idea. There was no chance of my poor Philippa's remaining unaccused or unsuspected of the deed she had unwittingly done; so her only hope of safety—indeed, considering all, I may also say my only hope of safety—was rapid flight. We must gain some land in which we could dwell without fear of being arrested. What land was there?

Many a one. The date of my story is before 1873, when nearly all the extradition treaties were made. At that time such treaties existed with only two foreign countries, France and the United States; so that our choice of a resting-place was not so limited as those who are flying from the clutches of the law find it today. However, in order to make certain, I paid a visit to a legal friend of mine; and, by quoting a supposititious case, managed to acquire a good deal of information respecting the dealings of one nation with another, so far as fugitives were concerned.

I found that although, with the two exceptions above-named, there was no settled international law on the subject, there was a kind of unwritten substitute, which was known by the name of the Comity of Nations. Under this code of courtesy, a notorious criminal, who had sought refuge in the arms of another country was not uncommonly, although there was no law under which he could be arrested, given up to his pursuers, by being simply driven across the frontier of the country in which he had hoped to find security. However, I gathered that this so-called comity was scarcely expected to be exercised by the most friendly state, unless the fugitive had fled almost red-handed, and so placed his guilt beyond doubt. No one exactly knew how far this obliging expulsion might be counted upon. It was generally supposed to be decided by the amount of influence or persuasion which one government exercised on the other.

This information rather upset my preconceived ideas as to the ease with which safety might be obtained; but reflection told me I had little to fear. The case against Philippa could be nothing more than one of suspicion. No one, not even I myself, had seen the deed done. A warrant would, no doubt, be issued for her arrest; but if our flight precluded its execution, I did not believe that any government would put itself out of the way to aid the English law. There was no one, save myself, who could positively swear that Sir Mervyn Ferrand had been killed by Philippa.

I learned that Spain was then, even as it is now, the land safest against English law. Perhaps the reason is that the grave, yet at times hot-blooded, Spaniard reckons human life at a lower value than more northernly nations. Anyway, it was to Spain that I turned my eyes; Spain that I resolved to reach without an hour's unenforced delay.

The very next day I broached the subject of foreign travel to my mother. Although so short a time had passed since they first met, I was overjoyed to see the terms upon which she and Philippa stood. The girl seemed to cling to her as to a natural protector—seemed ready to install her in the place of the mother she had lost. After all, the love of her own sex is indispensable to a woman's happiness. It did my heart good to see the two together. Philippa talked to my mother as she had never yet talked to me; and I knew that when the day came upon which I should ask for the only reward I wanted, my mother's kindness to the forsaken and shame-stricken girl would be an advocate that pleaded strongly in favour of my suit.

But, could it ever be? Could we know happiness in the face

of that dark night's work? Ah me! My heart sank as I thought that any day might bring the crushing blow. Let there be no delay. Let me not blame myself hereafter for any negligence or false security. Let us away from the peril.

'Mother,' I said, 'will you come abroad with Philippa and me?'

'Abroad, Basil! I have only just come home.'

'No matter; come with us at once. Let us go to some place where there is warmth and bright sunshine. Let us go to Spain.'

'Spain! Why Spain? Besides, surely Philippa is not fit for a long journey!'

'It will do her good. Her recollections of this country are but sad ones.'

'Well, in a week or two I will see about it.'

'No, at once. Let us start tomorrow or the next day. Mother, I ask it as a favour.'

'Give me some good reason, Basil, and I will do as you wish.'

'Look at me, and you will see the reason. Cannot you see that I am ill, worn out, nervous? I must have a change, and at once.'

She gazed at me with solicitude. 'Yes, I know you are not well; but why Spain?'

'A whim—a sick man's fancy. Perhaps because it is Philippa's father's country put it into my head. Mother, tell me, how do you like her?'

'She is the woman you love; she is very beautiful; she has been cruelly treated; she is blameless; to say more after so short an acquaintance would be exaggeration.'

'You will come to Spain with me—with her?'

She kissed me and gave in to my whim. Then I sought Philippa.

'My mother is going to take us abroad,' I said with a smile, which was forced, as all my smiles now were. 'She will see to everything for you.'

'She is kind—she is sweet,' said Philippa, clasping her

hands. 'Basil, I am beginning to worship your mother. But why are we going abroad?'

'To get away from sad thoughts, for one thing; for another, because I feel ill.'

She gave me a quick look of apprehension which brought the flush to my cheek. 'Oh, let us go at once!' she cried. 'Let us leave this land of ice, and I will nurse you and make you well. Where are we going? When are we going?'

'To Spain—tomorrow or the next day.'

She looked at me with the troubled gaze which I had so often noticed. 'Basil,' she said, 'you are doing this for my sake.'

'And my own, I fear.'

'I threw away your love—I spoilt your life. I came to you a shamed woman. You saved me! You did not scorn me. You brought me to your mother's arms. Basil, may God requite you: I never can.'

She burst into tears, and left the room hastily.

It was well I settled the matter of the foreign journey then. That afternoon the wind changed and a thaw set in—a thaw that slowly but surely drew away the thick white veil which covered the whole of England.

That night I had little sleep. I could do nothing but lie awake and picture that white tomb slowly melting away, until the white face beneath peered out of it and made the dread secret known to all. Who would be the first to discover it? Doubtless some country man or woman passing that way in the grey of the morning. I drew pictures of the discoverer's horror—the shriek of terror he or she would give. I scarcely dared to close my eyes; for I knew that if I dreamed, my dreams would take me to stand over the snowdrift, and force me to watch it melting away! It seemed to me that until Philippa was out of the range of pursuit I should not sleep again.

Faster and faster, now it had once begun, the thaw went on. Warm wind, heavy rain the next day, helped it. That tremendous fall of snow had, indeed, been the last effort of the winter. I dreaded what I might see in the morning's papers.

For it was the third day from that on which I spoke about going abroad; yet we were still in London. When it really came to making preparations for the projected trip, there were a thousand and one things to be done. There was the needful passport to be obtained; my mother had many purchases to make for both Philippa and herself. She was now fully contented with the prospect of a long sojourn on the continent; but she liked travelling in comfort, and objected very much to being hurried. So it was that, in spite of the pressing need for immediate flight, we were still in London.

The dangerous delay made me nervous, excitable and ill tempered. This state of mind was not without benefit to our cause, as my manner as well as my looks fully convinced my mother that my own health was the sole object of the journey. So, like a good creature, she set to work in thorough earnest to get everything ready for our departure.

Tomorrow morning we were to start. I prayed heaven that it might not be too late; that the next twenty-four hours might pass without what I dreaded taking place. For I knew that by now that ghastly object on the roadside must be lying with the light of day on its pale face!

With an effort I opened the morning's paper, and ran hastily up and down the columns. What cared I for politics, foreign news, or money-market intelligence? Here was the one paragraph which riveted all my attention. The white tomb had given up its secret! Read! To me those words were written in letters of fire!

'HORRIBLE DISCOVERY NEAR RODING

'The melting of the snow has brought to light what to all appearances is a fearful crime. Yesterday afternoon a labourer walking on the highway discovered the body of a gentleman lying by the roadside. His death had been caused by a pistol-shot. It is supposed that it must have occurred on the night of the great snow-storm, and that the body has lain ever since under the snow, which had drifted to the depth of some feet. The facts that death must have been instantaneous, and that no weapon can be found near the spot, do away with the theory of suicide. Letters and papers found upon the corpse tend to show it to be that of Sir Mervyn Ferrand, Bart. The unfortunate gentleman's friends have been communicated with, and the inquest will be opened tomorrow.'

For some minutes I sat like one stunned. Inevitable as it was that the discovery should be made, the shock seemed scarcely lightened by the foreknowledge; the danger seemed no less terrible. Oh, that we had started yesterday—were even to start today! What might not happen before tomorrow morning! My first impulse was to go to my mother and beg her to hasten our departure; but reflection showed me how unwise this course would be. I should alarm her—alarm Philippa! I could give no reason. My one longing was to keep the news from my poor love. Let her read that paragraph, and who could answer for the consequences? Looking as a medical man at her case, I knew that there was something about that night which troubled her; some dream, or semblance of dream, to which, fortunately, she could as yet give no coherence. Let her learn that Sir Mervyn Ferrand had ever since that night been lying dead where she met him, the fearful truth must come to her. No! Not a word to excite her suspicion. My task was a twofold one. I had to save her not only from what I suppose I must call justice, but also from herself. It seemed to me that the latter was the hardest part of my work; but I would do it—I swore I would do it. I would keep watch and ward, to see that nothing reached her—that she heard nothing which could awaken memories of those mercifully absent hours.

I tore the paper to pieces and burnt it. I think of all my dark days that one was the one I would be least willing to pass again. I trembled at every footstep on the stairs. Any man who paused for a moment outside our windows sent a cold chill over me. And in the midst of my misery I had to wear a cheerful face, and talk to Philippa and my mother about the pleasures of our projected journey! Ah! If we only reached the end of it in safety, the pleasure would not be altogether imaginary.

Once again I say, if you cannot feel with me, throw my tale aside. Heaven knows it is a sombre one! I was breaking the law; concealing what the law calls crime; doing all I could to save the criminal. But the criminal was Philippa, and I loved her! I myself would have stood face to face with Sir Mervyn Ferrand, and have freely given my own life if I could have assured his dying like the dog he was. Why then should I blame Philippa, who had done in her temporary madness what I would have done in cold blood? Yet why trouble to extenuate? I loved her! Those words sum up everything.

The morning dawned. No fatal messenger had arrived. I glanced hastily at the papers, which, however, contained no more information about the tragedy. Shortly after ten o'clock we started to drive to Charing Cross. The rattle of wheels over the stones seemed to send fresh life through my veins. We were off on the road to safety.

We started in plenty of time, as I wished to call at my bankers on the way. It was my intention to take with me a large sum in gold. Notes of any kind could be traced, but the bright sovereigns would tell no tale. I changed my cheque, and whilst doing so asked if there were any letters for me. Several persons addressed letters to me at my bankers. The spruce cashier sent to inquire, and, with my bag of gold, passed under the brass-wire railing a letter with a woman's handwriting on the envelope. I thrust it into my pocket, to read at my leisure.

We travelled by the tidal train for Paris, via Folkestone and Boulogne. It was not the pleasantest weather in the world for a journey; but I wrapped my charges up warmly, and did all I could to mitigate the hardships of the voyage, undertaken ostensibly for the sake of my health. My mother, who was by now an experienced and seasoned traveller, settled herself down to the journey, although she little guessed how short the rest I meant to give her until we reached our destination. She laughingly protested against the cruelty of dragging an old woman like herself away from England just as she had returned to it; but there was that in her voice and manner which told me she would for my sake make a far greater sacrifice of comfort than this.

I thought that Philippa's spirits, like mine, rose as we left London behind us. She smiled at my sallies and feeble attempts at making merry, which, now that we were fairly on our road to safety, were not quite so forced as they had been during the last few days. She listened with interest to the pictures I drew—imaginary ones, of course—of the beauties of the south; and I was glad to believe that the thought of visiting what might almost be called her native land was beginning to awaken her interest. Only let me be able to show her that life could still promise a pleasant future, and the moody memories of the past months might be banished for ever.

I am sure that no one who could have seen us that morning would have dreamt that out of that party of three, consisting of a comfortable pleasant-looking English matron, a strangely beautiful girl, and myself, two were flying from the hands of justice. Our appearance was certainly such as to disarm all suspicion.

'But where are we going?' asked my mother. 'I object to go wandering about without knowing where our pilgrimage is to end.'

'We are going to Paris first, then to Spain—to wherever we can find the warmth and sunshine which is necessary to my existence. If we can't find them in Spain, we will cross over to Africa, and, if needful, go down to the Equator.'

'Then you young people will have to go alone. I draw the line of my good nature at Europe.'

I glanced at Philippa. Her long curved lashes hid her eyes; but a tell-tale blush was on her cheek. I knew that the day was not so very distant when she would answer my appeal as I wished. I knew that, could I but sweep away the record of that one night, all might yet be well with her. Oh that she may never recall what I alone know!

As we were nearing Folkestone I remembered the letter which had been given me at the bank. I drew it from my breast, intending to read it; but the sight of the Roding post-mark on the outside made me change my intention. I remembered Mrs Wilson's half-promise to send me some communication. I longed and yet I dreaded to break the seal. I felt it would be better for me to read that letter alone. Whatever might be the tenor of its contents, I was sure it had some bearing on Philippa's relations with Sir Mervyn Ferrand.

We were soon on board the steamer and under weigh. Although the Arctic rigours of the last three weeks had departed, the air on the sea was too keen to make the channel passage an enjoyable one. I persuaded my mother and Philippa to take refuge in the saloon; and then I found a quiet spot where I was able to read my letter without fear of interruption, or of betraying myself by the emotion its contents might cause. It was well I did so, for the first words blanched my cheek. The letter began abruptly, so:

'I know or guess all. I know why Sir Mervyn Ferrand did not reach my house that night. I know the reason for her strange excited state. I know why she left my home before you came to seek her. I know how he met with the death he deserved.

'Ah! She is braver than I am. She has done what years ago I swore I would do; and yet I had not the courage. I was base enough to forego revenge for the sake of the beggarly maintenance he offered me—for the sake, perhaps, of my children. I sank low enough to become his tool—to do as he bade me, even to taking under my roof the woman who thought herself his wife. Yes, she has been braver than I. But her wrongs were greater than mine; for I had but myself to blame for being in such a degraded position that he could throw me aside like an old glove. He never married me.

'Fear nothing for your sister, if she be your sister. Tell her my lips are sealed to the death; and for the sake of her brave act tell her this:

'Sir Mervyn Ferrand's first wife *died on the 18th of June, 186-*, three months before the day on which he married your sister. She died at Liverpool, at No. 5 Silver-street. She was buried in the cemetery, under the name of Lucy Ferrand. She has friends alive; it will be easy to prove that she was the woman whom he married. Her maiden name was King. He hated her. They parted. He gave her a sum of money on condition that she never called herself his wife. He lost sight of her. I never did. For years I hoped she would die, and that he would marry me. She died too late for the hope to be realised. I told him of her death; but I changed the date. I would not tell him where she died. Part of his object in coming to Roding that night was to endeavour to wring the information from me. He would never have had it. No other woman should have been his wife so long as I could stop it.

'Now that he is dead, you can tell your brave sister that she may, if she likes, take the name, title, and what wealth she can claim. Fear nothing from me; I will be silent as death.'

CHAPTER VIII

FLIGHT

I READ the woman's letter again and again—read it with feelings in which joy and disgust were strangely mingled; but the former was the predominate sensations. In the first place, if Mrs Wilson kept her promise of secrecy, it seemed to me that all danger of suspicion falling upon Philippa was removed. There would be no one else to make known the fact, that upon the night of Sir Mervyn's death a wronged, distracted woman left her home—a woman whose life's happiness had been clouded by the villain's treacherous act—a woman of strong passions, who in her temporary delirium might easily be turned to take such vengeance for which I, at least, held her quite unaccountable. If I could but feel sure of the silence of the one person whom I dreaded, we might even return to London, and fear nothing. I wavered. After all there is something contemptible in flight. Should I trust to Mrs Wilson's promise, and return with my companions by the next boat from Boulogne?

No, a thousand times no! Philippa's welfare is far too precious to me to be trusted in the hands of one excitable woman—a woman, moreover, who has wrongs of her own calling for vengeance. Tomorrow her mind may change, and instead of furthering our safety, she may be urging on the pursuit. Let me trust no one save myself.

For my love's sake, I was overjoyed to hear that, supposing the woman's statement and dates were correct, Philippa was the dead man's lawful wife. Not that this fact for one moment palliated the guilt of his intention, or lessened the contempt and hatred I bore towards him; not that it changed in my eyes by one iota my love's position. Married or unmarried, to me she

76

was all that a woman could be. Though a blackguard's craft had wrought what would be her shame in the eyes of the world; though her hands were unconsciously red with a man's blood, to me she was pure as a vestal, innocent as a child.

Yet for her sake the news gladdened me. I knew that if ever the time should come when I could place proofs in her hands that she was a wife—that she could, if she chose, bear her worthless husband's name, and face the world without fear of scorn, the restoration of her self-respect would bring with it a joy which only a woman can rightly comprehend. And Philippa, with all her pride and passion, was a true woman, full of the softness and delicate dread of shame which characterises the best of her sex.

Yet when should I be able to tell her? Whenever I did so I must also reveal the fact of her husband's being dead, and my doing so must bring the whole story of his death to her knowledge. I trembled as I thought what this might mean. Surely its dramatic surroundings must suggest something to her mind— must bring back the night and its horrors; must, in fact, tell her what she had done in her madness! Rather than risk this, I must let her continue to bear the cruel weight of what she thought her shame. My aim must be to make her believe that Sir Mervyn Ferrand is still alive, and troubling nothing as to what has become of the woman whom he once falsely swore to love and cherish until death. I cursed the wretch's memory as I thought of him.

The sending of Philippa to live under the charge of one of his own discarded mistresses was but another proof of the man's revolting cynicism. Mrs Wilson's acceptance of the charge showed me to what a level a woman could sink. It told me, moreover, that in spite of her letter she was not to be trusted. A woman who could lend herself to her former lover's purposes in such a way as this must have parted with every atom of pride. It seemed to me that the woman and the man were well matched in baseness.

Still her letter lifted a load from my mind. I felt that for a while there could be no pursuit; yet I resolved to risk nothing, but hurry on with all possible speed. Only when we crossed the frontier of Spain should I sleep in peace.

All researches, with a view to obtaining evidence of the first Lady Ferrand's death, I postponed indefinitely. Some day, if all went well, I would return to England and procure the documents necessary to prove the validity of Philippa's marriage. There was no pressing hurry. As to any money which should be hers, never with my consent should she touch a penny which had belonged to the dead man.

Protracted as my meditations seem on paper, they were in reality much longer; indeed, they were not at an end when the boat steamed in Boulogne harbour. I went in search of my companions, who, I was glad to find, had borne the voyage well. We were soon in the train, and, without any event occurring worth recording, at eight o'clock stood on the Gare du Nord, Paris.

We drove through the brightly lit streets to the Hôtel du Louvre. The stains of travel washed away, my mother gave a sigh of satisfaction as she seated herself at the dinner table. Like a sensible woman, she was no despiser of the good things of this life. There were other late diners in the great coffee-room, and many a head was turned to look at the beautiful girl who sat on my right hand; for every day which brought her new health and strength, brought also to my love an instalment of her former rich beauty. In a very short time she would be to all appearances the Philippa of old.

'How long shall we stay in Paris, Basil?' asked my mother.

'It is now half-past nine; our train starts at 8.45 in the morning. Calculate the time.'

'Oh, nonsense! It is years since I have been in Paris. I want to look at the shops. So does Philippa, I am sure.'

'My dear mother, the man, much more the woman, who lingers in Paris is lost. If you are going elsewhere, the only way is to go straight through, or else you get no further. I have proved this, and mean to run no risk.'

'But remember we are only weak women. This poor child is far from strong.'

She smiled at Philippa, whose eyes thanked her for the affectionate appellation.

'Don't be merciless, Basil,' she continued; 'give us at least one day.'

'Not one. I am just going to look after a courier, so that you may travel in all possible comfort.'

My mother seemed almost annoyed, and again said I was merciless. What would she have said had she known that, unless I had received that letter, instead of going to our present comfortable quarters, we should have driven to the Orleans Railway, and taken the first train to the south? How little she knew—how little, I trusted, Philippa knew—from what we were flying!

I felt I must give my mother some reason for my haste; so, before going in quest of my courier, I took her aside.

'It is not well for Philippa to stay in Paris,' I said. 'Someone whom she ought not to meet was here a short time ago.'

I blamed myself for the deception; but what could I do? Alas! It seemed to me that my life, which once was fearlessly open to the inspection of all, was now full of little else save deceptions. Should I ever again be my true self?

My mother raised no further objection. I found a courier—a bearded gentleman of commanding presence, who spoke every European language with impartial imperfection. I gave him instructions to see to everything the next morning; to collect our luggage, save the small quantity we carried with us, and to register it through to Burgos. I had no particular reason for choosing Burgos, but it seemed a convenient place at which to take our first thorough rest.

The next day's journey was a dull, dreary, wearisome affair. My companions had not shaken off the fatigue of the previous day, and now that I felt Philippa's safety was, comparatively speaking, assured, a reaction set in with me. No wonder! I shudder now as I think of the strain to which both body and mind had been subjected during the last fortnight. I was moody and listless. The air was full of fog and mist. The so-called express train pounded along after the well-known style of French railways. Orleans, Blois, Tours, Poictiers, Angoulême, Coutras, and other stations passed me as one in a dream. The dull day crept on until dark evening was upon us, and we were all thoroughly glad when our day's journey ended at Bordeaux.

My mother, who was rather great at guidebooks, had beguiled part of the journey by a Murray, which somehow made its appearance from her travelling bag. As she knew we were to sleep at Bordeaux she had been laying down the law as to what we were to look at. We were to see the curious high wooden fifteenth-century houses of the old town; the cathedral, with its fine towers; the very old churches of St Croix and St Seurin, and a variety of other interesting objects. It needed all the assurance I possessed, all the invalid's querulousness and insistence I could assume, to induce her to consent to resume our journey the first thing in the morning. Even Philippa pleaded for delay, and gave me to understand that she thought I was using my mother unfairly. But I was firm. If I could I would have hurried on by the midnight train. Anyway, now that we were within a few hours journey of the frontier and of safety, I would leave no more than I could help to chance.

So, in the early morning, I got my party together and before it was light led them to the train. I believe that by now my mother looked upon me as rather out of my senses. She frankly owned she could not see the necessity for making such a toil out of what might be a pleasure. She little knew that nothing could have made that journey a pleasure to me; that even finding Philippa's eyes now and again fixed on my face with what I almost dared to think was tender interest—that even the blush which crossed her cheek when I caught those glances—was not sufficient to reward me for my anxiety.

A slow, a painfully slow train. Innumerable stoppages. A country which under the circumstances would have given me no interest even if we had been in summer instead of winter; and then, after nearly five hours' slow travelling, Bayonne at last. Bayonne, with its strong fortifications. Bayonne, with the welcome Pyrenees towering above it. In less than two hours we should be in Spain.

A curious dread seized me—a presentiment so strong that ever since then I have lost faith in presentiments. Something seemed to tell me that all my efforts had been in vain; that at the frontier there would be certain intelligence received which would lead to our arrest; that Philippa, with one foot, as it were, in the land of refuge, would be seized and carried back to face the horrors and the shame of a trial for murder. It was, as events showed, an absurd fancy, and only the increasing tension of my nerves can account for the hold it gained upon me.

I grew so pale, trembled so in every limb, that my companions were thoroughly alarmed. We had brandy with us, which was duly administered to me. After a while I recovered, and although the fear was still with me, sat with the stoicism of an Indian at the stake, awaiting what might happen at the frontier. I had done all I could. If, at the last moment, disaster overtook us, I had at least striven by every means within my power to avert it.

We have passed Biarritz, the merry bright watering-place. We have passed Hendaye, the French frontier station. We leave the towering Pyrenees on our left. We are at Irun, where all baggage must be jealously scrutinised. We are in Spain! Nobody has troubled us. No suspicious-looking stranger has watched us. The stoppage has been long, for the custom-house officers are annoyingly particular in the discharge of their duty; but our noble-looking courier has saved us all personal trouble. He has done us yeoman's service. At last we are in another train, a train which runs on a line of another gauge. The very time of day has changed. We have lost or gained—I forget which—some twenty minutes. We now count by Madrid time. We are fairly on Spanish ground, and I have saved my love. Saved her from others—now to save her from herself. Never, never shall she know the secret of that dark night. We will speed away to the south—to the sun; the colour; the brightness; the flowers. All shall be forgotten. The dark remembrance shall be swept from my mind. I will call it a dream. I will win Philippa's love—the love that I dare to believe is already almost mine. We will live for ever in bright, sunny, glowing lands. Who cares for dull, dark, dismal England? Have we not youth, wealth, and, oh blessed word! Love? Before my love and me lie years and years of sweetness and joy. Shake off black gloom and be merry, Basil North. You have conquered fate!

We have passed St Sebastian. The sluggish train is wearily winding up the valley of the Urumea. We are in wild and glorious scenery. The railway is carried at a great elevation, from which we get now and again peeps of far-away valleys. Yes, I could now find time to admire the wonderful scenery which lasted until we passed Miranda.

My mood changed with the country. I laughed; I jested. Each of the many stations at which we stopped furnished materials for my new-born merriment. I laughed at the solemn-looking Spanish railway officials, and drew pictures of the doleful fate of imaginary nobly-born hidalgos whom poverty forced to descend to such employment. I grumbled not at the slowness of the train, although an ordinary traveller might well, when on a Spanish line, sigh for the comparatively lightning speed of the much-maligned French trains. Time was nothing to me now. Was there not a lifetime stretching before me—and Philippa? My gaiety was contagious. My mother laughed until the tears came, and Philippa smiled as I had not seen her smile since we picked up under such sad circumstances that long-dropt thread of friendship.

Those who have travelled in Spain will scarcely credit me when I say we had the compartment to ourselves. We were troubled by no cloaked Spaniard who, as is the wont of his kind, insisted upon smoking like a furnace and keeping both windows shut. Our noble courier had been given his instructions. His arguments were venal, and had I troubled about money I should have found them costly. But they carried the point, and no one intruded on our privacy.

The hours went by. My mother slept, or pretended to sleep. I seated myself near Philippa, and whispered words of thinly-veiled love. She answered them not—I expected no answer—but her eyes were downcast and her cheek was blushing. She sighed. A sad smile played around her sweet mouth; a smile that spoke of a world of regret. That sigh, that smile, told me that she understood me, but told me also that, ah, it could never be! The past never forgives! But all the same she let her hand rest in mine; and although, considering what had happened, I scarcely dare to say so, for once, for many, many months, I was all but happy.

For me that journey ended only too soon. At night we reached Burgos, the capital of the old Castilian kingdom, and I laid my head on my pillow and enjoyed sleep such as I had not known since the night before that one, when Philippa, with the snow-flakes falling around her, stood outside the window of my cottage and gave me something to live for—something to hope for!

CHAPTER IX

SAFE—AND LOVED!

Now that we are safe in Spain; now that Philippa's arrest is a matter of impossibility, and her expulsion from a country so lax in its observance of international obligations highly improbable, when her guilt can at the utmost be only suspected, if indeed suspicion ever points to her, I may pass rapidly over the events of the next two months; the more so as my record of them would differ very little from the description of an ordinary tour in Spain. To me, after the feverish anxiety, the horrible dread as to what any hour might bring forth, which had characterised our flight from England, it seemed something very much like bathos my dropping at once into the position of the everyday tourist taking a couple of ladies on a round of travel; but for the time I was outwardly neither more nor less.

From Burgos we went to Valladolid; from Valladolid to Madrid—Madrid, the high-perched city, with its arid, uninteresting surroundings and abominable climate. Not long did we linger here. Bad and trying as the English winter may be, the cold of Madrid is a poor exchange for it. I had almost thrown aside the assumed character of an invalid; but I felt it would be the height of inconsistency, after forcing my companions to accompany me in the search of warmth, to make any stay in the Spanish capital. Right glad I was to leave it, and turn my face southwards. Philippa was by now in apparently good health, both bodily and mental; but whilst at Madrid I trembled for her, as I should tremble for anyone I loved who made that city a resting-place—a city swept from end to end by crafty, treacherous, icy winds blowing straight from the

Guadarrama mountains; insidious blasts in which lurk the seeds of consumption and death.

So at our leisure we went southwards, halting at such places and seeing such sights as we thought fit; lingering here and there just so long as it suited us; travelling by easy stages, and in such comfort as we could command. At Malaga we spent weeks revelling in the balmy, delicious air; at Granada we were days and days before we could tear ourselves from the interesting, absorbing glories of the departed Moor. We were in a new world—a world which I had always longed to see. At last—it was just at the end of April, when the land was full of roses, when vegetation was breaking into that rich luxuriance unknown in northern lands—we turned our steps to the city which I had in my own mind fixed upon as the end of our wanderings, the half Spanish, half Moorish, but wholly beautiful city of Seville; brilliant, romantic Seville, with its flower-bedecked houses, its groves of orange and olive trees, its luxuriant gardens, its crooked narrow streets, its Moorish walls, its numerous towers, all of which sink into insignificance under the shadow of the lofty Giralda. All I wanted seemed to be here.

Here was everything for the sake of seeking which I had professed to leave foggy England—sun, warmth, colour, brightness. Here, I thought, if in any place in the world, will the one I love forget what she knows of the cruel past. Here, it may be, our new life shall begin!

Glorious, wonderful Seville! The magic charm of the place fell on my companions as it fell upon me, as indeed it falls upon all who visit it. By common consent we arranged to stay our course for an indefinite time. Perhaps by now we all thought that we had endured enough of hotel life, and wanted some place which might bear the name of home; so, although such things are not very easy to find, I hired a furnished house. Such a house!

From the narrow street—the need of shade makes narrow streets indispensable to Seville—pass through a light open-work iron gate into a spacious white marble-lined courtyard or, as the Spaniards call it, *patio*; a courtyard open to the sky, save for the gaily-coloured awning which is sometimes spread over it; a space fragrant to the four corners with the perfume of orange and other sweet-smelling blossoms, bright with glowing oleanders, and musical with the murmur of fountains. Around the walls statues, some of the fair works of art, paintings and mirrors. Every sitting-room in the house opening on to this cool central fairyland—a fairyland which, for many months of the year, is almost the only part of the house used in their waking hours by the Sevillaños. Add to this a garden, not large but exquisite, full of the rarest and choicest blooms, and if you are not hopelessly bigoted, and enamoured of English fogs, you must long for such a home in courtly, beautiful Seville!

With such surroundings—almost those of a Sybarite—who can blame me for being lulled into security, if not forgetfulness, and for telling myself that my troubles were nearly at an end? Who can wonder at the castles I built as hour after hour I lounged in the *patio*, with its fragrant, soothing atmosphere, and gazed at Philippa's beautiful face, and now and again meeting her dark eyes, and sometimes surprising in those thoughtful depths a look which thrilled my heart—a look which I told myself was one of love?

True, that often and often in my sleep I saw the white, dead face, with the snow-heap forming over it. True, that often and often Philippa's wild cry, 'The wages of sin—on, on, on!' rang through my dreams, and I awoke trembling in every limb; but in the day-time, in the midst of the sweet shaded repose, I could almost banish every memory, every thought which strove to lead me back to grief and horror.

The days, each one sweeter than its forerunner, passed by. Each day was passed with Philippa. We wandered for hours through the marvellous gardens of the Alcazar; we drove under the shading trees of Las Delicias; we made excursions to Italica and other places, which the guide-book tells you every visitor to Seville should see; but I think we found in the ordinary sights, which were at our very door, as much pleasure as in any of the stock shows. We loved to watch the people. We delighted in the picturesque, ragged-looking, black-eyed Andalusian boy-rascals who played and romped at every street corner. We noted the exquisitely graceful figures of the Sevillañas; I, moreover, noted that the most graceful of these figures could not be compared to Philippa's own. We strolled up the awning-roofed Calle de las Sierpes, and laughed at the curious windowless little shops. Everything was so strange, so bright, so teeming with old-world tradition, so full of intense interest, that no wonder I could for the time send painful memories to the background.

And Philippa? Although there were times when her face grew sad with sad remembrances; although at times her eyes sought mine with that troubled, enquiring look; although I trembled as to what might be the question which I seemed to see her lips about to form; I did not, could not believe she was entirely unhappy. The smile—a quiet, thoughtful one, yet a smile—was oftener seen on her face. It came now of its own accord. More and more certain I grew that, if nothing recalled the past, or I should say, if nothing filled the blank, so merci-fully left, of that one night, the hour was not far distant when my love would call herself happy. Oh, to keep that fatal knowledge from her for ever!

Such was my life. So, in calm, peace, all but happiness, the days passed by, until the hour came when for the third time I dared to tell Philippa that I loved her—to tell her so with the certainty of hearing her re-echo my words. Yes, certainty. Had I not for many days seen her eyes grow brighter, the grave, thoughtful look leave her face, her whole manner change when I drew near? Such signs as these told me that the crowning moment of my life was at hand.

Here for one moment I pause. I scorn to excuse myself for wishing to marry a woman who had been, or supposed herself

to have been, the innocent victim of a scoundrelly man of the
world; I have nothing in common with those who think such
an excuse is needed. Mrs Wilson's statement that the marriage
was valid might be true or false. It gave me the impression that
it was true, and I believed that Philippa could lay claim to bear
the man's accursed name. But whether she was Lady Ferrand
or a trusting woman betrayed, for my own sake I cared little.
She was Philippa!

As to my intention of marrying, my one wish to marry a
woman who, in her temporary and fully accounted for delirium,
had killed the man who so cruelly wronged her, I have but this
to say. My tale, although I give it to the world, is not written
for the purpose of fiction. It is the story of myself—a story
which seemed to me worth telling—of a man who loved one
woman passionately, blindly, and without consideration. Such
was my great love for Philippa that I feel no shame in telling
the truth, and saying that had I seen her, in full possession of
her senses, level that pistol and shoot her betrayer through his
black heart, I should have held that only justice had been
done, I should have regretted the act, but, nevertheless, I would
have pleaded for her love as fervently and reverently as I was
now about to plead for it.

Once more I say, if you condemn me throw the book aside.

Philippa, with her eyes half closed, was, as was usual at that
hour, sitting in the *patio*. In her hand she held a sprig of orange
blossom, and ever and anon inhaled its delicious perfume; an
action, by-the-by, scarcely needful, as the whole air was redolent
of the fragrance thrown from the great tree in the centre of the
marble space. She was, or fancied she was, alone, as some little
time before I had left the court to obtain a fresh supply of
cigarettes; and my mother, who could never quite adapt herself
to the semi-open-air life, was taking a siesta in the drawing-
room. As I saw Philippa in all her glowing beauty, the white
marble against which she leant making as it were a suitable
foil to the warm colour of her cheek—the long curved black

downcast lashes—the bosom rising and falling gently—like an inspiration the thought came to me that in a minute my fate would be decided. Heavens! How could I have waited so long to hear the words which I knew she would say?

I crept noiselessly to her side. I placed my arm round her waist and drew her to me. I whispered words of passionate love in her ear—words the confidence of which startled me; but then this time I knew that my love of years was to be rewarded.

She did not shrink away; she did not struggle to free herself, but she trembled like a leaf in my embrace. She sighed deeply, even hopelessly, and I saw the tears welling in her dark eyes. Closer and firmer I held her, and kissed her cheek again and again. Had that moment been my last I should have said I had not lived in vain.

'Philippa,' I whispered, 'my queen, my love, tell me you love me at last.'

She was silent. The tears broke from her eyes and ran down her cheeks. I kissed the signs of sorrow away.

'Dearest,' I said, 'it is answer enough that you suffer these kisses, but I have waited so long—been so unhappy; look at me and satisfy me; let me hear you say, "I love you!"'

She turned her tearful eyes to mine, but not for long. She cast her looks upon the ground and was still, silent. Yet she lay unresisting in my arms. That, after all, was the true answer.

But I must have it from her lips. 'Tell me, dearest—tell me once,' I prayed.

Her lips quivered; her bosom rose and fell. The blush spread from her cheek and stole down her white neck.

'Yes,' she murmured; 'now that it is too late, I love you.'

I laughed a wild laugh. I clasped Philippa to my breast.

'Too late!' I cried. 'We may have fifty years of happiness.'

'It is too late,' she answered. 'For your sake I have told you that I love you, Basil. My love, I will kiss you once—then loose me, and let us say farewell.'

'When death closes the eyes of one of us we will say farewell—not until then,' I said, as my lips met hers in a long and rapturous kiss.

Then with a sigh she gently but firmly freed herself from my arms. She rose, we stood on the marble floor, face to face, gazing in each other's eyes.

'Basil,' she said softly, 'all this must be forgotten. Say farewell; tomorrow we must part.'

'Dearest, our lives henceforth are one.'

'It cannot be. Spare me, Basil! You have been kind to me. It cannot be.'

'Why? Tell me why.'

'Why! Need you ask? You bear an honoured and respected name; and I, you know what I am—a shamed woman.'

'A wronged woman, it may be, not a shamed one.'

'Ah! Basil, in this world, when a woman is concerned, wronged and shamed mean the same thing. You have been as a brother to me. I came to you in my trouble; you saved my life—my reason. Be kinder still, and spare me the pain of paining you.'

By look, by word, by gesture, she seemed to beseech me. Oh, how I longed to tell her that I firmly believed she was the dead man's wife! I had much difficulty in checking the words which were forming on my lips. But I dared not speak. Telling her that the marriage was a valid one meant that I must tell her of her husband's death, and, it might be, how he died.

'Philippa,' I said, 'the whole happiness of my life, my every desire, is centred upon making you my wife. Think, dearest, how when I had no right to demand this gift my life was made desolate; think what it will be when I know you love me and yet refuse to be mine! Have I been true to you, Philippa?'

'Heaven knows you have.'

'Then why, now that you love me, refuse me my reward?'

'Oh, spare me!—I cannot, I will not give it. Basil, dear Basil,

why with your talents should you marry the cast-off—mistress—
of Sir Mervyn Ferrand? Why should you blush to show your
wife to the world?'

'Blush! The world! What is my world save you? You are all
to me, sweetest. You love me—what more do I want? Before
this time next week we will be married.'

'Never, never! I will not wrong the man I love. Basil, farewell
for ever!'

She clasped her hands and fled wildly across the court. I
caught her at the door, which she had reached and half opened.
'Promise me one thing,' I said; 'promise you will wait here until
my return. I shall not be five minutes. It is not much to ask,
Philippa.'

Philippa bent her head as in assent. I passed through the
door, and in a few minutes returned to the *patio*, accompanied
by my mother, who glanced from Philippa to me in a surprised
way.

'What is the matter?' she asked, with her cheerful smile.
'Have you two young people been quarrelling?'

Philippa made no answer. She stood with her fingers inter-
laced; her eyes cast on the ground.

'Mother,' I said, 'I have today asked Philippa to be my wife.
I have told her that all my happiness depends upon her consent
to this. I have loved her for years; and at last she loves me. Yes,
she loves me.'

My mother gave a little cry of pleasure, and stepped forward.
I checked her.

'I love her, and she loves me,' I continued. 'But she refuses
to marry me. And why? Because she fears to bring shame on
an honourable name. You know her story; you are my mother.
You, of all people in the world, should be the most jealous as
to the honour of my name. You should know whom you would
choose for my wife. Tell her—'

I said no more. My mother advanced with outstretched arms,
and in a moment my poor girl was weeping in her embrace,

whilst words which I could not hear, but whose purport I could well guess, were being whispered to her. I had indeed been right in trusting to my mother's noble nature.

'Leave us for a little while, Basil,' she said, as Philippa still sobbed upon her shoulder. 'Come back in a quarter of an hour's time.'

I turned away, went past the screen which is sometimes put up to ensure privacy, out of the iron gate, into the narrow street. I watched the lounging, dignified-looking men and the dark-eyed women who went by; I looked at the merry urchins at play; and after what seemed an interminable quarter of an hour, returned to learn how my gentle counsel had succeeded with my suit.

My mother and Philippa were sitting with their arms around each other. Philippa, as I entered the *patio*, raised her eyes to mine with a look of shy happiness. My mother rose and took the girl by the hand.

'Basil,' she said, 'I have at last been able to persuade her that you and I, at least, rise above the conventionalities of what is called the world. I have told her that, knowing all I know, I see nothing to prevent her from being your wife. I have told her that simply for her own sweet sake I would rather see you marry her than any woman in the world. And, Basil, I fancy I have made her believe me.'

With her soft eyes full of maternal love, my mother kissed me and left the court, I opened my arms to close them round the fairest woman in the world; and all the earth seemed bright and glorious to me. My great love had conquered! And yet, even in that moment of bliss, my thoughts involuntarily flew away to a snow-heaped road in England—to a white drift, under which for days and days a ghastly object had once been lying. A dream! A dream! It must have been a fearful dream! Forget it, Basil North, and be happy in the happiness you have at last won!

CHAPTER X

THE SWORD FALLS

ONCE conquered—once convinced that the obstacles which her solicitude for my welfare raised against my wish were not insuperable—Philippa offered no further resistance; whilst as for me, every day that might be counted before I called her my wife seemed a day spoilt, if not entirely wasted. With my mother's arguments to back my own fervent persuasion, I had no difficulty in winning Philippa's consent to our marriage taking place as soon as the needful formalities could be complied with. And yet, although the day was fixed, it was at my instance changed, and the ceremony postponed for a while.

My reason for deferring my crowning happiness was this. Knowing all that I knew, the question arose; under what name was Philippa to be married? Under her own maiden name; under the false name which for some time Sir Mervyn Ferrand, for reasons best known to himself, had made her assume; or under that name which, supposing Mrs Wilson had spoken the truth, she was legally entitled to bear? So anxious, so resolved was I that there should be no shadow of doubt as to the validity of her second and happier marriage, that after due consideration I determined to sacrifice my own inclinations, and postpone our wedding long enough to give me time to pay a flying visit to England, where I could do my best to obtain such evidence as would show that Philippa was the dead man's widow.

I made the excuse that I found many matters of business connected with my property that must be attended to before I could be married. I travelled to England—to Liverpool—as fast as I could. I stayed there for a week, and during that time made full researches into the life and death of a woman who, as Mrs

Wilson said, had died on a certain date, and been buried under the name of Lucy Ferrand.

The information I acquired as to her antecedents is of no consequence to my story. Whatever her faults may have been, her history was a sad one; indeed it seemed to me that the history of any woman who had been cursed by Sir Mervyn Ferrand's love was a sad one. However, the result of my investigations was, in short, this: Ferrand had married the woman many years ago. They had parted by mutual consent. With his cynical carelessness, he had troubled no more about her; and, stranger still, she had not troubled him. She died on the date given by my informant. The question of identity could be easily settled; so that if ever Philippa chose to claim the rights appertaining to Sir Mervyn Ferrand's widow, she would have no difficulty in making that claim good. But I trusted that years might pass before she learned that the man was dead.

I made my presence in England known to no one; in fact, I felt that in returning to my native country I ran a certain amount of risk. For all I knew to the contrary, there might be a warrant out against me. If suspicion as to the author of that night's work had in any way been directed to Philippa, I, the partner of her flight, could not hope to escape free. However, I comforted myself by thinking that if danger menaced us I should have heard something about it, as after our first hurried start I had made no attempt to conceal our whereabouts. It would have been useless. My mother had friends in England, with whom she exchanged letters. I had an agent and lawyers, with whom, if only for financial reasons, I was bound to correspond. I had been obliged to write to my stolid William, and instruct him to get rid of the cottage as best he could, and to look out for a fresh place for himself. But all the same I did not care to let it be known that I was now in England.

Whilst engaged upon raking up evidence on Philippa's behalf, I did not neglect to make such enquiries as I could respecting the event which had happened that night near

Roding. I found that, so far as the general public knew, the crime was still veiled in mystery. No one had been arrested; no one had been accused; no reason for the deed had been discovered, and as yet suspicion pointed to no one. Indeed, in spite of the hundred pounds reward offered by Government, it seemed that Sir Mervyn Ferrand's murder was relegated to swell the list of undiscovered crimes. By this I knew that Mrs Wilson had kept her promise of silence; and now that months had gone by; now that public attention had been turned from the thrilling affair; now that Philippa seemed as far or farther than ever from giving any token, which suggested the awakening of recollection of what her wrong, her frenzy, had prompted her hand to do unknowingly, I dared to hope that any chance which remained of a revelation of the truth was reduced to a minimum. These results of my investigations and enquiries gave me immense relief, and my heart was all but gay as, armed with the proofs of the first Lady Ferrand's death, I hurried back to Seville, Philippa, and the happiness which I vowed should be mine.

We were married. Philippa and I were married! Married; and a few months ago I sat lonely, miserable and heart-broken, deeming that the one I loved was lost to me for ever! What matters the things which have filled those months, and made them the most painful of my life? Today we are man and wife, joined together till death us do part!

I said no word as to the result of my enquiries in Liverpool. I had no difficulty in persuading Philippa, who in some things was as simple and trusting as a child, that it was necessary, or at least advisable, she should be married under the name which her first certificate of marriage affected to bestow upon her. She signed her name for the last, it may, for aught I know, have also been the first time, as Philippa Ferrand; and I noticed that she shuddered as she formed the letters.

Although my bride was by birth half a Spaniard, and although I had by now in many ways conformed to the Spanish mode of life, we were still English enough to look upon going away somewhere for a honeymoon as indispensable. It would be but a short trip; and as my mother in our absence would be left at Seville alone, or with servants only, we did not care to go very far away. It so happened that, although so close to Cadiz, we had not yet paid that town a visit, and thought the present a capital opportunity for so doing.

To Cadiz we went, and stayed several days at the Hôtel de Paris. We liked the white-walled town, rising and shining above the dark-blue sea, like, as I have somewhere seen it described, a white pearl in a crown of sapphires; or, as the Gaditanos call it, *tazita de plata*, a silver cup. We liked the rows of tall terrace-topped houses. We liked the movement and bustle on the quays and in the port. We liked the walks on the broad granite ramparts, and the lovely views of the busy bay and country beyond it; but all the same we agreed that Cadiz bore no comparison to our beautiful Seville, and the sooner we returned to that gay city the better.

Now that I had gained my desire, was I happy? After all that had past, could I have been happy during those early days of our wedded life? As I look back upon them, I sit and muse, trying in vain to answer the question to my own satisfaction. Philippa loved me—she was my wife; come good, come evil, she was mine for ever. In so much I was happy, thrice happy. Could I have lived but for the present, my bliss would have known no ally.

But there was the past! I could not altogether forget the path which had led to such happiness as now was mine. I could be thankful that I alone knew all the horrors and dangers with which that path was studded. I alone knew the secret of that one night. Although I could keep it for ever, would it be always a secret?

Yes, and there was the future. Behind the happiness which was mine at present lurked a dread as to what the future had in store for me—for us. It was a dread which day by day grew stronger. The greater my happiness, the more dreadful the thought of its being wrecked. The feeling that my house of joy was built upon sand was always obtruding on my most blissful hours, and not, I knew, without good reasons.

Philippa's very avoidance of speaking of her past life lent some justification to my gloomy forebodings. Not once did Sir Mervyn Ferrand's name pass between my wife and me. Not once did she ask me for any further particulars concerning the events of that night upon which, in the height of her short-lived mania, she reached my cottage. True that upon becoming my wife, and beginning a new and happier stage of life, it might be but natural for her to wish to consign to oblivion the wrong, the shame, the suffering wrought by a villain's craft; yet I was so mixed up in the catastrophe that silence on the subject seemed strange. Her reticence alarmed me. I fancied it must be caused by some vague uneasiness connected with that night—some doubt which she dared not seek to set at rest. It is, I know, not unusual for women, after their recovery from that mysterious disease which had for a while driven my poor girl distraught, to be able to recall and accurately describe the delusions which had afflicted them during those wandering hours. I myself had in one or two cases noticed this peculiarity, and the authorities which I had studied during Philippa's illness mention it as an indisputable fact. My great dread was that at some moment, perhaps when our happiness was as perfect as it could be, some simple chance, some allusion to certain events, even the bare mention of a name, might supply the missing link, and the fearful truth would be revealed to my wife.

Our return journey to Seville was made by water. Although the Guadalquiver is not a very interesting river, we thought travelling by steamer would be a pleasant change from the journeys in the hot, stuffy, slow trains, full from end to end with the odour of garlic and tobacco; so early one morning we left Cadiz and were soon steaming up the sluggish, dull,

turbid river, with the great flat stretches of swampy land on
either hand.

There were not many passengers on board the steamer. The
boat itself was a wretched affair, and before an hour was over
we wished we had chosen the train as a mode of transit. Mile
after mile of the level deserted land through which the river
flows passed by, and presented no objects of interest greater
than herds of cattle or flights of aquatic birds. Save that Philippa
was by my side, it was the dullest journey I ever made.

Of course there were English tourists on board; no spot is
complete without them. Two of them, young men, and apparently gentlemen, had seated themselves near us; and after the
usual admiring glances at my beautiful Philippa, commenced a
desultory talk with each other.

From the unrestrained way in which they spoke, and from
the strength of some of their unfavourable comments on the
scenery, or lack of scenery, it was clear that they took us for
natives, before whom they could speak without being understood. Philippa, of course, looked a thorough Spaniard, and
my own face had become so tanned by the sun that I might
have been of any nationality.

The young fellows chatted on, quite oblivious to the fact
that two of their neighbours understood every word they
spoke. For some time I listened with great amusement;
then the lulling motion of the steamer, the sluggish muddy
flow of the stream, the monotonous banks past which we
stole, exercised a soporific effect upon me, and I began to
doze and dream.

Through my dreams I heard a name, a hated name, spoken
clearly and distinctly. I started and opened my eyes,
Philippa's head was stretched forward as if she was intent
upon catching some expected words spoken by another. 'Sir
Mervyn Ferrand,' I heard one of our fellow-voyagers repeat.
'Yes, I remember him; tall, good-looking man. Where is he
now? He was a bad lot.'

'Surely you read or heard about it?' said his companion in a tone of surprise.

I touched my wife's arm. 'Come away, Philippa,' I said.

She made a motion of dissent. Again I urged her. She shook her head pettishly.

Ah! I forgot where you have been for months,' said the second tourist, laughing; 'out of the pale of civilisation and newspapers. Well, Ferrand was murdered—shot dead!'

'Philippa, dearest, come, I implore you,' I whispered.

It was too late! The look on her face told me that nothing would now move her—nothing! She would hear the dreadful truth, told perhaps with distorted details. I groaned inwardly. The moment I had so long dreaded had come. If I dragged her away by force—if I interrupted the speakers—what good could it do? She had heard enough. She would force me to tell her the rest. I could only pray that she would not in any way associate herself with the man's death.

'Murdered! Poor fellow! Who murdered him?' I heard the first speaker say.

'No one knows. He was shot dead on a country roadside, just as that fearful snow-storm of last winter began. It seems almost incredible, but the snow drifted over him, and until it melted the crime was not discovered. In the interval the murderer had, of course, got clean away.'

'Poor devil! I never heard any good of him; but what an end!'

I was not looking at the speakers. I was noting every change in my wife's face. I saw the colour fly from her cheek. I saw her lips and throat working convulsively, as though she was trying to articulate. I saw her dark eyes contract as in anguish. I knew that she was clasping her hands together, as was her way when agitated. Suddenly she turned her eyes to mine, and in her eyes was a look of horror which told me that the very worst had come to pass—that the dread which had haunted me was realised! Then with a low moan she sank, white and senseless, on my shoulder.

Though in a whirl of despair, I believe that I assumed a kind of mechanical calm. I seem to remember that the two English tourists offered their assistance; that, as we bore Philippa to an extemporised couch in the shadiest and coolest place we could find, I smiled, and attributed my wife's fainting-fit to the heat of the sun, the smell of engines, or something of that kind. Little did those young men guess what their chance words had wrought. Little could they think that in speaking of Sir Mervyn Ferrand's death they had, perhaps, wrecked the happiness of two lives. My heart was full of grief and fear, but I believe I bore myself bravely.

In spite of such restoratives as we could administer, Philippa's swoon lasted for a considerable time. I troubled little about that fact. Indeed, to me it seemed well that syncope should have supervened, and for a time banished the dreadful memories which had so suddenly invaded her brain. Could such a thing have been possible, I would almost have wished that her insensibility would continue until we reached Seville. But it was not to be so. By-and-by she sighed deeply, and her eyes opened. Consciousness and all its dreaded sequence was hers once more.

I spoke to her, but she made no reply. She turned her eyes from mine; she shunned my gaze; she even seemed to shrink from the touch of my hand. During the remainder of that dreary journey not one word passed her lips. She lay with her face turned to the side of the vessel, needless of curious glances from fellow-passengers; heedless of my whispered words of love; heedless of all save her own thoughts—thoughts which led her, I trembled to picture whither.

Through all those long sultry hours whilst the wretched steamboat ploughed its way up the broad muddy stream. I sat beside her, trying to find some way out of our sorrow. Alas! Every road was stopped by the impassable obstacle of Philippa's knowledge of what she had done. For she knew it, I was certain. That look in her eyes had told me so much.

The duration of her insanity had been so short that I could gather no comfort from the fact that by some merciful arrangement maniacs who recover their erring senses are troubled little by the deeds they have done in their moments of madness. I felt that in my wife's case my only hope was to endeavour by argument to bring her to my own way of thinking; that is, to consider herself unaccountable by any law, human or divine, for her actions at the time. But I doubted if her sensitive, impulsive nature could ever be induced to take this view of her act. I doubted, had she not been the woman I loved with a passionate love, if I could have quite absolved her from the crime, with the remembrance of her words, 'Basil, did you ever hate a man?' still with me.

Yet, strange anomaly, I would, in fair fight of course, have shot that man through the heart and have gloried in the deed. But then Philippa was a woman, and had she not been the woman I loved I might have shrank from the one who, even in her madness, was urged to take such fearful vengeance.

I smiled bitterly as I thought how a chance breath of wind had tumbled my house of cards to the ground. I smiled almost triumphantly as I told myself that, come what might—misery—shame—death—I had won and held for a week the one desire of my life. Nothing could deprive me of that memory.

Home at last! Still silent, or answering my questions by monosyllables, Philippa was brought by me to our once happy home in Seville. My mother, with arch smiles of welcome on her comely face, was at the gate of the *patio* ready to receive us. As she saw her a kind of shiver ran through my poor love's frame. She let my mother embrace and caress her without any display of reciprocal affection.

'Philippa is ill,' I said, in explanation. 'I will take her to her room.'

I led her to the apartment which my mother had in our absence fitted up for us. It was gay and beautiful with flowers, and there were many other careful little evidences of the hearty welcome which was waiting us. Philippa noticed nothing. I closed the door and turned towards my wife.

She looked at me with those wondrous dark eyes, which seemed to search my very soul. 'Basil,' she said, in a low, solemn voice, 'tell me—tell me the truth. What had I done that night?'

CHAPTER XI

SPECIAL PLEADING

IT was over! She knew! The hope which may have buoyed my spirits, that Philippa's agitation at learning of Sir Mervyn Ferrand's death was but due to the fact that once she loved the man, entirely vanished. I could see no loop-hole of escape, no possibility of persuading her that she was fancying horrors which had never taken place. Moreover, although I would have given my life to have saved her from the knowledge of this thing, I could not meet the eyes of her I loved and lie to her.

I did indeed, if but for the sake of gaining time, attempt to stammer out some evasive answer; but she interrupted me before I had spoken five words.

'Why do I ask?' she echoed. 'I knew it all—all—all! In dreams it has come to me—the whitened road—the dull dead face—the whirling snow! In dreams I have stood over him, and said to myself, "He is dead!" But, Basil, my love, my husband, I thought it was but a dream. I drove it away. I said, "It must be a dream. I hated him, and so I dreamed that I killed him." Basil, dearest Basil, tell me, if you can, that I dreamed it!'

Her voice sank into accents of piteous entreaty. She looked at me yearningly.

'Dearest, it must have been a dream,' I said.

She threw out her arms wildly. 'No, no! It was no dream. Even now I can see myself standing in the night over that motionless form. I can feel the cold air on my cheek. I can see myself flying through the snow. Basil, I hated that man, and I killed him!'

The tears were streaming down my cheeks. I seized her hands, and strove to draw her to me. She tore herself from my grasp, and, throwing herself wildly on the bed, broke into a paroxysm of sobs. As I approached her she turned her head from me.

'I killed him! Killed him!' she whispered in awe-struck tones. 'Oh, that fearful night! It has haunted me ever since. I knew not why. Now I know! He wronged me, and I killed him! Killed him!'

I placed my arm around her neck, and my cheek against hers. As she felt my touch she started up wildly.

'No, no!' she cried. 'Touch me not! Shun me! Shrink from me! Basil, do you hear? Do you understand? I have murdered a man!'

Once more she threw herself on the bed, her whole frame quivering with anguish.

'A shamed—a ruined woman!' she muttered. 'A villain's forsaken toy, and now a murderess! You have chosen your wife well, Basil!'

'Sweetest, I love you,' I whispered.

'Love me! How can you love me? Such love is not holy. If you love me, aid me to die, Basil! Give me something that will kill me! Why did you save my life?'

'Because I loved you then, as I love you now.'

She was silent, and I hoped was growing calmer. I was but waiting for the first shock of her newly-born knowledge to pass away, in order to reason with her, and show her that by every moral law she was guiltless of the fearful crime. Suddenly she turned to me.

'How did I kill him?' she said, with a shudder.

'Dearest, rest. We will talk again presently.'

'How did I kill him?' she repeated with vehemence.

'He was found shot through the heart,' I answered, reluctantly.

'Shot through his heart—his wicked heart! Shot by me! How could I have shot him? With what? Basil, tell me all, or I shall go mad! I will not have the smallest thing concealed. I will know all!'

'He was shot with a pistol.'

'A pistol! A pistol! How did I come by it? Where is it?'

'I threw it away.'

'You! Then you knew!'

I bowed my head. I felt that concealment was useless. She must know all.

I told her everything. I told her how she had promised to come for me; how, as she did not keep that promise, I went in search of her. I told her how she had swept past me in the snow-storm; how I had overtaken her. I repeated her wild words, and told her how the fatal weapon had fallen at my feet, and how I had, on the impulse of the moment, hurled it away into the night; how she had broken away from me, and fled down the lonely road; how, excited and terrified by her words, I had gone on to learn their meaning; how I had found the body of Sir Mervyn Ferrand; how, without thought of concealing the deed, I had laid the dead man by the roadside; how I had rushed home, and found her, Philippa, waiting for me, and in the full height of temporary insanity. I told her all this, and I swore that from the moment I discovered that her senses had gone astray I held her, although she had done so dreadful a deed, as innocent of crime as when she slept, a baby, on her mother's breast.

She listened to me with fixed dilated eyes. She interrupted me neither by word nor gesture; but when I had finished speaking she covered her face with her hands, and great tears trickled through her fingers. 'No hope! No hope!' she cried. 'Oh, Basil, I dared to hope that something you would tell me would show me it was not my hand which did this thing! My love, my own love, we have been so happy whilst I could persuade myself all this was a dream! We shall be happy no more, Basil!'

Although she still shrank from me, by force I drew her to me, and laid that poor head on my shoulder. I stroked the smooth black silky hair, I kissed the white forehead, and used

every endearing and soothing expression that love such as mine
could suggest. In vain! The moment I loosened my hold my
wife fled from my side.

'Basil,' she cried, 'you knew it! You knew the blood of a man
was on my hands! Again I say such love is not holy!'

'Dearest, again I tell you that in my eyes—if the truth were
known, in the eyes of all—you are innocent as a babe.'

She shook her head hopelessly. I saw that nothing at present
could move her. Perhaps it was more than I had a right to
expect. So for the time I gave up arguing. I begged her for my
sake to retire to rest. I gave her a soothing draught. I sat by her
for hours, and held her hand, until at last, her eyelids fell, and
worn out by grief, she slept.

Oh, how right I had been in choosing flight! Although a
cursed chance had revealed what I fondly hoped would be for
ever buried in oblivion, how right I had been! Had the hands
of Justice grasped my sweet wife, although she might no doubt
have been found guiltless, the trial, the exposure, would have
killed her. Thank heaven, she was safe, and amenable only to
the tribunal of her own sensitive conscience!

When I heard her breathing grow regular, and knew that
she was in a deep sleep, I pressed my lips gently to her fair
cheek, and left her. I went in search of my mother, and made
the best tale I could think of to account for Philippa's indis-
position. I forced myself to wear a smiling face, and to listen
with a show of interest to the account my mother gave me of
certain difficulties which had during my absence arisen with
some of the native servants. But there was nothing which could
really interest me when I thought of my poor love lying there
sleeping, to awake, alas, to sorrow and remorse. No wonder
that, as soon as I had spent with my mother the smallest portion
of time which filial duty and gratitude exacted, I flew back to
Philippa's bedside.

I watched beside her until she awoke—until her splendid
dark eyes unveiled themselves. I leant over and kissed her

passionately. Between sleeping and waking, while consciousness was yet in abeyance, she returned my caresses. Then came back memory and its terrors.

'Leave me,' she said; 'I am a murderess!'

Once more I denied it; once more I told her she was innocent. My only hope was, that by continued argument I might in time ease her mind. She listened almost apathetically. I grew eloquent and passionate. Was I not pleading for my own sake as well as hers? If I could but persuade her she was unaccountable for what she had done, some remnant of the happiness which a few days ago I had promised myself might even now be left.

'Basil,' she whispered, 'I have been dreaming horrible things. Will they try me—and hang me?'

'We are in Spain, dearest. Even if you were guilty, the English law would not reach you.'

She started. 'And it was for this you hurried to Spain? To save me from a felon's death?'

'To save you from what, in your state at the time, you could not bear. I say again you are innocent, but I dare not risk the trial.'

She was silent for some minutes; then she spoke.

'I am proud, passionate, wicked,' she said; 'but I could never have meant to do this. I was mad! I must have been mad! Basil, you could tell them I was mad. They would believe you, and forgive me.'

She looked at me imploringly.

'I could stand up,' I said, 'and state on oath that you were at the time in a raging delirium. I could pledge my professional reputation that your actions were the result of madness. Fear nothing on that score, my wife.'

I spoke boldly; but as I spoke a thought shot through me—a thought which blanched my cheek and brought the beads of perspiration to my brow. I knew enough of law to be aware that a husband could not in a criminal case give evidence for or against his wife. My marriage with Philippa had deprived her of the benefit of my testimony as to her insanity. I trembled like a leaf as I pictured what might happen in the event of her being tried for the murder of Sir Mervyn Ferrand. The very nurses had but seen her sane. No one but myself and perhaps my servant had seen her in her madness.

My dismay was such that I was bound to leave the room, in order to recover my presence of mind. Again and again I thanked heaven that we were on foreign soil. The thought that my unreasoning love might have destroyed her I loved was almost more than I could bear.

I fancy I have lingered long enough over that terrible time, when my wife first learnt that the dream which had haunted her was reality—that her hand had unknowingly avenged her supposed and premeditated wrong. Let me but say that the mental anguish into which the knowledge plunged her was not unattended by physical evil. In fact, for many days my poor girl was ill, very ill. My mother and I nursed her with every care, and by-and-by youth and a splendid constitution reasserted themselves, and, a shadow of her former self, she was able to leave her bed. My mother was tenderness itself to her daughter. She knew nothing of the true cause of her illness; indeed, she blamed me roundly for not having taken proper care of my beautiful bride, and vowed laughingly that for the future nothing should induce her to trust Philippa out of her sight.

Now that Philippa knew all she had done, I thought it better to tell her that, although he had no intention of so doing, Sir Mervyn Ferrand, in causing a mock marriage to be celebrated, had by a strange chance really made her his wife. This gave her little comfort. 'It makes my crime the greater,' she said bitterly. 'I have killed my husband instead of my seducer! I am not fit to live!'

Weeks went by. Philippa gradually grew stronger, and, what was even more a cause of joy to me, calmer and more reasonable on a certain subject. With all the power I could bring to bear, I had never ceased to impress upon her that morally she was innocent, and I believed my words were bearing fruit. Her fits of mental anguish and self-reproach grew of less frequent occurrence. She did not, whenever we were alone, continually harp upon her crime. Calm seemed to settle upon us once more, and I ventured to hope that the great physician, Time, would one day bring to my wife's heart something that might be called sorrowful happiness; but I knew I must wait years and years for this.

She was changed, greatly changed. Her lips seldom smiled; her eyes never brightened, unless when she saw me drawing near. She seemed older and graver. But I knew, in spite of all, she loved me with a deathless love.

Although at last we had ceased to discuss the sorrow of our life, I suspected it was seldom absent from her mind. Sometimes as I lay beside her I heard her moaning and talking in her troubled dreams, and too well I knew the cause. As my arm stole round her, and assured her of the safety and certainty of my great love, in my heart I cursed the dead man whose evil deed had brought such lasting woe on the fair head pillowed on my bosom. Ah me! What life might have been for us two, now that love reigned between us!

Once—it was shortly after Philippa began to creep, a weak invalid, about the fragrant *patio*—she said to me, with evident meaning in her voice,

'Basil, do you see the London papers?'

'Sometimes—not always. I have almost forgotten England.'

'Promise me you will see them every day.'

'I will, if you wish; but why?'

Her voice sank. 'Can you not guess? Basil, listen. I have consented to be guided by you. I am praying that the day may come when I shall think as you think. But what if an innocent person were accused of the crime I have committed? Then there is but one course; you could urge nothing against it. Promise me you will see the paper of every day as soon as it reaches here. I shall have no peace unless you do.'

I promised fearlessly. Justice does sometimes make mistakes, but not such a mistake as the one hinted at by Philippa. No; Sir Mervyn Ferrand's death was a mystery never to be solved. So, to set my poor wife at ease on the matter, I wrote and ordered that the *Times* should be posted to me every day.

CHAPTER XII

TEMPTED TO DISHONOUR

I HATE looking back and re-reading words which I have written whilst the impulse was upon me; but I fancy I have somewhere called this tale a confession; if not, I should have done so. It claims no more to be ranked as a work of art than as a work of imagination. How could it? It holds only two characters—a man and a woman. It treats but of their love and of a few months of their lives. Nevertheless, in telling it I have endeavoured to conceal nothing. I have tried to describe my thoughts, my hopes, my fears, my sorrows and my joys, as they really were. I have, I believe, suppressed nothing which could lead anyone to condemn my actions more strongly than, it may be, they now condemn them. My wish has been to show myself as I was then—no doubt am now—a weak, selfish man; yet, for the love which he bore a woman, one willing to risk fortune, life, even honour. If I have failed in my attempt to represent myself as such a one, believe it is not from intention, but from sheer inability.

But whether I have so far succeeded or failed in my purpose I know not; but I know that in this chapter I must, perforce, fail. The language rich and powerful enough to serve my needs has yet to be invented. The writer who could in any fitting way reproduce my thoughts has yet to be born.

And yet the chapter will be a short one. It will be but the record of a few hours; but such hours! Hours during which I struggled against a temptation to commit, not only crime, but base cowardly crime; a temptation stronger, I dare to think, than poor human nature has as yet been subjected to. My words sound bold; but listen.

Oh, that one morning! How well I can remember it! Our breakfast was just over. The quaint-shaped little table, with its snowy cloth throwing into relief the deep colours of the luscious fruit upon it, still stood in the awning-roofed *patio*. I was alone, my mother and Philippa having retired indoors to see about some domestic economy. I lounged lazily and at my ease. I rolled and lighted a cigarette, blaming myself as I did so for my barbarity in profaning the blossom-scented air with tobacco smoke. Then I took from my pocket the London *Times*, which had arrived by the last post, and listlessly set to work to skim its lengthy columns.

I had no fear as to what the paper might contain. It was not from newspaper reports that I apprehended danger. I had, however, noticed that Philippa, when she saw me with a newspaper in my hand, eyed me anxiously and inquiringly; so that generally I contrived to glance through it when she was absent. I never permitted her to touch it until I had read it; but my only reason for this prohibition was that I feared lest some chance allusion to the mysterious and undiscovered crime might distress her. Her own far-fetched fancy that another might be accused of it gave me not a moment's uneasiness.

So I turned and doubled back the broad sheets. I ran down the topics of the day. I skimmed the leading articles. I glanced at the foreign news; paid scant attention to law reports, and disregarded altogether the money-market intelligence. At last I turned my attention to the provincial news column. A name caught my eye; a cold shiver of dread ran through me. My cigarette fell on the marble pavement, and lay there unheeded, as, with agitation which no words can describe, I read a short paragraph placed under the heading of Tewnham, the principal town of the county in which Roding was situated. Read!

'William Evans, the man accused of the murder of Sir Mervyn Ferrand, Bart., in January last, will be tried at these Assizes, which open on the twentieth. The case, which excites considerable interest, will be taken on the first day. It is reported that although fresh evidence against the prisoner will be forthcoming, it will be of a purely circumstantial nature.'

Every word of that accursed paragraph seemed like a blow falling upon my head. For some minutes I sat as one stunned. I felt my teeth chattering. I knew that my cheek was blanched. Philippa's fanciful dread had come to pass! Another—an innocent man—was bearing the blame of her own mad act! Dazed, stupid, scarcely able to comprehend what must be the full effect of what I had just read, I sat motionless, with my eyes fixed upon that fatal sheet.

The sound of my mother's pleasant voice calling to Philippa at last awoke me from my stupor. They were coming. I could not face them. I doubled up the newspaper, thrust it into my pocket, and rushed out into the street. As yet I had not dared to imagine what this intelligence might mean to us. I must have long hours of solitude, in order to decide what course should be adopted to face this, the last, the worst peril.

I passed swiftly through the iron gate. I went up the narrow street at a pace which must have made all who saw me think me mad. Whither did I go? I scarcely remember. I think it must have been to one of the public gardens; but in that hour all sense of locality left me. I went instinctively in search of solitude. I found, I know not how or where, some shady deserted spot. There, in the anguish of my heart, amid the wreck of my sand-founded happiness, I threw myself on the ground, and dug my finger-nails into the dry soil.

At first I thought I was going or had gone mad. The thoughts which rushed through my mind were disjointed, and wanted coherence. An innocent man accused of the crime! To be tried on the twentieth! The twentieth! And now it is the sixteenth! Fresh evidence forthcoming! The fools—the utter fools! This the boasted detective skill! To arrest on suspicion, to bring

to trial a man who must be ignorant of everything connected
with the murder! What is to be done? What can be done? Oh,
my wife! My poor darling wife!

Then, I believe, I cried like a child. It seemed to me that all
was lost. There was but one thing to be done—one course to
be taken. My darling must give herself up to justice, and by her
confession free this luckless wretch who now stands in peril of
his life. She must bear the shame of the trial, and trust to human
justice and the mercy which she had a right to expect. Oh, it
was pitiful, pitiful! For a long while no alternative course
suggested itself to me.

Human justice! What is justice? See how it can err! It can
arrest, try, and—oh, horrible thought!—perhaps condemn to
death an innocent man! How then would it fare with Philippa?
Who, now that marriage has sealed my lips, was there to prove
her madness when she slew that man? I raged at the thought. It
seemed to me that we were hard and fast in the toils. I might,
it is true, call William, my servant, to swear that her manner
was strange and wild upon that night. I might call the nurses
to prove that when first they saw her she was recovering from
an attack of mania. But would they be credited? Would not a
clever lawyer soon convince twelve ordinary men that it was
not her madness which prompted the crime, but the crime
which produced the madness? We were indeed meshed and
bound; hemmed in on every side; helpless and, it seemed,
hopeless!

And Philippa must be told this! I must tell her! How could
I nerve myself to make the truth known to her—now, of all
times, when her health was all but restored; when a kind of sad
but placid acquiescence in what fate had wrought seemed to
be gradually coming over her; now, when I was once more
building up hopes of happiness for her as well as for me? For
I knew—ah, think of this, and pity me!—that before another
half-year should pass there might be given to my wife and me
a gift which would go far towards sweeping away the memories

of gloom and horror which had of late spread over our lives. I even dared to hope, to feel certain, that as she gazed into baby eyes, as she pressed a tiny head to her bosom, some, nay, much of the lost sweetness and glory of life might return to my love.

Think of this, and picture me lying on the ground that day, with the damning intelligence fresh on my mind! Think that in a few hours I must return to my home, and tell my wife that the bolt had fallen! There was no alternative!

No alternative? Stay, there is an alternative! The blood seemed to course wildly through my veins, my heart beat fiercely, my lips grew dry, and a choking sensation came over me, as for the first time the simple yet certain way of cutting the knot of my difficulties flashed across my mind. So simple, so easy it at first appeared, that I laughed at my stupidity in not having seen it at once.

Tear that accursed paper to pieces, Basil North! Scatter those pieces to the winds. Forget what you have read. Go back to your luxurious flower-bedecked home. Meet the one you love with a smile upon your face: you have forced smiles before now! Greet her as usual. Say nothing of this morning's news. Keep your own counsel; bury all you have learnt in your secret heart. Do this, and be happy for evermore!

But the man—the man who in a few days' time is to be tried for another's act? Well, what of him? The fool will doubtless be acquitted. Fool! Yes, it is the right term for one who can bring himself under suspicion. But if Justice runs on the wrong track until the end—if that man dies?

What then? What is his miserable life, what are a hundred lives, when weighed against Philippa's happiness? What is conscience? What is right and wrong? What is the phantom which men call honour? What, after all, is crime? Be silent, and forget. You are asked to do no more. You have riches, youth, health, and a strong will. The fairest woman on the earth adores you. Why hesitate? Why let one boor's life weigh in the scale?

Argue the matter in another way. Are not thousands of men slain every year by the whim of a monarch or a statesman? The thought of their deaths troubles not those who send them forth to fight. Men kill each other for revenge, for money, for a point of honour, and the killer lives on like other men live! Trust this man to the vaunted array of Justice. He is innocent, and will come from the ordeal unscathed. If found guilty, let him die. He will not be the first innocent man who has died, nor will he be the last to die. It is but one life! He is nothing to you; think of him no more. Come what may, you will always have your sunny home and the woman you love. Her children will grow up around you. Why hesitate? A life's happiness is to be won by simply sealing your lips. Its cost is but, supposing Justice blunders, to bear the burden of one man's death. A paltry price!

This was the temptation with which I wrestled during those long hours. Again and again I was on the point of yielding. Once or twice I rose to my feet with the fixed determination of destroying that paper, and letting things take their own course. Once or twice I even forced my steps some distance in the direction of home, but each time I turned, went back to the sheltered spot, threw myself again on the ground, and fought the battle anew.

No, I could not do this thing. I was a gentleman and a man of honour. Paltry as the price was when compared with what it might buy, I could not pay it. Although my whole soul was merged in Philippa's welfare, I could not, even for her sake, suffer an innocent man to be done unjustly to death. The crime was too black, too base, too contemptible! I felt sure that, with the man's blood morally on my head, the supremest joys which life could give would not lull my conscience to rest. I knew it would not be long before remorse and shame drove me to commit suicide.

Let the preachers say that sin is easy; that wrong is more alluring than right. There may be some sins which are easily committed, but I dare to say that there are others which the average man, educated by the code of honour, and dreading shame and cowardice, finds it far easier to avoid than to bring himself to commit. No, every sin is not easy!

But all the same my struggle was a mortal one. At times I fancy—it may be but fancy—that even now my mind bears some traces of that conflict; a conflict in which my victory meant ruin to my nearest and dearest. Was I not right when I said that my temptation was an all but unparalleled one? Yet in reasserting this let me humbly disclaim all credit for not having yielded. I strove to yield, but could not.

It was only when I had conquered, and put the temptation from me, that I was able to see how utterly useless such a crime as that urged upon me would have been. Doubtless Philippa, sooner or later, would have learnt that Sir Mervyn Ferrand's supposed murderer had paid the penalty of the crime. How would it have fared with us then—then, when reparation was placed out of the question? Knowing as I did every thought of my wife's, every turn of her impulsive, sensitive nature, I was fain to tell myself that such news would be simply her death-blow.

But what was to be done? Finding that I could not compass the treachery which I dared to meditate, I cast about for another loop-hole of escape. What if I were to return to England, and accuse myself of the crime? To ensure Philippa's safety I would right willingly give away my own life. It showed the state to which my mind was reduced when I say that I considered this scheme in all its bearings, and for a while thought it furnished a solution to my difficulties! I wonder if my brain was wandering?

I laughed in bitter merriment as the absurdity of my new plan forced itself upon me. I had forgotten Philippa, and what the effect of such a sacrifice would be upon her. I had forgotten that she loved me, even as I loved her; that my dying for her sake—for the sake of saving her from the consequences of that gruesome night—would make an expiation, if any were due from her, the most fearful which human or diabolical ingenuity could devise.

No! Neither by sinning against my fellow-man nor by a voluntary sacrifice of my own life could I save her. After all my protracted mental struggles, all my lonely hours of anguish and wild scheming, I was forced to return to the point from which I started. Philippa must surrender herself, and free this innocent man. There was, indeed, no alternative!

And a day gone, or all but gone! The trial on the twentieth! To reach England—to reach Tewnham in time to stop that trial, we must travel day and night. Day and night across sunny or starlit Spain—across pleasant France—we must speed on, until we reached our own native land, now lying in all the rich calm of the early autumn. I must lead my wife, my love, to her doom!

I rose from the ground. I felt weary, and as if I had been cudgelled in every limb. I dragged myself slowly back to my home. 'She must be told; she must be told. But how to tell her?' I muttered as I went along. My appearance must have been wretched; for I received the impression that several grave-looking Sevillaños turned and looked after me as I passed by. Even as a cowardly felon who drags himself slowly to the scaffold, I dragged myself to the gate of our pleasant home, and on tottering feet passed into that fragrant space in which the happiest hours of my life had been spent.

As I entered, the remembrance of some tale which once I had read flashed through my mind—a tale of the ferocity of a bygone age. It was of a prisoner who was forced by his captors to strike a dagger into the heart of the woman he loved. I know not where the tale is to be found or when I read it.

But it seemed to me that mine was a parallel case.

Pity me!

CHAPTER XIII

THE LAST HOPE

THEY were sitting in the courtyard, my mother and my wife. They looked the embodiment of serene happiness. Their large fans—the use of the fan came like an inspiration to Philippa, my mother acquired it after much practice—were languidly waving to and fro. Philippa's rounded arm was outstretched; her fair left hand was in the clear water which fell from the fountain and filled a white marble basin, in which the gold carp darted about in erratic tacks. She was moving her fingers gently backwards and forwards, startling the timid fish, and half smiling at their terror. It seemed to me that my mother was remonstrating at the uproar she was creating in the brilliant-coated republic.

That picture is still in my mind. That picture! I can sit now in my chair, lay down my pen, and call up every picture of that time. Nothing, save the grief, has ever, or ever will, fade from my memory.

It was well for both of us that I had fought out the battle with myself in solitude, where no eye could see me, where I could see no one. Even as it was, knowing what a change my news must work, I paused, and a ghost of the day's temptation rose before me. But it rose too late. The die was cast. Philippa had seen me, and my mother's eyes followed hers. I braced myself up, and went towards them with as jaunty a manner as I could assume. My mother began a mock tirade on my shameful desertion of Philippa and herself. Her words carried no meaning to my ears. My eyes met those of my wife.

With her I made no attempt at concealment. Where was the good? The worst, the very worst, had come. My eyes must have told her the truth.

I saw her sweet face catch fire with alarm. I saw her lips quiver. I saw the look of anguish flash into her eyes; yet I knew that I was helpless, utterly helpless.

She rose. I made some conventional excuse, and went to my room. In a moment Philippa was at my side.

'Basil, husband, love,' she whispered, 'it has come!'

I laid my head on the table and sobbed aloud. Philippa's arms were wreathed around my neck.

'Dearest, I knew it must come. I have known it ever so long. Basil, do not weep. Once more I tell you I am not worth such love as yours.'

I covered her dear face with kisses. I strained her to my heart. I lavished words of love upon her. She smiled faintly, then sighed hopelessly—a sigh which almost broke my heart.

'Tell me all, my love,' she said calmly. 'Let me know the very worst.'

I could not speak; for the life of me the words would not come. With trembling hands I drew out the newspaper, and pointed to the fatal lines. She read them with a calm which almost alarmed me.

'I knew it must be,' was all she said.

I threw myself on my knees before her. I embraced her. I was half distraught. Save for my wild ejaculations of undying love, there was silence for many minutes between us.

Presently, with gentle force, she raised my head and looked at me with her sweet and sorrowful eyes.

'Basil, my dearest, you have been wrong. The right is right, the wrong is wrong. See what you have done! Had you not striven to save me, only I should have had to answer for this. Now it is you and me, and perhaps a third—an innocent, stainless life, that will be wrecked.'

'Spare me! Spare me!' I said. 'As you love me, spare me!'

She kissed me. 'Dearest, forgive me. I should not blame you. Only I am to blame.' Then, with a sudden change in her voice, 'When do we start for England, Basil?'

Although I expected this question, I trembled and shuddered as I heard it. Too well I knew what England meant. It meant Philippa's standing in open court, in a prisoner's dock, the centre of a gaping crowd, self-accused of the murder of her husband! And as I pictured this, once more, and for the last time, the temptation shook me.

I spoke, but I averted my eyes from hers. I could not meet them. My voice was husky and strange; it sounded like the voice of another man. A sort of undercurrent of thought ran through me, that if Philippa would but share it, I could bear any burden, any dishonour.

'Listen!' I said, in quick accents. 'We are far away; safe. We love each other. We can be happy. Let the man take his chance. What does anything matter, so long as we love and are together?'

I felt that her eyes were seeking mine. I felt a change in the clasp of her hand. I knew that she was nobler and better than I.

'Basil,' she said softly, and speaking like one in a dream, 'it was not my husband, not the man I love, who said that. I forgive you for the sake of your great love, for the sake of all you have done, or tried to do, for me. Tell me now, when do we start for England?'

Her words brought back my senses. Never in the wildest height of my passion had I loved Philippa as I loved her at that moment. I besought her pardon. She gave it, and once more repeated her question.

With the calm of settled despair I consulted the railway-guide, and found that if we left Seville tomorrow morning by the first train, we might, by travelling day and night, early on the morning of the twentieth reach the town in which the trial was to be held. I made the result of my researches known to my wife; and upon my assuring her that we should have time to spare, she left all the arrangement of the journey to me.

After this, another painful question arose. Was my mother to be told? Philippa, who may, perhaps, in her secret heart have

craved for a woman's support and sympathy in her approaching
trial, at first insisted that my mother should be taken into our
confidence—a confidence which, alas, in a few days' time would
be gossip to the world. I besought her to waive the point, to
spare my mother's feelings until the very last moment. We could
not take her with us on our hurried journey. We were young;
she was old. The fatigue, combined with the grief, would be
more than her frame could endure. I could not bear to think
of her waiting lonely in Seville for the bad news which she
knew must come in a day or two from England. Let us say
nothing respecting the wretched errand on which we are bound.
Let us depart in secret, and leave some plausible explanation
behind us.

To my relief, Philippa at last consented to this. Then, after
a long, tearful embrace, we steeled ourselves to join my mother
at the evening meal, and to bear ourselves so that she should
suspect nothing of the tempest within our hearts. We did not
for very long subject ourselves to this strain upon our nerves.
It seemed to me now that every moment spent otherwise than
alone with my wife was a precious treasure wasted, a loss which
I should for ever regret. So very early we pleaded fatigue, and
retired to our rest. Such rest!

Philippa bade my mother good-night with an embrace so long
and passionate that I feared it would awaken alarm, especially
when it was succeeded by my own veiled, but scarcely less
emotional, adieu. For who could say that we should ever meet
again? I do not believe it struck Philippa that in accompanying
her I was running the slightest risk. Had she thought so, she
would have insisted upon going alone. But I knew that the part
I had played in that night's work would probably bring a severe
punishment upon my own head. What did I care for that?

Silently and sadly in the retirement of our room we made
our preparations for the journey, which began with the morn.
There was no need to cumber ourselves with much luggage.
We should rest in no bed until the trial was over. What

resting-place might then be Philippa's, heaven only knew! So our packing was soon completed.

Then I wrote a letter, to be given to or found by my mother in the morning. I told her that an important matter took me post-haste to England; that Philippa had determined to accompany me; that I would write as soon as we reached London. I gave no further explanation. I hoped she would attribute my sudden flight to the erratic nature which she often averred I possessed.

After all, the deception mattered little. In a week's time nothing would matter. Grief, overwhelming grief, would be my portion; a portion which, by her affection for me and for Philippa, my poor mother would be forced to share.

All being now ready for our start, we strove to win some hours of sleep. Our efforts were mocked to scorn. Through that, the last night we might spend alone together, I believe neither my wife nor myself closed an eyelid. Let me draw a veil over my wild distress and Philippa's calm acquiescence in her fate. Some grief is too sacred to describe.

Morning! Bright, broad, clear, cool, odorous morning! Our sleeplessness had at least spared us the anguish of awaking, and, whilst for a moment glorying in the beauty of the world, to remember what this morning meant to us. Giving ourselves ample time to reach the railway-station, we crept from our room, and, with eyes full of blinding tears, crossed the pleasant *patio*. I paused in the centre, and plucking a lovely spray from the great orange tree, kissed it and gave it to my wife. Without a word she placed it in the bosom of her dress. As she drew her mantle aside to do so, for the first time I noticed that she wore the very dress which clad her on that fatal night. Although it was utterly unsuited to the almost tropical heat through which we should have to travel, I dared not remonstrate with her. Now, of all times, her slightest wish should be my law.

Noiselessly I undid the massive studded wooden gate, which at night-time closed the entrance to the *patio*. Unseen, we stepped into the shady, narrow street. Our luggage was light. I could carry it with ease to the station, which was not a great distance off. We were there only too soon.

We had to wait some time ere the train, which, following the example of the true Spaniard, declines on any consideration to be hurried, made its appearance. We took our seats in silence. At last the dignified train condescended to move onwards. We sat side by side, and gazed and gazed in the direction of the beautiful city from which we were flying; gazed until we saw the very last of it, until even the great towering Giralda was lost to view. Then, and only then, I think we fully realised to what end we were speeding.

The next three days and nights seem now little more to me than a whirling dream. On and on we went to work out our fate; over the same ground which I had traversed, with scarcely less agitated feelings, some months ago. I ground my teeth when I thought how little my strenuous and seemingly successful efforts had availed. Now, not from any omission of precaution; not because the law compelled: not by the exercise of force; but simply on account of the great dictum of right and wrong, we were, of our own accord retracing our steps to face the danger from which we had fled. Oh, bitter irony of destiny!

What was money to me now? Nothing but so much dross! It could do one thing, only one, that gold which I lavished so freely on that journey. It could assure that Philippa and I might travel alone. It could give us privacy for the time that journey lasted, that was all!

Yet, although alone, we spoke but little. Our thoughts were not such as can be expressed by words. Her hand in mine, her head on my shoulder—sleeping when we could sleep, waking and looking into each other's faces—knowing that every mile of sunny or starlit country over which we passed brought us nearer to the end. Ah! I understood then how it is that lovers who are menaced by some great sorrow can kill themselves, and die smiling in each other's arms! We might have done so;

but our deaths would have left to perish that stranger whom we were speeding to save.

So, as in a dream, the hours, the days, the nights, went by. We might have been travelling through the fairest scenery in the world, or through the most arid desert. I scarcely troubled to glance out of the carriage window. The world for me was inside.

It was after we left Paris—Paris, which today seemed all but within a stone's-throw of London—that I aroused myself, and braced my energies to discuss finally with Philippa our proper plan of action. I felt that my right course would be to go straight to some solicitor, tell the tale, and ask him to put matters in train. But I could not bring myself to do this. Our secret was as yet our own. Moreover, through the misery of those hours, one ray of hope had broken upon me. If Philippa could be brought to yield to my guidance, to follow my instructions, it was not beyond the bounds of possibility that we might be saved, and saved with clean hands.

'Dearest,' I whispered, 'tonight we shall be in London.'

Her fingers tightened on mine. 'And at Tewnham?' she said. 'We shall be in time?'

'In ample time. But, Philippa, listen—'

'Basil, as you love me, not one word to tempt, to dissuade me!'

'Not one; but listen. Sweetest, if you will be guided by me, even now all may go well. This man—'

'The poor man who is standing in my place?'

'Yes; listen. Heaven forbid that I should tempt you. Think; he is, no doubt, a man of a lowly station in life. Philippa, I am rich, very rich.'

'I do not understand you,' she said, pressing her hand to her brow.

'Money will compensate for anything. Let him stand his trial. He is innocent. If there is justice in the land, he may, he must be found not guilty.'

'But the agony of mind he must pass through!'

'For that I will pay him over and over again. He may be but a country boor, to whom a thousand pounds would be inexhaustible wealth. But, whatever his station, the compensation sent to him by an unknown hand shall make him bless the day which laid him under the false accusation. Reflect, look at the matter in every light. I swear to you that in my opinion we may, with a clear conscience, await the result of the trial.'

She sighed, but made no answer. Her silence was a joy to me. It told me that my specious argument carried weight. I took her hands and kissed them. I told her again and again that I loved her; that my life as well as hers depended on her yielding.

It was long before she yielded. The thought of a fellow-creature lying in prison, perhaps for months, and tomorrow to stand in shame before his judges, on account of a deed which she herself had done, was anguish to her noble nature. Then, growing desperate at seeing the only plank which could save us from the wreck spurned for the sake of what, in my present mood, I was able to believe too finely-strained a scruple, I used my last and, as I rightly judged, my most powerful argument. I told her that it would be not only she who would suffer for that unconscious act, but that I, her husband, must pay the penalty due from an accessory after the crime.

Heaven forgive me for the anguish my words caused that loving heart! Philippa, on whom the intelligence of my danger fell like a thunderbolt, sank back in her seat, pale and trembling. Had I ever doubted that my wife's heart-whole love was my own, that look would have dispelled the doubt.

She prayed and besought me to leave her at the next station; to let her finish the journey and make her avowal alone. My reply was short, but sufficiently long to put all hope of my consenting to such a course out of her head. Then, for my sake, she yielded.

'On one condition—one only,' she said.

'Be guided by me in this. In all else you shall do as you like.'

'I must be in the court, Basil. I must hear the trial. If the worst happens, there must not be the delay of a moment; then and there I must proclaim the truth.'

'You shall be at hand—close at hand. I will be present.'

'No! I must be there. I must hear and see all. If the man is found guilty, I must, before his horrible sentence is pronounced, stand up and declare his innocence.'

'All that could be done afterwards.'

'No; it must be done then. Basil, fancy—put yourself in his place! Nothing could atone for his anguish at hearing himself condemned to death for a crime he knows nothing of. I must be there. Promise me I shall be there, and for your sake I will do as you wish.'

It was the best concession I could get. I promised. I concealed the fact that if, when sentence was pronounced, a woman rose in the body of the court, and asserted the prisoner's innocence and her own guilt, the probabilities were she would be summarily ejected. This made no difference. Let Philippa be silent; let the man be found not guilty, and the next train could bear us back to Seville.

Yes, even now there was hope!

CHAPTER XIV

THE CRIMINAL COURT

WE reached Charing Cross at four o'clock on the morning of September 20th. The first train by which we could get to Tewnham was timed to leave Liverpool Street at seven, so that we had an hour or two to spare for such refreshment as we cared to take, such rest as we dared to allow ourselves. What with the fatigue of continuous travel, and the dread of what this day was to bring forth, it may be easily believed that we were thoroughly worn out. We were, indeed, more fitted to go to bed and sleep for a week, than to proceed upon the last stage of our dismal journey.

But there was no help for it. If we meant to be in time, we must go on by the early morning train. I begged my wife to lie down, and endeavour to snatch an hour's sleep. She refused firmly. Much of that calm which had characterised her since the moment when I broke the fatal news to her had vanished. Its place was now taken by an excitement, suppressed, but nevertheless clearly manifest to my eyes. The fear that we should not reach Tewnham in time for the trial seemed to haunt her unceasingly. It was for this reason she so peremptorily refused to lie down and court sleep. She feared lest, our eyes once closed, we should from sheer exhaustion, sleep for hours, and so miss the morning train. She was ever picturing the horror of that poor unknown man's being led from the dock, with the death sentence ringing in his ears.

So the time which elapsed before we started for Tewnham we spent in the hotel. I bespoke rooms by telegram, sent when we reached Folkestone. We made an apology for a meal; in fact, what we could get at that time of night was of itself little more than an apology. We sat all but silent, watching the hands of the clock, which told us how fast the precious moments were passing away. We saw the grey morning struggle with, and at last conquer, the yellow gas-light. We heard the hum of traffic growing louder and louder in the streets below us. Then we turned to make what may be rightly called our last adieus. Who could say that today my wife and I might not be parted for ever?

Whilst at the hotel I tried to obtain the file of the *Times*. I wanted to look back and see if I could find the account of magisterial proceedings against this unlucky William Evans. He must, of course, have appeared before the lesser tribunal, and could I see the account of his appearance, I should be able to judge as to the strength of the case against him. But the file was not forthcoming. Perhaps it did not exist; perhaps the sleepy-eyed Teutonic waiter did not understand what I wanted; so, still in the dark as to why suspicion should have fallen upon this innocent man, we left the hotel and drove to Liverpool Street Station.

At nine o'clock our journey was ended. We stood on the platform of Tewnham railway-station. My poor wife wore a thick black veil, so her face I could not see; but I knew it was as pale as death. Now and again her hand, which rested on my arm, pressed it convulsively. I think we were the most unhappy pair on the earth!

We were even denied the time for any more farewells or expressed regrets. The hour was chiming from the old cathedral tower. The business of the Courts, I knew, always began at ten o'clock, and, considering the crowd which would most surely be attracted by so interesting a case as this trial for a murder committed so many months ago, I felt sure that unless we proceeded at once to the Shirehall, our chance of gaining entrance would be but a small one. I hailed one of the closed cabs which were waiting outside the station.

As I did so I felt a heavy hand laid upon my shoulder, and

heard a rich, pleasant-sounding, and not unfamiliar voice exclaim, 'Basil North, as I'm a sinner!'

That anyone should at this moment address Basil North in a merry way seemed a positive incongruity. I turned round almost angrily, and found myself face to face with an old friend. He was a barrister named Grant; a man four or five years my senior, but one with whom, before I forswore the society of my fellow-men, I had been on intimate terms. I had not seen him for a considerable time; but had heard, casually, that he was making great strides in his forensic career.

In spite of my distress, I returned his greeting, and grasped his hand warmly. After all it seemed a relief to find that I had a friend left in the world.

'What brings you here?' I asked.

'The only thing that could bring me to such a place—circuit work. I have an important case on today. That's the worst of a place so near London as this one. One is tempted to spend the nights in town, which means getting up at an unholy hour in the morning. But you! Why are you here? I heard you were as rich as Midas, and living abroad in luxury.'

'I have been abroad for some time. I hope to go back again very soon.'

'Happy man!' he ejaculated. I could scarcely keep the bitter smile from my lips, as I thought how ill-applied were his words.

As he spoke he glanced at Philippa, whose grace and beauty of form defied the concealment attempted by thick veil and sombre garments.

'But what brings you to this sleepy old town?' continued Grant.

I hesitated for a moment. Then, thinking that truth, or at least half-truth, was the best, told him I had come down to witness the trial for murder.

'I should doubt you're getting into court,' he said. 'The morbid interest excited round about here is, I am told, very great. The sheriff is besieged by applications for tickets.'

'Couldn't you help me? The fact is, I have a particular

reason, not mere curiosity, for wishing to be present at this trial.'

'I don't think I can,' said Grant. 'Does your—the lady wish to go with you?'

'My cousin—yes,' I said, seeing that he expected an introduction. He raised his hat, and made some courteous and pleasant remark, to which Philippa, to my surprise, replied in a calm and fitting way.

Grant knew I had no sister. I called her cousin because I had a wild hope that, if the worst happened, I might be able to conceal the true relationship in which we stood, and so be permitted to give evidence on her behalf. I trusted my wife would guess that I had a good reason for this deception.

'Try and manage this for me, Grant,' I said so earnestly that my friend made no further demur.

'Take me in your cab, and I will see what I can do.'

During our drive to the Shirehall I asked Grant what he knew about the impending trial.

'Nothing,' he said frankly. 'I hate murder cases—hate even to read about them. Of course I know that Sir Mervyn Ferrand was killed, and hidden in the snow for days and days. But I know no more.'

'Who is the accused?'

'I don't know. I thought, from your anxiety, you must know him.'

'Will he be found guilty?'

'I don't know. Stay, I heard someone who ought to be well informed say yesterday that the case for the prosecution was most feeble. He seemed to doubt if the grand jury would return a true bill.'

As I heard this I pressed Philippa's hand secretly. I felt that she was trembling.

The drive to the Shirehall occupied only a few minutes. We did not go to the public entrance, in front of which I could see a crowd of people nearly blocking up the street. We stopped at another door, and Grant, after looking round, caught sight of what appeared to be an inspector of police. He entered into a little conversation with him, the result of which was that we were given into his care.

'This is a breach of the law,' whispered my friend as he bade me good-bye. 'You will have to atone for it by a handsome gratuity.'

We followed our guide. Philippa, although walking with a firm step, leant heavily upon my arm. I scarcely know by what door we entered that palace of justice. The stalwart policeman led us through stone corridors and passages, which re-echoed with the tread of our feet, and at last we found ourselves before a double swinging plain oak door, over which in old English letters was written 'Criminal Court'.

I felt Philippa shudder, and knew that the sight of those words brought the horror of the situation fully home to her. Mechanically I pressed a sovereign in the hand of the venal inspector, or whatever he was; then, holding my wife's hand, I passed through the noiseless swinging door into the all but empty court.

A few policemen and other officials were lounging about. Two or three people, who had no doubt gained admittance in the same way as we had done, were seated in various coigns of vantage. I led Philippa up the broad steps, and pointed to one of the hard wooden benches provided for the accommodation of the general public. These benches were raised step by step, one above another. We chose our position about half-way up, on the right-hand side of the court. Philippa, with her thick veil falling down to her chin, and so defying recognition, sank wearily into her seat. I placed myself beside her; my hand crept under the cloak she wore and held her hand.

Surely it was all a dream—a dreadful realistic dream! I should wake and find myself under the great orange tree in that courtyard in gay Seville, my half-smoked cigar and the book which I had been lazily reading lying at my feet; my mother opposite me, laughing at my somnolency, and Philippa's grave dark eyes looking with calm everlasting love into my own. I should wake and find the cool of the evening had succeeded to the glare of the afternoon. We should walk through the merry streets, lounge in the Alameda, wander through the glowing Alcazar gardens, or drive out miles and miles over the fertile smiling plains. Or I should even wake and find myself nodding over my fire in my lonely cottage, the stolid William the only human creature within hail; Philippa's return, the snowstorm, the dreadful discovery, the flight, Seville, the marriage, all, all a dream!

In a kind of stupor—the temporary reaction, I suppose, consequent upon such fatigue and trouble—I gazed round me, and wondered where I was.

What is this great empty building, lit from one side by large clerestory windows of ecclesiastical design? What are these dull grey vacant walls; that lofty ceiling, crossed and cut into small squares by dark rafters; this leaded floor, on which feet fall all but noiselessly? What are those raised boxes on either side of the building—those small railed platforms all but adjoining them, and all but adjoining that panelled oak structure at the end facing me? What is that rectangular box-shaped erection with overhanging carved cornice? Let us away from this dismal colourless place! Let me wake and find myself amid the flowers, orange trees, the fair sights and surroundings of our Spanish home.

No! I have but to turn my dazed eyes to the centre of space in which we sat, to know that I am dreaming no dream; that we must wait here and learn our fates. That oblong wooden enclosure with high sides, topped by a light iron railing, brings reality back to me. It is the prisoner's dock. In an hour's time a man will stand there. He will be brought up those stone steps which lead to it from below, the topmost flag of which I can just see. He will stand there for hours. As he leaves the dock, declared innocent or guilty, so will our lives be declared happy or miserable.

My hand holds my wife's yet closer; for the last minutes which may be ours to spend together are slipping by so fast, so very fast!

See, the clock under the balcony marks half-past nine. The all but deserted court begins to assume the appearance of preparing for business. Policemen and other officials pass to and fro, some arranging papers, some replenishing ink-bottles, and placing quill pens ready for the barristers and solicitors who will soon fill those front seats. Someone, with what seems to me bitter irony, places a magnificent bouquet of flowers on either hand of the judge's vacant chair. What have flowers in common with such a scene as this? Flowers, too, which are beautiful enough to recall to my mind the fair Spanish home which, may be, we shall see no more. Flowers in this den of sorrow! Rather should every seat, every beam, be draped in black.

Now the doors on each side of the court open, and remain open. I hear a shuffling of many feet. People, in a continuous stream, pass through the entrance, and wend their way to the portion of the court allotted to the general public. So fast, so thick they come, that in ten minutes this space is thronged almost to suffocation. Philippa and I are pressed closer and closer to each other, as every inch of the bench on which we are seated is appropriated. The court is full.

Crowded by respectable-looking, well-dressed people, who have gained admission, as I heard, by favour of the Sheriff. Yet, respectable as they are, each man, each woman, rushes in eagerly and strives for the best available seat. And for what reason? To see and hear a poor wretch tried for his life! In my bitter mood I look with hate on these sensation-seekers. I hate them even more when I think that their morbid craving for excitement may be satisfied with such food as they little expect;

and I clench my teeth as I picture the scene at that moment when Philippa, in pursuance of her immovable resolution, rises, and makes her effort to proclaim her own guilt and the convicted man's innocence. Although I strive to force the picture from my mind, by telling myself that justice cannot err, that the man will be acquitted, yet again and again the dread of the worst seizes me, and I hate every face in that crowd, which may by-and-by be gaping, with looks of wonder and curiosity, at the woman I love!

As in a haze, I see some faces which are familiar to me. A number of gentlemen enter, and seat themselves on the benches which counsel usually occupy. Some few of these I knew by sight. They are country gentlemen from the neighbourhood of Roding, who are now called to serve on the grand jury. I see also the thin-faced, hawkish looking woman who calls herself Mrs Wilson. I am thankful that she takes a seat in front of us and does not see us. She, like ourselves, must know that an innocent man is this day about to be tried.

So for half an hour I sit, gazing now at the crowd of people, now at the empty dock and vacant bench in front of me; listening to the hum of conversation which rises from the packed court; longing for the moment to come when this dreadful suspense may end; yet all the same dreading and willing to put off that moment. And all the while Philippa, in her black garb, close to me and, unseen by our neighbours, holding my hand.

Hush! The door at the back of the bench opens, and at ten o'clock to the minute the red-robed judge appears. He bows to the court, seats himself, and by his action signifies that he is ready to begin the business of the day. No trembling prisoner in the dock ever scanned a judge's face with more anxiety than I scan his lordship's at this present moment.

An old man, too old, it seems to me, for such a responsible post; an amiable, pleasant-looking man—not, I venture to think, one who can bear the reputation of being a 'hanging judge'. I breathe a prayer that he may this day be able to direct aright the course of justice.

Hush! Hush! Silence in the court! Oh, my poor, sweet wife, let me grasp that hand yet closer, for the moment which for days and nights has never been absent from our minds has come! What will it bring us?

CHAPTER XV

THE BLACK CAP

THERE is silence, or all but silence, in the court. The buzz of suppressed conversation sinks almost to nothing—absolutely to nothing as the judge's marshal rises, and after gabbling through the mysterious proclamation which begins 'Oyez! Oyez! Oyez!' declares the court open.

Philippa, still closely veiled, sits like a statue. Her hand, which ever grasps mine, scarcely responds to the pressure by which again and again I endeavour to bid her hope for the best. I would give much if even now I could get her to consent to my leading her away. I dare not suggest this. I know that doing so would be waste of words.

The court is open. The red judge is perusing letters and papers which lie in front of him as calmly and unconcernedly as if the life's happiness of, at least, one man and woman, did not greatly depend upon the view he takes of the case about to be tried. He raises one of his bouquets and inhales the perfume of the flowers. How can one in his position behave like an ordinary mortal? Were we not here, he might condemn an innocent man to a shameful death! I wonder if, with such horrible responsibility resting on him, a judge can ever really be a happy man?

These thoughts seem trivial; but my mind is by now in a strange state; it is, indeed, so sensitive that every slight incident, every small ceremonial of today seems to be impressed for ever upon it.

A bewigged gentleman—the clerk of assize, the man next me tells his neighbour—rises and calls name after name, until he has fixed upon the twenty-three gentlemen needed to form the grand jury. They stand up in their places, and, in batches of four, are rapidly sworn. The absurd proclamation against vice and immorality is read; much good may it do everyone present! Then the clerk sits down, and the judge, forsaking his papers, begins his work.

He arranges his robes to his satisfaction, leans forward, and, placing the tips of his long white fingers together, addresses—charges, I am told, is the right term—the grand jury in a pleasant colloquial manner. I strain every aural nerve to catch the purport of his glib words. He is sure to say something about this important murder case. I shall, perhaps, be able to learn how it was that the man fell under suspicion.

Alas! The judge is one who by dint of years of practice has acquired the knack of using his voice only just so much as is absolutely necessary. The grand jury is close to him, and can, no doubt, hear him; but to those who, like ourselves, are far away in the background of the court, his remarks are inaudible. All I can catch is a closing caution to the grand jury, to bear in mind that it is not within its province to determine the innocence or guilt of the prisoners, but simply to decide whether there is or is not sufficient evidence for the cases to go to trial.

The grand jury files out of court to conduct its solemn deliberations in the place appointed. The judge addresses a few smiling words to the sheriff and other magnates who, by right or favour, occupy seats on the bench; then he returns to the perusal of his papers.

For the first time since we entered the court Philippa speaks to me. 'Are they trying him now?' she asks in a low awed whisper, yet in a voice so changed that I know what the suspense is costing her. Briefly I explain the procedure of the law, so far as I know it. She sighs, and says no more.

More monotonous calling of many names, to which summons, however, another class of men respond. The common jurymen are now being called. Probably, to save time, twelve men are sent into the box, where they sit, some appearing to enjoy the

dignity of the position, some with stolid indifference, others
with acute unhappiness plainly manifested. I look at these
men with scarcely less interest than I look at the judge. On
them, or on some of them, our fate rests as much, perhaps
more, than it rests on him. Those men are trying us—not only
the man who will by-and-by stand in that rail-topped enclosure
into which we look down.

Twenty long weary minutes pass by. All eyes turn to a
wooden gallery in the right-hand corner of the court. A door
in the wall opens. The members of the grand jury emerge and
fill the gallery. The foreman arms himself with a gigantic
fishing-rod, to which he attaches a paper, which is conveyed
by this clumsy method to that busy gentleman, the clerk of
assize. What idiotic foolery all this seems to me!

The clerk detaches the document, glances at it, and looks
up at the gallery.

'Gentlemen of the grand jury, you return a true bill against
William Evans for murder?'

'We do,' answered the foreman with shy solemnity.

I grind my teeth. Fools! If men of culture and standing err
like this, what can be expected from a common jury? It is well
for me that I heard the caution just now given by the judge. I
take such comfort as I can by thinking they have tried the
evidence, not the man. What can the evidence be? Ah! We shall
soon know.

The clerk turns, and, addressing no one in particular, says,
'Bring up the prisoner.' Once more I set my teeth. I feel my
wife's arm tremble; her hand grows cold. I hear a buzz, as of
expectation, run through the crowded court. Every eye turns
in one direction—towards the empty dock. For a moment a
species of dizziness comes over me; objects swim before my
eyes. The sensation passes away. I recover myself. The dock is
no longer untenanted. In the centre, with a stalwart policeman
on either side of him, stands the accused! The man who, if
needs be, must be saved by such a sacrifice!

From my place, far back in the public gallery, I can, of course, see nothing more of the prisoner than his back. I gaze at this with intense curiosity, endeavouring to determine the station of the man who is now about to be tried for his life. I can but gather this much: He is tall and slight. His dress is of a semi-respectable nature, but seems to have seen much service. He might be anything from a broken-down clerk to a gentleman's servant out of elbows. I rejoice at his poverty-stricken appearance. Judging from it, money will be welcome to him. Let the jury but assert his innocence, and I feel certain that the liberal pecuniary compensation which it is my intention to mete out will repay him a hundred times for the ordeal which he is undergoing.

Ordeal! Yes, it is the right word. It is easy to see it is a terrible ordeal to the poor fellow. No need to look at his face to be told that much. Even as he emerged from the cells below he seemed to quake with fear. Now he absolutely falls forward in the dock, supporting himself by grasping the iron railing which runs round the top. I notice that his fingers, as they cling to the iron bars, open and close convulsively. Every movement of his back and shoulders betrays fear and anguish of mind. His state is pitiable, so pitiable that one of his custodians places his hand under the wretched man's arm, and gives him the physical support which he so sorely needs. He bends his head as in shame, and I know that could I see his face, it would be white as my own or my wife's.

In spite of the strain upon my mind, I was able to wonder at the prisoner's hopeless demeanour. Although I had, as it were, torn my very heart out by the roots to ensure this man's safety in the event of things going wrong with him; although I did not even now regret the course I had taken, I am bound to say that his cowardly behaviour took away much of the sympathy which I should otherwise have felt for him in his unmerited predicament. It is, of course, very easy to say what one would do if in another's place. I certainly felt sure that, were I in that poor fellow's plight, the consciousness of my own innocence would give me strength enough to raise my head, and face boldly all the judges, juries, and prosecuting counsel in the world. I was willing to make every allowance for the nervousness natural to such a position; but I groaned inwardly as I gazed upon that miserable, limp, half-standing, half-reclining form.

Why does he not stand upright? Too well I know that another is watching that abject wretch with interest even more intense than mine. I know that every attitude of shame or fear is understood by Philippa, and adds to the scruples which she feels at following my advice and awaiting the result of the trial. Every agonised movement of the prisoner in the dock seems to be faintly reproduced by the hand within my own. Every pang he suffers runs through the frame of the woman who knows that he is suffering for her deed.

The clerk reads over the indictment: 'That he, William Evans, did feloniously, wilfully, and of malice aforethought kill and murder Sir Mervyn Ferrand, Baronet.' As the reading proceeds Philippa draws me towards her. 'Basil,' she says in a low whisper, 'this is more dreadful than I dreamed of. I cannot bear it longer. Think of that poor man's anguish! Basil, he also may have a wife who loves him; she may be in the court. Think of her! Oh, what can I do? What can I do?'

'Nothing—nothing but wait and hope,' I answer.

'Could you not go down and speak to him, or send a message in some way? Tell him not to be so wretched; that even at the last moment he will be saved; that the real murderer will confess and free him. Basil, you must do this.'

'I cannot. I dare not. It would ruin us. Hush, dearest; be calm, and listen.'

The reading of the indictment is now over. The clerk turns to the prisoner. 'Are you guilty, or not guilty?' he asks in a clear voice. Although everyone in that court knows what the answer will be, there is a silence so profound that a pin might be heard drop. Everyone seemed desirous of hearing the prisoner's voice. Even I, myself, lean forward, and strain every nerve to hear his plea.

There is a long, dead pause. It may be that the prisoner does not understand that he is expected to reply. It may be that his collapsed state deprives him of the power of speech. I notice that one of the policemen touches him on the shoulder, and whispers to him. Still for a moment there is silence.

It is broken, but not by the prisoner. Philippa gives a low, soft wail, heard only, I think, by me. 'I can bear it no longer,' she whispers. She snatches her hand from mine. She throws back her thick, dark veil, and stands erect in the body of the court. I cast one glance at her pale but determined-looking face, then bow my head upon my hands, and wish that death might at that moment smite us both. All is over! I am conquered!

Even as I hide my face I see every eye in that thronged court turning to the tall, majestic, dark-robed figure which rises in the midst of that motley throng. Then, clear and loud, I hear her beloved voice ring out.

'My lord,' I hear her say. I raise my head at the sound. The eyes of bench, bar, jury, and public are fixed upon her. The very prisoner turns in the dock and gazes straight at her.

She gets no farther than those two words. 'Order in the court! Order in the court!' is shouted so sternly and fiercely that she all but loses her presence of mind. She falters, she hesitates, and glances helplessly around. I seize the moment. By sheer force I drag her back to her seat. I pray her by the love she bears me to wait in silence. I draw the veil over her face, to hide it from the hundreds of curious eyes which are turned upon it. Whilst so doing, I hear the sharp mandate, 'Turn that person out of court.'

Had any serious attempt been made to put the order in force, I believe that Philippa would have resisted, and once more attempted to assert the prisoner's innocence and her own guilt—if it was guilt. Fortunately the policeman who draws near us to carry out the order is my friend of the morning who had accepted my gold. It may be on this account he favours us. It may be, when a momentary disturbance subsides, and the perpetrator does not seem bent upon repeating it, that the expulsion is not insisted upon. It may be that Philippa's accosting the judge was looked upon as a solecism brought about by the excitement of a weak woman who was in some way connected with the prisoner. I suppose such a scene does sometimes occur; and perhaps, if its repetition is guarded against, a humanely-minded judge will not deny the offender the sorry comfort of seeing her friend's trial to the end. Perhaps the judge who this day presides is unusually good-natured and easy-going. Anyway, our friendly policeman does not carry out his instructions, and the court resumes its business.

But many curious looks are cast at the veiled woman by my side. I notice that the hawk-faced Mrs Wilson turns in her seat, and looks always at us; and, strange to say, I notice that the prisoner in the dock is still staring fixedly in our direction. The policemen take him by the arms; face him round towards the bench. Once more the solemn question, 'Are you guilty, or not guilty?' is asked.

A short excited pause. The prisoner answers. Well I know what he says, although he speaks so faintly that I do not hear his voice. Strange to say, his answer seems to create considerable agitation. People who are near to him look back and whisper to those in the rear. A barrister turns in his seat, and stares in a dumbfounded way at a gentleman behind him. This gentleman rises up fussily, and bustles round to the dock, where for a minute he seems to be engaged in earnest conversation with the prisoner. The latter shakes his head sullenly and hopelessly. In an apparently highly-excited state, the gentleman, whom I rightly judge to be solicitor for the defence, hurries

back, whispers to the barrister, and seems by his gesture to
be washing his hands of some responsibility.

What does it all mean? Why do they not go on with
the trial? The suspense is growing more than I can bear.
Hush! The judge speaks.

The excitement is spreading through the court. In spite
of the warning looks of the authorities, people are whispering
to each other. The judge is speaking earnestly to the prisoner.
He seems to be explaining something, counselling something.
Still the man shakes his head sullenly. What does it all mean?

Mean! The next solemn action, the next solemn words
of the red-robed judge answer my question, and tell me that
a thing has come to pass which never entered within the
range of probability. Or have I been asleep? Has the trial been
gone through, and the worst, the very worst, happened? No;
five minutes ago I pulled Philippa back to her seat, and forced
her to withhold her damning words. Even now my grasp is
on her to prevent her from rising.

Ha! Look! The judge places a square of black silk upon his
head. The prisoner cowers down. He would fall, were it not
for the arms which support him on either side. A rustle of
intense feeling runs through the court. Men catch their breath;
women's eyes are distended. The sensation-seekers are
rewarded. Hark! The judge speaks. I can hear him plainly now,
although there is deep emotion in his voice.

'Prisoner at the bar, you are guilty, by your own confession,
of an atrocious, cold-blooded murder, the motive for which is
known but to yourself and your God. For me only the painful
duty remains—'

Guilty! On his own confession! The man guilty! The man
to save whom we have travelled night and day—he the criminal!
Philippa, my peerless Philippa! My wife! My love! Innocent!
Innocent! This—this revulsion of feeling is more than human
nature can bear!

'Order in the court! Order in the court!' What is it? Who

is it? Only a woman in a dead faint. She is borne out tenderly, lovingly, proudly, by a man who clasps his precious burden to a heart full of such rapture as few of his fellow-creatures can ever have known.

But let it also be hoped that few have ever endured such grief and anguish!

CHAPTER XVI

'WHERE ARE THE SNOWS THAT FELL LAST YEAR?'

ALTHOUGH, whilst engaged in the labour of writing this story, I have many times regretted that I am nothing more than a plain narrator of facts and incidents, not a master of fiction, I think I have not yet felt the regret so strongly as at the moment when I begin this chapter. The sombre acts of the life drama in which Philippa and I played parts so painful, so full of grief, and even if brightened by a ray of joy, of joy fallacious and of uncertain tenure—these acts I have found little difficulty in describing; I had simply to throw my mind back to the pictures of the past and reproduce them in words. The task, whether well or ill done, was not a hard one.

But now, when in one moment and as if by magic, everything changed; when sorrow seemed to be simply swept out of our lives; when that poor abject wretch's confession of guilt, forced from him in some mysterious way, not only left our whole future bright and cloudless, but consigned to rest all the ghosts of the past, whose shadowy forms had hitherto dogged our steps and denied us the happiness rightly due to those who love as we loved; now it is that I feel my shortcomings acutely, and wish my pen was more powerful than it is.

And yet a word will describe the state of my own mind as, when the last solemn words were spoken by the judge—spoken in a voice which showed emotion and distress at being compelled to condemn a fellow-creature to death—I carried my fainting wife from the crowded, reeking court. The momentary sense of rapture passed away; bewilderment, sheer bewilderment, is the word for what was left. I could not think. All my reasoning faculties had left me. In fact, I believe that had

Philippa not swooned, and so needed my mechanically given care, I myself should have fallen senseless on that threshold which an hour before we crossed, thinking we were going to endless misery.

I remember this much. As I laid Philippa on one of the hard wooden benches in the stone corridor I kept repeating to myself, 'Innocent, my love is innocent; that man is guilty.' I suppose this continual reiteration was an endeavour to impress the tremendous fact upon my brain, which for a time was incredulous, and refused to entertain it.

I threw up my wife's veil and bathed her face with water, which was brought me by a kindly policeman. Presently her eyes opened, and consciousness returned; she strove to speak.

My presence of mind was fast returning. 'Dearest,' I whispered, 'as you love me, not a word in this place. In a minute we will leave it.'

She was obedient; but I knew from the wild look of joy in her eyes that obedience tasked her to the utmost. She was soon able to rise, and then we walked from the court, pushed our way through the crowd who waited in the street, busily discussing the sudden termination to the trial, threw ourselves into a cab, and in another moment were alternately weeping and laughing in each other's arms.

It was, however, but for a moment. The inn to which we drove was close at hand. There we were shown into a room, and were at last free to give the fullest vent to our pent-up feelings.

It would be absurd for me to attempt to reproduce our words, our disjointed exclamations. It would be sacrilege for me to describe the tears we shed, the embraces, the loving caresses we lavished on each other. Think of us an hour, one short hour ago! Think of us now! The curse laid upon us by that awful night removed for ever! Our secret kept, or secrecy, if still advisable, no longer absolutely needful. Philippa, in spite all I had seen, in spite of all she had told me on that night when I found her, a wild distracted woman, in a storm the wildest that years have known, guiltless of her husband's death! Innocent, not only as she had in my eyes always been, but also, what was far more, innocent in her own eyes!

Small wonder that for nearly an hour we sat with our arms twined around each other, and used few words which were more than rapturous exclamations of love and joy.

There! I cannot, will not describe the scene more fully. I will say no more, except this: when at last we grew calmer, Philippa turned to me, and once more I saw terror gathering in her eyes.

'Basil,' she said, 'it is true—it must be true?'

'True! Of course it is.'

'That man, the prisoner, could not have pleaded guilty when he was innocent.'

'Why should he? It meant death to him, poor wretch.'

'But why did he confess?'

'Who can tell? Remorse may have urged him to do so.'

Philippa rose, and her next words were spoken quickly and with excitement.

'No, I did not do it. The thought, the dream haunted me, but I did not believe it until I heard those men talk of the way he died. Then it all came back to me. The mad storm, the dead man over whom I stood; even then I don't think I actually believed it. It was when you told me how you found me, that I lost all hope.'

'Dearest, forgive me. I should have believed in the impossibility of the act even in your delirium, even if I had seen it done. Philippa, say you forgive me.'

She threw her arms around me. 'Basil, my husband,' she whispered, 'you have done much for me, do one thing more; find out the whole truth—find out why this man killed him, how he killed him; find out, satisfy me that his confession was a true one; then, Basil, such happiness as I have never even dreamed of will be mine!'

'And mine,' I echoed.

I promised to do as she wished. Indeed, the moment I had recovered my senses, I resolved to learn everything that could be learned. Once and for all I would clear away every cloud of doubt, although that cloud might be no bigger than a man's hand.

But Philippa must not stop in Tewnham. Her strange conduct during the trial, her fainting-fit after it, were bound to have attracted the attention of those present. No doubt she was looked upon as a friend of the prisoner, who was overpowered by the sudden and awful ending of the case. Still, she must not stay at Tewnham.

We went to London by an afternoon train. The next morning I again ran down to the place at which the trial was held. I ascertained the name of the convict's solicitor, and as soon as I found him at leisure requested the favour of an interview.

I found him apparently a worthy, respectable man, but of a nature inclined to be choleric. I told him I called on him because I was much interested in the case of the convict William Evans. Mr Crisp, that was his name, frowned and fidgeted about with some papers which were in front of him.

'I would rather not talk about the case,' he said sharply. 'Nothing for many years has so much annoyed me.'

'Why? Your client only met with his deserts.'

'True—true. But I am a lawyer, sir. Our province is not to think so much of deserts as of what we can do for a client. It is hard to try and serve a fool.'

'No doubt; but I scarcely understand your meaning.'

'Meaning! I could have saved that man. There was no evidence to speak of against him. What did it amount to? A pistol of a peculiar make found in a field half a mile away from the scene of the murder; one man who could swear that the pistol was my client's property—a pawnbroker, to whom he wanted to sell it. Positively, sir, that was the whole case for the Crown. Never so disgusted in my life—never!'

The excitable little man's looks showed that his disgust was not assumed.

So the pistol which I had thoughtlessly hurled away had, after all, furnished the clue and brought the criminal to justice. Although I was now quite satisfied that the right person was to suffer for the dark crime, I resolved to get all the additional information I could.

'But why did he plead guilty?' I asked.

'Because he was a fool,' rapped out Mr Crisp. 'It was like committing suicide. I don't care a button for the man himself; but I confess I was annoyed at seeing my case all knocked to pieces by his obstinacy. I went to him; if you were in court, you no doubt saw me. I begged him to withdraw his plea. I told him I could save him. Yet the fool insisted.'

'Did penitence or remorse urge him?'

'I don't know. He could have had more time for penitence and remorse if he had let me save him from the gallows. No; he says, "It's no good—not a bit of good. You don't know all I know. There's someone in court who knows all about it—saw it all done. She's come to hang me." I have no idea what he meant.'

I started. I knew what the man meant. He, in common with everyone else in that court, had turned and looked at Philippa as she rose from her seat and addressed the judge. It was the sight of Philippa that had taken away the wretch's last hope of escape.

'I washed my hands of the fellow, of course,' continued Mr Crisp; 'but I did take the trouble to enquire if any witnesses for the prosecution had been allowed to enter the court. I am assured they were all kept in waiting outside.'

I sat for some moments in deep thought. The solicitor looked at me, as if he fancied I had already taken up as much of his valuable time as he could spare.

'Is there any way of gaining access to the condemned man?' I said. 'Could you, for instance, get an order to see him?'

'No doubt I could; but I have no object in seeing him.'

'I will give you an object,' I said. 'I want you to see that man, and, if possible, get a written, or at least dictated, confession from him—not of the bald fact that he is guilty, but of all particulars connected with the murder.'

Mr Crisp looked surprised, and expressed his opinion that it was all but impossible to obtain what I wanted.

I had taken rather a fancy to the brisk-spoken, sharp little man. He seemed to me trustworthy; so that, after consideration, I determined to confide to him my reason for making this request. Under the assurance of professional secrecy, I told him briefly so much as I thought fit of Philippa's and my own connection with the events of that night. He listened with an interest which augured well for the reception which awaits the sombre tale I now give to the world. His curiosity seemed excited, and he promised to see the convict, and, if possible, learn all I wanted to know. I left my address, and bade him good-day.

I did not care to linger at Tewnham; so I walked down to the railway-station, intending to return to town by the next train. As I waited on the platform a down-train came in. A sudden impulse seized me. The day was still young. I had time to spare. I crossed the bridge, entered the train, and in a quarter of an hour was at Roding. I went there because I was impelled by a desire to once more visit the actual scene of the beginning of all these troubles.

I walked that road which Sir Mervyn Ferrand had walked that dark night. But oh, how changed everything was! Yet not more changed than our own lives. It was a glorious afternoon in September. The rain of the preceding day had left the earth moist and fresh. The fields, on either side of the road, were gleaming with that bright, pure emerald which they wear after the ruthless scythe has swept away the ripe grass and the marguerites and other flowers which grow among it; or else they were filled from hedge to hedge with a golden sea of waving corn, or sheaves waiting to be garnered; for the harvest that year was not early. The wild roses were long over, but fragrant honeysuckle and other wild flowers still made gay the hedgerows and banks. The birds had awakened from their August silence, and were singing once more. The great sleepy cows lay under the shade of the trees. The large mows of new hay stood side by side with their dingy-looking, but more valuable, elder brothers. The whole land seemed wrapped in happy autumnal repose. The scene was calm, peaceful, and thoroughly typical of England. So beautiful it was, so full I now felt of love for my native land, that had these pages been then written, I should, upon my return home, have erased all my glowing description of Seville.

A breath of soft but fresh air came blowing from the far-away downs. I drew in a deep draught; I threw back my shoulders and stood erect. I laughed aloud in my great happiness as a comical picture, familiar to my childhood, of Christian losing his burden, rose before my mind, and seemed to be the exact thing wanted to illustrate my own case. Yes, the burden I had borne had fallen from my back for ever!

Ah! Here is the spot—the very spot where Sir Mervyn fell. It was here, just under that cluster of ragged-robins, I must have placed his corpse, little thinking that the kind white snow would hide it, and save my love and me. Oh, how I prayed in those days that the bitter weather might last; that its iron grip would hold the world fast until Philippa's health and strength returned! It did so, and saved us!

'Where are the snows that fell last year?' Ah! Should I not rather sing 'Where is the grief of yesterday?' Gone like the snow. Other snow may fall, other grief may come, but last year's snow and yesterday's grief are gone for ever!

Nevertheless, that spot was too suggestive of horrible reminiscences for me to linger long over it. I turned away, and in my great happiness could whisper to myself that I forgave the dead man for the ill he had wrought. May his bones rest in peace! I walked along the road, right on until I came to the cottage in which, like a coward who could not face his troubles, I had spent those aimless, miserable months. It was untenanted. Half-defaced auction bills were in the windows and on the doorposts; for some months ago the furniture had been sold. I paused and looked at the window by which Philippa had entered, and felt that since that night I had passed through more grief, passion, fear, hope and joy than would fill an ordinary lifetime. Then I turned and shook the dust off my feet. Never again would I come within twenty miles of this place.

On the road back, to my annoyance, I encountered Mrs Wilson. I tried to pass without sign of recognition, but she was too quick for me. She stood in front of me, and I was bound to stop.

She was more haggard, more drawn, more aquiline-looking than ever. Her eyes alone looked young. They at least had spirit and vitality in them. They positively blazed upon me.

'She did not do it, after all!' she said fiercely.

At first I thought of affecting surprise, and asking her what she meant; but I felt that any attempt at equivoque would be but vain.

'She did not,' I answered shortly.

'Fool that I was!' she cried. 'Fool, to be led away by an impulse! Why did I tell her? I swear to you, Dr North, that had I not felt sure it was her act, she should never have known. She should have gone to her grave a shamed woman, as I shall go!'

Her look was venom itself.

'Remember,' I said sternly, 'Lady Ferrand is now my wife. I will not hear her name coupled with yours.'

She laughed scornfully. 'Your wife! She soon forgot her first love. Why did I speak? I wish my hand had withered before I wrote that letter. Do you know why I wrote it?'

'No; nor do I care.'

'I wrote it for vengeance. She had, I thought, served that man as I ought to have served him; but I hated her for it, for

I loved him still. So I thought it would be so sweet for her to know that she had killed her husband, and for you, her lover—I knew you were her lover—to know that I could at any moment give her up to justice! I was a fool. Why did that man plead guilty? When I saw your wife rise in court I laughed. I knew what was coming. Now, instead of harming her, I have done her good.'

'You have,' I said curtly, and turning upon my heel. The malignity of this woman was so intense that I felt thankful she could in no way work Philippa harm.

A quarter of a mile up the road I turned. Mrs Wilson, a black spot on a fair scene, was standing gazing after me. I hurried on until a bend in the path hid her from sight. I hurried on back to Philippa and happiness!

CHAPTER XVII

CLEAR SKIES

ALTHOUGH England was now to me and to my wife a land very different from the one we quitted some eight months ago, we were anxious to get back to Seville, if only to set at rest my mother's fears. She, poor woman, as a letter showed, was much exercised as to what manner of business could have made us leave her in so unceremonious a way. The moment the glad truth had become known to me, I had telegraphed, saying that all was well with us, and that we should soon join her. Two things only detained us.

The first was that we wanted the convict's confession. Although Philippa said little on the subject, I knew that until it arrived she would not be quite happy. There was with her a haunting dread that the man, in the hopes of mitigating his sentence, had pleaded guilty to a crime of which he was innocent. Even the accurate account which I gave her of my interview with the solicitor did not quite satisfy her. So we waited impatiently for the full explanation, which might or might not come.

The second thing which kept us in London was this. I determined that before I left I would have the fact that when I married Philippa I married Lady Ferrand fully acknowledged. I found my way to the gentlemen who were winding up the dead man's affairs, and stated my case to their incredulous ears. At first they treated me as an impostor.

But not for long. Indeed, my task was half done. They had already, without any assistance from Mrs Wilson, ferreted out the date and particulars of the death of the first Lady Ferrand. They had but to assure themselves that the marriage-certificate which I laid before them was no forgery, and surrender at discretion.

It was a poor estate, the administrators told me. Sir Mervyn had died intestate. He had during his lifetime made away with nearly all he could alienate. Still, there was some personal property, of which my wife could claim a share, and a certain amount of real property, on which she was entitled to dower. But it was a very poor estate.

I cut them very short. I told them that, let the deceased's wealth be great or little, not one penny-piece of it should soil my wife's fingers. If Sir Mervyn Ferrand's heir was in want of the money, it should, provided he was a different stamp of man from his immediate predecessor, be given to him a free gift. If not, some hospital should be benefited by it. All I wanted was that it should be clearly understood that Sir Mervyn Ferrand left a widow.

The administrators, one of whom was, by-the-by, the heir, evidently looked upon me as a most eccentric personage. Perhaps it was for this reason, or—as I do not wish to cast unmerited blame—perhaps it was because the estate wound up to nothing—well, anyway, even to this day we have received no communication, much less remittance, from the administrators; nor, to tell the truth, have I troubled them again. Philippa's marriage admitted, I washed my hands of all the Ferrand brood.

The confession did not arrive; but I persuaded Philippa to leave England. Mr Crisp could send whatever he had to send to Seville just as well as to London. So once more, and this time in all but perfect happiness, we took that long journey which was by now quite familiar to us.

The joy, the wild joy, with which Philippa threw herself into my mother's arms checked all the upbraidings and reproach which we apparently merited. Our return was like the return of a prodigal son and daughter. Laughter, tears, and happiness!

Although I told my mother nothing as to the object of our mysterious journey; although she asked me nothing; although no word evidencing her knowledge of what had passed has ever crossed her lips, I know that all has been revealed to her; that Philippa has sobbed out the whole strange tale on her breast. I know it by this, that since the day of our return my mother's deep love for my wife has shown itself even tenderer, sweeter, and deeper. Yes, I was spared the telling of the tale. My mother's eyes the next day showed me that Philippa had given her the history, as I have given it here, from beginning to end.

No, not quite the end. Sit by me once more, as I asked you at the beginning of my story to sit by me; but this time, not by the side of a smouldering fire, but out in the fair, gay *patio* of our Andalusian home. Philippa and I are side by side. The post has just come in, and brought me a bulky packet, on which, in a clerkly hand, is written my name and address. I tear the wrapper open with eagerness. I know what it contains; Philippa knows. I wish to read it first alone, but the appealing look in her eyes turns me from my purpose. After all, there is nothing to fear, there can be nothing which she should not know. So, with our cheeks all but touching, we read together. Sit by us, lean over my shoulder, and read with us.

'THE CONFESSION OF WILLIAM EVANS, NOW LYING IN TEWNHAM GAOL UNDER SENTENCE OF DEATH:
'On the fifth of January, this year, I returned from New Zealand. I worked my passage home. When I reached London I had but a few shillings in my pocket. I had no articles of value which I could sell. All I owned, except my clothes and the little bit of money, was a pistol which a man on board the ship had given me. It was a pistol of his own invention. He had several with him, and said he wanted to get the sort known. Why he gave it to me God knows; but he did, and a couple of cartridges.

'I spent my money—all but a shilling or two. I tried to get work, but none was to be had. Then I remembered that I once had a friend who lived near Roding. I went there by train. I had just enough money to pay my fare. I found that the man I knew had left the place two years ago. I walked back to the town penniless and desperate.

'The first thing I did was to go the pawnbroker's, and try and sell the pistol. The man wouldn't buy it at any price. He said his shop was full of pistols. I went away, and walked to the railway-station to try and earn a few pence somehow. I was in despair—all but starving.

'About seven o'clock the train from London came in. A tall gentleman came out of the door of the station. I asked him if he had any luggage I could carry for him. He told me to be off. Then I asked him, for pity's sake, to give me a shilling to buy some food. He cursed me, and I began to hate him.

'He stood under the gas-lamp, and drew out a great gold watch and looked at the time. Then he asked a man near which road he must take to get to a village named Cherwell. The man told him. I saw him walk away, and I knew where he was going.

'I shall be hanged next week; there is no hope for me. But I tell the truth when I say that, bad fellow as I have been, I had never committed such a crime as the one which at that moment entered my head. That tall man had money, jewellery and good clothing; I had nothing. I was starving. So I ran on, got before him, went miles up the road, and sat down in the bitter cold on a heap of stones, waiting for him to come, and making up my mind to kill and rob him. I knew I must kill him, because he was so much stronger and bigger than I was. My pistol was loaded.

'He came. I saw him in the moonlight. I stood up as he came near and, God forgive me, pulled the trigger, and shot him through the heart. He fell like a stone, and I knew I was a murderer.

'Oh, if I could I would have undone the deed! I stood for a long time before I dared to go to the body and steal the things for which I had committed the crime. Then I nerved myself and went to take the price for which, unless God is merciful, I had sold my soul.

'I never took a farthing. Just as I was about to begin I heard the sound of feet. I looked up, and saw a woman or a spirit coming to me. I dropped the pistol in terror. I felt sure she saw me. I looked at her under the moon. Her face was white, her lips were moving, her hair was all flying about. She came straight to where the dead man lay, then stopped and wrung her hands. I fled away in deadly fear. I ran across several fields. I dared not stop. I thought that spirit of ghost was following me.

'I ran on until the snow began. I must have died in that snow-storm if I had not found a half-roofed cowshed. I crept into this, and lay all the night and part of the next day. I was the most wretched being in the world.

'Hunger at last drove me out. I got through the snow somehow, and reached a house, where the people saved me from dying of starvation. But nothing could make me go again to the spot where I had done the murder. My life since then has been one of agony. Even now that I am going to be hanged I am happier than I have felt for months. May God forgive my crime!

'I pleaded guilty at the trial because I turned round in the dock, and saw the woman who I thought was a spirit standing up and ready to denounce me to the judge. I knew that she saw me that night, and I was bound to be found guilty.

'I have confessed all. Every word of this is truth. As I hope for mercy, it is all true!

'WILLIAM EVANS

'P.S.—I took the above confession down from the prisoner's dictation. It should be all you want. The man seems thoroughly penitent, but I do not trouble you with his expressions of remorse and regret.

'I remain, dear sir, yours faithfully,

'STEPHEN CRISP'

We read the last lines; the paper fluttered down from our hands; we turned to each other. Tears of deep thankfulness were in my wife's sweet eyes. Down to the smallest detail, the wretched man's confession made everything clear. Nothing was left unexplained, except, perhaps, the motive which induced Philippa to go that night to meet her would-be betrayer once more. This we shall never know, but her temporary madness may amply account for it. We need seek no further; the faintest doubt as to her own perfect innocence is removed from my wife's mind. Hand in hand, heart to heart, lip to lip, we can stand, and feel that our troubles are at last over.

Our troubles over! Shall those words be the last I write? No, one scene more—the scene that lies before me even now.

An English home. Outside, green shaven lawns, trim paths, and fine old trees. Inside, the comfort and the peace which make an English home the sweetest in the world. For when the need was gone; when sunny Spain no longer was for us the one safe land, its charms diminished, and we pined to see once more England's fair fields and ruddy honest faces. So back we came, and made ourselves a home, far, far away from every spot the sight of which might wake sad thoughts. And here we live, and shall live till that hour when one of us must kiss the other's clay-cold brow, and know that death has parted those whom naught but death could part.

Look out; look through this shaded window. There she sits, my wife; a tall son at her side, fair daughters near her. Years, many years have passed, but left no lines upon her brow; brought no white threads to streak that raven hair. The rich bright beauty of the girl is still her own. To me, now as of yore, the sweetest, fairest woman in the world!

The children see me as I gaze with thoughtful happy eyes upon that group beneath the trees. They call and beckon me. My wife looks up; her eyes meet mine, just raised from these sad pages. Ah! Love, sweet love, in those dear eyes what was it once my fate to read? Shame, sorrow, dread, despair and love. All these, save love, have vanished long ago; and as I turn to pen these lines—the last, that look of calm, assured, unclouded joy keeps with me, telling me that from her life has past even the very memory of those dark, dark days!

THE END

MUCH DARKER DAYS

BY

A. HUGE LONGWAY

[ANDREW LANG]

CONTENTS

I	THE CURSE (REGISTERED)	169
II	A VILLAIN'S BY-BLOW	174
III	MES GAGES! MES GAGES!	178
IV	AS A HATTER!	181
V	THE WHITE GROOM	185
VI	HARD AS NAILS	188
VII	RESCUE AND RETIRE!	194
VIII	LOCAL COLOUR	201
IX	SAVED! SAVED!	205
X	NOT TOO MAD, BUT JUST MAD ENOUGH	208
XI	A TERRIBLE TEMPTATION	211
XII	JUDGE JUGGINS	215
XIII	CLEARED UP	220

PREFACE

A BELIEF that modern Christmas fiction is too cheerful in tone, too artistic in construction, and too original in motive, has inspired the author of this tale of middle-class life. He trusts that he has escaped, at least, the errors he deplores, and has set an example of a more seasonable and sensational style of narrative.

A.H.L.

PREFACE (REVISED EDITION)

PARODY is a parasitical, but should not be a poisonous, plant. The Author of this unassuming jape has learned, with surprise and regret, that some sentences which it contains are thought even more vexatious than frivolous. To frivol, not to vex, was his aim, and he has corrected this edition accordingly.

A.H.L.

CHAPTER I

THE CURSE (REGISTERED)

WHEN this story of my life, or of such parts of it as are not deemed wholly unfit for publication, is read (and, no doubt, a public which devoured *Scrawled Black* will stand almost anything), it will be found that I have sometimes acted without prim cautiousness—that I have, in fact, wallowed in crime. Stillicide and Mayhem (rare old crimes!) are child's play to *me*, who have been an 'accessory after the fact'! In excuse, I can but plead two things—the excellence of the opportunity to do so, and the weakness of the resistance which my victim offered.

If you cannot allow for these, throw the book out of the railway-carriage window! You have paid your money, and to the verdict of your pale morality or absurd sense of art in fiction I am therefore absolutely indifferent. You are too angelic for me; I am too fiendish for you. Let us agree to differ.

I say nothing about my boyhood. Twenty-five years ago a poor boy—but no matter. *I* was that boy! I hurry on to the soaring period of manhood, 'when the strength, the nerve, the intellect is or should be at its height' (or *are* or should be at *their* height, if you *must* have grammar in a Christmas Annual), if the patient has led, as I did, a virtuous and contemplative life, devoted to extending popular culture. *My* nerve was at its height: I was thirty.

Yet, what was I then? A miserable moonstruck mortal, duly entitled to write M.D. (of Tarrytown College, Alaska) after my name—for the title of Doctor is useful in the profession—but with no other source of enjoyment or emotional recreation in a cold, casual world. Often and often have I written M.D. after my name, till the glowing pleasure palled, and I have sunk back asking, 'Has life, then, no more than this to offer?'

Bear with me if I write like this for ever so many pages; bear with me, it is such easy writing, and only thus can I hope to make you understand my subsequent and slightly peculiar conduct.

How rare was hers, the loveliness of the woman I lost—of her whose loss brought me down to the condition I attempt to depict!

How strange was her rich beauty! She was at once dark and fair—*la blonde et la brune!* How different from the Spotted Girls and Two-headed Nightingales whom I have often seen exhibited, and drawing money too, as the types of physical imperfections! Warm Southern blood glowed darkly in one of Philippa's cheeks—the left; pale Teutonic grace smiled in the other—the right. Her mother was a fair blonde Englishwoman, but it was Old Calabar that gave her daughter those curls of sable wool, contrasting so exquisitely with her silken-golden tresses. Her English mother may have lent Philippa many exquisite graces, but it was from her father, a pure-blooded negro, that she inherited her classic outline of profile.

Philippa, in fact, was a natural arrangement in black and white. Viewed from one side she appeared the Venus of the Gold Coast, from the other she outshone the Hellenic Aphrodite. From any point of view she was an extraordinarily attractive addition to the Exhibition and Menagerie which at that time I was running in the Midland Counties.

Her father, the nature of whose avocation I never thought it necessary to inquire into, was a sea cook on board a Peninsular and Oriental steamer. His profession thus prevented him from being a permanent resident in this, or indeed in any other country.

Our first meeting was brought about in a most prosaic way.

Her mother consulted me professionally about Philippa's prospects. We did not at that time come to terms. I thought I might conclude a more advantageous arrangement if Philippa's *heart* was touched, if she would be mine. But she did not love me. Moreover, she was ambitious; she knew, small blame to her, how unique she was.

'The fact is,' she would observe when I pressed my suit, 'the fact is I look higher than a mere showman, even if he can write M.D. after his name.'

Philippa soon left the circuit 'to better herself'.

In a short time a telegram from her apprised me that she was an orphan.

I flew to where she lodged, in a quiet, respectable street, near Ratcliff Highway. She expressed her intention of staying here for some time.

'But alone, Philippa?'

(She was but eight-and-thirty).

'Not so much alone as you suppose,' she replied archly.

This should have warned me, but again I passionately urged my plea.

I offered most attractive inducements.

A line to herself in the bills! Everything found!

'Basil,' she observed, blushing in her usual partial manner, 'you are a day after the fair.'

'But there are plenty of fairs,' I cried, 'all of which we attend regularly. What can you mean? Has another—?'

'He *hev*,' said Philippa, demurely but decidedly.

'You are engaged?' She raised her lovely hand, and was showing me a gold wedding circlet, when the door opened, and a strikingly handsome man of some forty summers entered.

There was something written in his face (a dark contusion, in fact, under the left eye) which told me that he could not be a pure and high-souled Christian gentleman.

'Basil South, M.D.' said Philippa, introducing us. 'Mr Baby Farmer' (obviously a name of endearment), and again a rosy blush crept round her neck in the usual partial manner, which made one of her most peculiar charms.

I bowed mechanically, and, amid a few dishevelled remarks on the weather, left the house the most disappointed showman in England.

'Cur, sneak, coward, villain!' I hissed when I felt sure I was well out of hearing. 'Farewell, farewell, Philippa!'

To drown remembrance and regret, I remained in town, striving in a course of what moralists call 'gaiety' to forget what I had lost.

How many try the same prescription, and seem rather to like it! I often met my fellow-patients.

One day, on the steps of the Aquarium, I saw the man whom I suspected of not being Philippa's husband.

'Who is that cove?' I asked.

'Him with the gardenia?' replied a friend, idiomatically. 'That is Sir Runan Errand, the amateur showman—him that runs the Live Mermaid, the Missing Link, and Koot Hoomi, the Mahatma of the Mountain.'

'What kind of man is he?'

'Just about the usual kind of man you see generally here. Just about as hot as they make them. Mad about having a show of his own; crazed on two-headed calves.'

'Is he married?'

'If every lady who calls herself Lady Errand had a legal title to do so, the "Baronetage" would have to be extended to several supplementary volumes.'

And this was Philippa's husband!

What was she among so many?

My impulse was to demand an explanation from the baronet, but for reasons not wholly unconnected with my height and fighting weight, I abstained.

I did better.

I went to my hotel, called for the hotel book, and registered an oath, which is, therefore, copyright. I swore that in twenty-five years I would be even with him I hated. I prayed, rather inconsistently, that honour and happiness might be the lot of her I had lost. After that I felt better.

CHAPTER II

A VILLAIN'S BY-BLOW

PHILIPPA was another's! Life was no longer worth living. Hope was evaluated; ambition was blunted. The interest which I had hitherto felt in my profession vanished. All the spring, the elasticity seemed taken out of my two Bounding Brothers from the Gutta Percha coast. For months I did my work in a perfunctory manner. I added a Tattooed Man to my exhibition and a Two-headed Snake, also a White-eyed Botocudo, who played the guitar, and a pair of Siamese Twins, who were fired out of a double-barrelled cannon, and then did the lofty trapeze business. They drew, but success gave me no pleasure. So long as I made money enough for my daily needs (and whisky was cheap), what recked I? My mood was none of the sweetest. My friends fell off from me; aye, they fell like ninepins whenever I could get within reach of them. I was alone in the world.

You will not be surprised to hear it; the wretched have no friends. So things went on for a year. I became worse instead of better. My gloom deepened, my liver grew more and more confirmed in its morbid inaction. These are not lover's rhapsodies, they merely show the state of my body and mind, and explain what purists may condemn. In this condition I heard without hypocritical regret that a distant relative (a long-lost uncle) had conveniently left me his vast property. I cared only because it enabled me to withdraw from the profession. I disposed of my exhibition, or rather I let it go for a song. I simply handed over the Tattooed Man, the Artillery Twins, and the Double-headed Serpent to the first-comer, who happened to be a rural dean. Far in the deeps of the country, near the little town of Roding, on a lonely highway, where no man ever came, I took a 'pike. Here I dwelt like a hermit, refusing to give change to the rare passers-by in carts and gigs, and attended by a handy fellow, William Evans, stolid as the Sphynx, which word, for reasons that may or may not appear later in this narrative, I prefer to spell with a *y*, contrary to the best authorities and usual custom.

It was midwinter, and midnight. My room lay in darkness. Heavy snow was falling. I went to the window and flattened my nose against the pane.

'What,' I asked myself, 'is most like a cat looking out of a window?'

'A cat looking in at a window,' answered a silvery voice from the darkness.

Flattened against the self-same pane was another nose, a woman's. It was the lovely organ of mixed architecture belonging to Philippa! With a low cry of amazement, I broke the pane: it was no idle vision, no case of the 'horrors'; the cold, cold nose of my Philippa encountered my own. The ice was now broken; she swept into my chamber, lovelier than ever in her strange unearthly beauty, and a new sealskin coat. Then she seated herself with careless grace, tilting back her chair, and resting her feet on the chimney-piece.

'Dear Philippa,' I exclaimed politely, 'how is your husband?'

'Husband! I have none,' she hissed. 'Tell me, Basil, *mon Bijou*, did you ever hate a fellow no end?'

'Yes,' I answered, truly; for, like Mr Carlyle, I just detested most people, and him who had robbed me of Philippa most of all.

'Do you know what he did, Basil? *He insisted on having a latch-key!* Did you ever hate a man?'

I threw out my arms. My heart was full of bitterness.

'He did more! He has refused to pay my last quarter's salary. Basil, didn't you ever hate a man?'

My brain reeled at these repeated outrages.

'And where are you staying at present, Philippa? I hope you are pretty comfortable?' I inquired, anxiously.

Philippa went on: 'My husband as was has chucked me. I was about to have a baby. I bored him. I was in the way—in the family-way. Basil, did you ever hate a fellow? If not, read this letter.'

She threw a letter towards me. She chucked it with all her old gracious dexterity. It was dated from Monte Carlo, and ran thus:

'As we don't seem quite to hit it off, I think I may as well finish this business of our marriage. The shortest way to make things clear to your very limited intelligence is to assure you that you are not my wife at all. Before I married you I was the husband of the Live Mermaid. She has died since then, and I might have married you over and over again; but I was not quite so infatuated. I shall just run across and settle up about this little affair on Wednesday. As you are five miles from the station, as the weather is perfectly awful, as moreover I am a luxurious, self-indulgent baronet and as this story would never get on unless I walked, don't send to meet me. I would *rather* walk.'

Here was a pretty letter from a fond husband. 'But, ha! proud noble,' I whispered to my heart, 'you and me shall meet tomorrow.'

'And where are you staying, Philippa?' I repeated, to lead the conversation into a more agreeable channel.

'With a Mrs Thompson,' she replied; 'a lady connected with Sir Runan.'

'Very well, let me call for your things tomorrow. I can pass myself off as your brother, you know.'

'My half-brother,' said Philippa, blushing, 'on the mother's side.'

The brave girl thought of *everything*. The child of white

parents, I should have in vain pretended to be Philippa's full brother. They would not have believed me had I sworn it.

'Don't you think,' Philippa continued, as a sudden thought occurred to her, 'that as it is almost midnight and snowing heavily it would be more proper for me to return to Mrs Thompson's?'

There was no contesting this.

We walked together to the house of that lady, and at my suggestion Philippa sought her couch.

I sat down and awaited the advent of Mrs Thompson. She soon appeared.

A woman of about five-and-thirty, with an aquiline face, and a long, dark, silky beard sweeping down to her waist. Whatever this woman's charms might have been for me when I was still in the profession, she could now boast of very few. Doubtless she had been in Sir Runan's show, and was one of his victims.

I apologised for the lateness of my call, and entered at once on business.

Mrs Thompson remarked that 'my sister's health was not as it should be'—not all she could wish.

'I do not wish to alarm you; no doubt you, her brother, are *used* to it; but, for a girl as mad as a hatter—well, I'll trouble you!'

'I myself can write M.D. after my name,' I replied—'*She* can write M.A.D.,' interrupted my hostess—'and you,' I went on, 'are related, I think, to Sir Runan Errand?'

'We are connections,' she said, not taking the point of my sarcasm. 'His conduct rarely astonishes me. When I found, however, that this lady, *your* sister, was his wife, I own, for once, I *was* surprised.'

Feeling that this woman had the better of it, with her calm, polished, highbred sarcasms, I walked back to the 'pike, full of hopes of a sweet revenge.

As, however, I had never spoken to a baronet before, I could not but fear that his lofty air of superior rank might daunt me when we met tomorrow.

CHAPTER III

MES GAGES! MES GAGES!

NEXT morning came, chill and grey, and reminded me that I had two duties. I was to wait at home till Philippa came over from Mrs Thompson's, and I was also to hang about the road from the station, and challenge Sir Runan to mortal combat.

Can duties clash?

They can. They did!

The hours lagged slowly by, while I read Sir Runan's letter, read and re-read it, registered and re-registered (a pretty term of my own invention) this vow of vengeance.

Philippa's 'things'—her boxes with all her properties—arrived in due time.

Philippa did not.

I passed a distracted day, now bounding forth half-way to the railway station to meet Sir Runan, now speeding back at the top of my pace to welcome Philippa at the 'pike.

As I knew not by what train Sir Runan would reach Roding, nor when Philippa might be looked for, I thus obtained exercise enough to make up for months of inaction.

Finally the last train was due.

It was now pitch-dark and snowing heavily, the very time which Philippa generally chose for a quiet evening walk.

I rushed half-way to Roding, changed my mind, headed back, and arrived at the 'pike.

'Has a lady called for me?' I asked the Sphynx.

'Now, *is* it likely, sir?' answered my fellow, with rough humour.

'Well, I must go and meet her,' I cried, and, hastily snatching a bull's-eye lantern and policeman's rattle from the Sphynx, I plunged into the darkness.

First I hurried to Mrs Thompson's, where I learned that Philippa had just gone out for a stroll after a somewhat prolonged luncheon. This was like Philippa. I recognised that shrinking modesty which always made her prefer to veil her charms by walking about after nightfall.

Turning from Mrs Thompson's, I felt the snow more sharply on my face. Furiously, blindly, madly it whirled here and drifted there.

Should I go for Sir Runan? Should I wait where I was? Should I whistle for a cab? Should I return to the 'pike?

Suddenly out of the snow came a peal of silvery laughter. Philippa waltzed gracefully by in a long ulster whitened with snow.

I detected her solely by means of my dark lantern.

I rushed on her, I seized her. I said, 'Philippa, come back with me!'

'No, all the fun's in the front,' shrieked Philippa. 'My quarter's salary! Oh, my last quarter's salary!'

With these wild words, like bullets from a Gatling gun rattling in my ears, I seized Philippa's hand.

Something fell, and would have rattled on the hard high road had it not been for the snow.

I stooped to pick up this shining object, and with one more wild yell of 'My quarter's salary!' Philippa waltzed again into the darkness.

Fatigued with the somewhat exhausting and unusual character of the day's performances, and out of training as I was, I could not follow her.

Mechanically, I still groped on the ground, and picked up a small chill object.

It was a latch-key! I thrust it in my pocket with my other keys.

Then a thought occurred to me, and I chucked it over the hedge, to serve as circumstantial evidence. Next I turned and went up the road, springing my rattle and flashing my bull's-eye

lantern on every side, like Mr Pickwick when he alarmed the
scientific gentleman.

Suddenly, with a cry of horror, I stopped short. At my very
feet, in the little circle of concentrated light thrown by the
lantern, lay a white crushed, cylindrical mass.

That mass I had seen before in the warm summer weather—
that mass, once a white hat, had adorned the brows of that
masher!

It was Sir Runan's topper!

CHAPTER IV

AS A HATTER!

YES, the white hat, lying there all battered and crushed on the white snow, must be the hat of Sir Runan!

Who else but the tigerish aristocrat that disdained the homely four-wheeler and preferred to walk five miles to his victim on this night of dread—who else would wear the gay gossamer of July in stormy December?

In that hat, thanks doubtless to its airy *insouciant* grace, he had won Philippa; in that hat he would have bearded her, defied her, and cast her off! The cruelty of man! The larger and bulkier crumpled heap which lay on the road a little beyond the hat, that heap with all its outlines already blurred by snow, that heap must be the baronet himself!

Oh, but this was vengeance, swift, deadly vengeance!

But how, but how had she wreaked it? *She*, already my heart whispered *she!*

Was my peerless Philippa then a murderess?

Oh, say not so; call hers (ye would do so an she had been an Irish felon) 'the wild justice of revenge', or the speedy execution of the outraged creditor.

Killed by Philippa!

Yes, and why? The answer was only too obvious. She must have gone forth to meet him, and to wring from him, by what means she might, that quarter's salary which the dastard had left unpaid. Then my thoughts flew to the door-key, the cause of that fierce family hatred which burned between Philippa and her betrayer. That latch-key she had wrested from him, it had fallen from her hand, and I—I had pitched it into space!

Overcome with emotion, I staggered in the direction of the

'pike. All the way, in the blinding, whirling snow, I traced the unobliterated prints of a small fairy foot.

This was a dreary comfort! Philippa had gone before me; the prints of the one small foot were hers. She must, then, have hopped all the way! Could such a mode of progression be consistent with a feeling of guilt? Could remorse step so gaily?

My man William, the Sphynx, opened the door to me. Assuming a natural air, I observed:

'Miss South is at home?'

'Yes, sir. Just come in, sir.'

'Where is she now?'

'Well, sir, she just is on the rampage. "I'll make 'is fur fly," she up and sez, sez she, when she heard as you was hout. Not a nice young lady for a small tea-party, sir,' he added, lowering his voice; 'a regular out-and-outer your sister is, to be sure.'

The Sphynx, in spite of his stolidity, occasionally ventured upon some slight liberty when addressing me.

I made a gay rejoinder, reflecting on the character of his own unmarried female relations, and entered the room.

Philippa was sitting on the lofty, dark oak chimney-piece, with her feet dangling unconventionally over the fireplace. The snow, melting from her little boots and her hair, had made a large puddle on the floor.

I came up and stood waiting for her to speak, but she kept pettishly swinging her small feet, as one who, by the action, means to signify displeasure.

'Philippa,' I said sternly, 'speak to me.'

'Well, here's a gay old flare-up!' cried Philippa, leaping from the chimney-piece, and folding her arms fiercely akimbo.

'Who are you? Where's the baby? *You* a brother; you're a pretty brother! Is *this* the way you keep 'pointments with a poor girl? Who killed the baby? You did—you *all* did it.'

Her words ran one into the other, as with an eloquence, which I cannot hope to reproduce (and indeed my excellent publisher would not permit it for a moment), she continued to dance derisively at me, and to heap reproaches of the most vexatious and frivolous nature on my head.

'Philippa,' I remarked at last, 'you frivol too much.'

A sullen look settled on her face, and, with the aid of a chair, she reseated herself in her former listless, drooping attitude upon the chimney-piece.

On beholding these symptoms, on hearing these reproaches, a great wave of joy swept over my heart.

Manifestly, Philippa was indeed, as Mrs Thompson had said, 'as mad as a hatter'. Whatever she might have done did not count, and was all right. We would plead insanity.

She had fallen a victim to a mental disease, the source of which I have no hesitation in saying has not yet been properly investigated. So far as I know there is no monograph on the subject, or certainly I would have read it up carefully for the purpose of this Christmas Annual. I cannot get on without a mad woman in my stories, and if I can't find a proper case in the medical books, why, I invent one, or take it from the French. This one I have invented, and not wholly without success, as every competent and learned Master in Lunacy ought to admit.

The details of Philippa's case, though of vast and momentous professional interest, I shall reserve for a communication to some journal of Science.

As for the treatment, I measured out no less than sixty drops of laudanum, with an equal amount of very old brandy, in a separate vessel. But preparing a dose and getting a patient like this to take it, are two different things. I succeeded by the following device.

I sent for some hot water and sugar and a lemon. I mixed the boiling element carefully with the brandy, and (separately) with the laudanum.

I took a little of the *former* beverage. Philippa with unaffected interest beheld me repeat this action again and again.

A softer, more contented look stole over her beautiful face. I seized the moment. Once more I pressed the potion (the *other* potion) upon her.

This time successfully.

Softly murmuring 'More sugar,' Philippa sank into a sleep—sound as the sleep of death.

Philippa might awaken, I hoped, with her memory free from the events of the day.

As Princess Toto, in the weird old Elizabethan tragedy, quite forgot the circumstance of her Marriage, so Philippa might entirely forget her Murder.

When we remember what women are, the latter instance of obliviousness appears the more probable.

CHAPTER V

THE WHITE GROOM

I SHALL, I am sure, scarcely be credited when I say that Philippa's unconsciousness lasted for sixteen days. I had wished her to sleep so long that the memory of her deeds on the awful night should fade from her memory. She seemed likely to do so.

All the time she slept I felt more and more secure, because the snow never ceased falling.

It must have been thirty feet deep above all that was mortal of Sir Runan Errand.

The deeper the better.

The baronet was never missed by anyone, curious to say. No inquiries were made; and this might have puzzled a person less unacquainted than myself with the manners of baronets and their friends.

Sometimes an awful fascination led me along the road where I had found the broken, battered mass.

I fancied I could see the very drift where the thing lay, and a dreary temptation (dating probably from the old times when I had some wild beasts in the exhibition) urged me to 'stir it up with a long pole'. I resisted it, and, bitterly weeping, I turned away towards Philippa's bedside.

In the night I met Mrs Thompson in a dress of phosphorescent material like patent match boxes.

'Does she hate him?' she asked suddenly.

'Forgiveness is a Christian virtue,' I answered evasively.

I could not trust this woman.

'Listen,' she said, 'and try to understand. If I thought she hated him, I would tell her something. If she thought you hated them, he would tell me something. If ye or you thought he hated her, I would tell him something. I will wait and see.'

She left me to make the best (which was not much) of her enigmatical words.

She was evidently a strange woman.

I felt that she was mixed up in Sir Runan's early life, and that we were mixed up in Sir Runan's early death—in fact, that everything was very mixed indeed.

She came back. 'Give me your name and college,' she said, 'not necessarily for publication,' and I divined that she had once been a proctor at Girton. I gave her my address at the public-house round the corner, and we parted, Mrs Thompson whispering that she 'would write'.

On reaching home I leaped to Philippa's apartment.

A great change had come over her.

She was awake!

I became at once a prey to the wildest anxiety.

The difficulties of my position for the first time revealed themselves to me.

If Philippa remained insane, how was I to remove her from the scene of her—alas!—of her crime?

If Philippa had become sane, her position under my roof was extremely compromising.

Again, if she were insane, a jury might acquit her, when the snow melted and revealed all that was left of the baronet.

But, in that case, what pleasure or profit could I derive from the society of an insane Philippa?

Supposing, on the other hand, she was sane, then was I not an accessory after the fact, and liable to all the pains and penalties of such a crime?

Here the final question arose and shook its ghostly finger at me: 'Can a sane man be an accessory after the fact in a murder committed by an insane woman?'

So far as I know, there is no monograph on this subject, or

certainly I would have consulted it for the purpose of this Christmas Annual.

All these questions swept like lightning through my brain, as I knelt by Philippa's bedside, and awaited her first word.

'*Bon jour, Philippine*,' I said.

'Basil,' she replied, 'where am I?'

'Under my roof—your brother's roof,' I said.

'Brother! Oh, stow that bosh!' she said, turning languidly away.

There could not be a doubt of it, Philippa was herself again!

I rose pensively, and wandered out towards the stables.

Covered with white snow over a white macintosh, I met by the coach-house door William, the Sphynx.

THE WHITE GROOM!

Twiddling a small object, *a door-key of peculiar make*, in his hand, he grinned stolidly at me.

'She's a rum un, squire, your sister, she be,' chuckled the Sphynx.

'William,' I said, 'go to Roding, and bring back two nurses, even if they have to hire twenty drags to draw them here. And, William, bring some drugs in the drags.'

By setting him on this expedition I got rid of the Sphynx. Was he a witness? (Where had I read of 'The White Witness'?— surely in some old mysterious back number of *Punch*!) *He was certainly acquainted with the nature of an oath!*

CHAPTER VI

HARD AS NAILS

OF course when I woke next morning my first thought was of Philippa; my second was of the weather. Always interesting, meteorological observation becomes peculiarly absorbing when it entirely depends on the thermometer whether you shall, or shall not, be arrested as an accessory after the fact, or (as lawyers say) *post-mortem*. My heart sank into my boots, or rather (for I had not yet dressed) into my slippers, when I found that, for the first time during sixteen days, the snow had ceased falling. I threw up the sash, the cold air cut me like a knife. Mechanically I threw up the sponge; it struck hard against the ceiling, and fell back a mass of brittle, jingling icicles, so severe was the iron frost that had bound it.

I gathered up a handful of snow from the window-sill. It crumbled in my fingers like patent camphorated tooth-powder, for which purpose I instantly proceeded to use it. Necessity is the mother of invention. Then I turned, as a final test, to my bath. Oh, joy! It was frozen ten inches thick! No tub for me today! I ran downstairs gleefully, and glanced at the thermometer outside my study window. Hooray, it registered twenty degrees below zero! It registered! That reminded me of my oath! I registered it once more, regardless of legal expenses.

My spirits rose as rapidly as the glass had fallen. The wind was due east, not generally a matter for indecent exultation.

But while the wind was due east, so long the frost would last, and that white mass on the roadside would remain *in statu quo*.

So long, Philippa was safe.

After that her fate, and mine too, depended on the eccentricities of a jury, the chartered libertinism of an ermined judge, the humour of the law, on a series of points without precedent concerning which no monograph had as yet been written; and, as a last desperate resource, on the letters of a sympathetic British public in the penny papers. The penny papers, the criminal's latest broadsheet anchor! Under the exasperating circumstances, Philippa remained as well as could be expected. She spoke little, but ate and drank a good deal. Day after day the brave black frost lasted, and the snowy grave hid all that it would have been highly inconvenient for me to have discovered. The heavens themselves seemed to be shielding us and working for us. Do the heavens generally shield accessories after the fact, and ladies who have shortened the careers of their lords? These questions I leave to the casuist, the meteorologist, the compilers of weather forecasts, and other constituted authorities on matters connected with theology and the state of the barometer.

I have not given the year in which these unobtrusive events occurred.

Many who can remember that mighty fall of snow, exceeding aught in the recollection of the oldest inhabitant, and the time during which the frost kept it on the earth, will be able and willing to fix the date.

I do not object to their thus occupying their leisure with chronological research.

If they feel at all baffled by the difficulties of the problem, I will give them an additional 'light': *Since that year (thank goodness!) there has been no weather like it.*

Answers may be sent to the Puzzle Editor of *Truth*.

Day by day Philippa grew better and better. This appears to be the usual result of excessively seasonable weather acting on a constitution previously undermined by bigamy, murder, and similar excesses.

I spare all technical summary of the case, sufficient to say that this was one of the rare instances in which the mind, totally unhinged, is restored to its balance by sixty drops of laudanum taken fasting, with a squeeze of lemon, after violent exercise on an empty stomach.

The case is almost unique; but, had things fallen out otherwise, this story could never have been got ready in time to romp in before the other Christmas Annuals.

Matters would have become really *too* complicated!

As Philippa recovered, it became more and more evident even to the most dilatory mind that the sooner she left the scene of her late unrehearsed performance the better.

The baronet had not yet been missed—indeed, he never *was* missed, and that is one of the very most remarkable points in the whole affair.

When he *did* come to be missed, however, he would naturally be sought for in the neighbourhood of the most recent and attractive of his wives.

That wife was Philippa.

Everything pointed to instant flight.

But how was I to get Philippa to see this? *Ex hypothesi* she knew nothing of the murder. On the other hand, all her pure, though passionate nature would revolt against sharing my home longer than was necessary. But would not the same purity prevent her from accompanying me abroad?

Brother and sister we had called ourselves but Philippa had never been the dupe of this terminology.

Besides, was not her position, in any case, just a little shady?

An idea now occurred to me for the first time. Many men would long ere now have asked their mothers to *chaperon* them. It flashed across me that I had a mother.

He who says 'mother' says '*chaperon*'.

I would take my Philippa to my mother. Philippa was now completely convalescent.

I can only attribute my lingering to the sense of fatality that all things would come round and be all square.

Love I had laid aside till I could see my way a little clearer in the certainly perplexing combination of circumstances.

Nevertheless, Philippa, I say it advisedly, seemed to me a good deal more pure and innocent than when we first met. True, she had been secretly married to a man under a name which she knew to be false.

True, she had given birth to a baby whose later fate remains a mystery even to this day. True, her hands were stained with the blood of Sir Runan Errand.

But why speak of Redistribution, why agitate for Woman's Suffrage, if trifles like these are to obstruct a girl's path in society?

Philippa's wrongs had goaded her to madness. Her madness was responsible for the act. She was not mad any longer. Therefore she was not responsible. Therefore Philippa was innocent.

If she became mad again, then it would be time to speak of guilt.

But would these syllogisms be as powerful with a British as they certainly would have proved with a French jury?

Once Philippa seemed to awaken to a sense of the situation.

Once she asked me, 'How she came to my home that night?'

'You came *out of* the whirling snow, and *in* a high state of delirium,' I answered, epigrammatically.

'I thought I came on foot,' she replied, dreamily.

'But, Basil,' she went on, 'what afterwards? What's the next move, my noble sportsman?'

What, indeed! Philippa had me there.

Clearly it was time to move.

In order to avert suspicion, I thought it was better not to shut up my house.

For the same purpose, I did a little in crime on my own account.

A man tires of only being an accessory.

William, the Sphynx, obviously 'was in the know', as sporting characters say. Was in the know of what was in the snow! I must silence William.

I took my measures quietly.

First I laid in two dozen of very curious pale sherry at half-a-crown.

I bought each bottle at a separate shop in a different disguise (making twenty-four in all), that my proceedings might not attract attention.

I laid down the deadly fluid with all proper caution in the cellar.

At parting from William I gave him five shillings and the cellar key, telling him to be very careful, and await my instructions.

I knew well that long before my 'instructions' could reach him, the faithful William would be speechless, and far beyond the reach of human science.

His secret would sleep with the White Groom.

Then Philippa and I drove townward through the dark, Philippa asking me conundrums, like Nebuchadnezzar.

'There was something I dreamed of. Tell me what it was?' she asked.

But, though better informed than the Wise Men and Soothsayers of old, I did not gratify her unusual desire.

On reaching town I drove straight to the hotel at which my mother was staying.

It was one of those highly-priced private hotels in the New Cut.

As, however, I had no desire to purchase this place of entertainment, the exorbitant value set on it by its proprietors did not affect my spirits.

In a few minutes I had told my mother all save two things: the business of the baby, and the fate which had overtaken Sir Runan.

With these trifling exceptions she knew all.

To fall into Philippa's arms was, to my still active parent, the work of a moment.

Then Philippa looked at me with an artless wink.

'Basil, my brother, you are really too good.'

Ah, how happy I should have felt could that one dark night's work have been undone!

CHAPTER VII

RESCUE AND RETIRE!

HITHERTO I have said little about my mother, and I may even seem to have regarded that lady in the light of a temporary convenience. My readers will, however, already have guessed that *my* mother was no common character.

Consider for a moment the position which she so readily consented to occupy.

The trifling details about the sudden decease of Sir Runan and the affair of the baby, as we have seen, I had thought it better *not* to name to her.

Matters, therefore, in her opinion, stood thus:

Philippa was the victim of a baronet's wiles.

When off with the new love, she had promptly returned and passed a considerable time under the roof of the old love; that is, of myself.

Then I had suddenly arrived with this eligible prospective daughter-in-law at my mother's high-priced hotel, and I kept insisting that we should at once migrate, we three, to foreign parts—the more foreign the better.

I had especially dilated on the charms of the scenery and the salubrity of the climate in *countries where there was no extradition treaty with England.*

Even if there was nothing in these circumstances to arouse the watchful jealousy of a mother, it must be remembered that, as a *chaperon*, she did seem to come a little late in the day.

'As you have lived together so long without me,' some parents would have observed, 'you can do without me altogether.'

None of these trivial objections occurred to my mother.

She was good-nature itself.

Just returned from a professional tour on the Continent (she was, I should have said, in the profession herself, and admirably filled the *exigeant* part of Stout Lady in a highly respectable exhibition), my mother at once began to pack up her properties and make ready to accompany us.

Never was there a more good-humoured *chaperon*. If one of us entered the room where she was sitting with the other, she would humorously give me a push, and observing 'Two is company, young people, three is none', would toddle off with all the alacrity that her figure and age permitted.

I learned from inquiries addressed to the *Family Herald* (correspondence column) that the Soudan was then, even as it is now, the land safest against English law. Spain, in this respect, was reckoned a bad second.

The very next day I again broached the subject of foreign travel to my mother. It was already obvious that the frost would not last for ever. Once the snow melted, once the crushed mass that had been a baronet was discovered, circumstantial evidence would point to Philippa. True, there was no one save myself who could positively *swear* that Philippa had killed Sir Runan. Again, though I could positively swear it, my knowledge was only an inference of my own. Philippa herself had completely forgotten the circumstance. But the suspicions of the Bearded Woman and of the White Groom were sure to be aroused, and the Soudan I resolved to seek without an hour's delay.

I reckoned without my hostess.

My mother at first demurred.

'You certainly don't look well, Basil. But why the Soudan?'

'A whim, a sick man's fancy. Perhaps because it is not so very remote from Old Calabar, the country of Philippa's own father. Mother, tell me, how do you like her?'

'She is the woman you love, and however shady her ante-cedents, however peculiar her style of conversation, she is, she must be, blameless. To say more, after so short an acquaintance, might savour of haste and exaggeration.'

A woman's logic!

'Then you *will* come to the Soudan with us tomorrow?'

'No, my child, further south than Spain I will *not* go, not this journey!'

Here Philippa entered.

'Well, what's the next news, old man?' she said.

'To Spain, tomorrow!'

> *'Rain, rain,*
> *Go to Spain,*
> *Be sure you don't come back again'*

sang sweet Philippa, in childish high spirits.

I had rarely seen her thus!

Alas, Philippa's nursery charm against the rain proved worse than unavailing.

That afternoon, after several months of brave black frost, which had gripped the land in its stern clasp, the rain began to fall heavily.

The white veil of snow gradually withdrew.

All that night I dreamed of the white snow slowly vanishing from the white hat.

Next morning the snow *had* vanished, and the white hat must have been obvious to the wayfaring man though a fool.

Next morning, and the next, and the next, found me still in London.

Why?

My mother was shopping!

Oh, the awful torture of having a gay mother shopping the solemn hours away, when each instant drew her son nearer to the doom of an accessory after the fact!

My mother did not object to travel, but she *did* like to have her little comforts about her.

She occupied herself in purchasing—

A water-bed.
A *boule*, or hot-water bottle.
A portable stove.
A travelling kitchen-range.
A medicine chest.
A complete set of Ollendorff.
Ten thousand pots of Dundee marmalade.

And such other articles as she deemed essential to her comfort and safety during the expedition. In vain I urged that our motto was *Rescue and Retire*, and that such elaborate preparations might prevent our retiring from our native shore, and therefore make rescue exceedingly problematical.

My Tory mother only answered by quoting the example of Lord Wolseley and the Nile Expedition.

'How long did *they* tarry among the pots—the marmalade pots?' said my mother. 'Did *they* start before every mess had its proper share of extra teaspoons in case of accident, and a double supply of patent respirators for the drummer-boys, and of snow-shoes for the Canadian boatmen in case the climate proved uncertain?'

My mother's historical knowledge, and the unique example of provident and exhaustive equipment which she cited, reduced me to silence, but did not diminish my anxiety. The delay made me nervous, excited, and chippy.

Tomorrow morning we were to start.

Tomorrow morning was too late.

With an effort I opened the morning paper—the *Morning Post*, as it happened—and ran hastily up and down the columns, active exercise having been recommended to me. What cared I for politics, foreign news, or even the sportive intelligence? All I sought for was a paragraph headed 'Horrible Disclosures', or, 'Awful Death of a Baronet'. I ran up and down the columns in vain.

No such item of news met my eye. Joyously I rose to go, when my eye fell on the *Standard*.

Mechanically I opened it.

Those words were written (or so they seemed to me to be written) in letters of fire, though the admirable press at Shoe Lane did not really employ that suitable medium.

'HORRIBLE DISCOVERY NEAR RODING.'

At once the truth flashed across me. The *Morning Post* had not contained the intelligence because

THE GOVERNMENT HAD BOYCOTTED
THE 'MORNING POST'!

Only journals which more or less supported the Government were permitted to obtain 'copy' of such thrilling interest!

And yet they speak of a free press and a free country!

Tearing myself away from these reflections, I bent my mind on the awful paragraph.

'The melting of the snow has thrown a lurid light on the mysterious disappearance (which up to this moment had attracted no attention) of an eccentric baronet, well known in sporting circles. Yesterday afternoon a gentleman's groom, wading down the highway, discovered the white hat of a gentleman floating on the muddy stream into which the unparalleled weather and the negligence of the Road Trustees has converted our thoroughfare. An inscription in red ink within the lining leaves no doubt that this article of dress is all that is left of the late Sir Runan Errand. The unfortunate nobleman's friends have been communicated with. The active and intelligent representative of the local police believes that he is in possession of a clue to the author of the crime. Probably the body of the murdered noble has been carried down by the flooded road to the sea.'

I tore that paper to pieces, and used it to wrap up sandwiches for the journey.

Once again I say, if you cannot feel with me, throw this tale aside. Heaven knows it is a sombre one, and it goes on getting sombrer and sombrer! But probably, by this time, you have either tossed the work away or looked at the end to see what happened to them all.

The morning dawned.

I filled my bag with Hanover pieces, which I thought might come in handy on the Spanish Turf, and packed up three or four yellow, red, green, and blue opera hats, so useful to the adventurous bookmaker.

At this very moment the postman arrived and gave me a letter in a woman's hand.

I thrust it in my breast pocket recklessly.

The cab rattled away.

At last we were off.

I am sure that no one who could have seen us that morning would have dreamt that out of that party of three—a more than comfortable-looking English matron, a girl whose strange beauty has been sufficiently dwelt upon, and a gentleman in a yellow crush hat and a bookmaker's bag—two were flying from the hands of justice.

Our appearance was certainly such as to disarm all suspicion.

But appearances are proverbially deceitful. Were ours deceitful enough?

'But where are we going?' said my mother, with the short memory of old age.

'To Paris first, then to Spain, and, if needful, down to Khartoum.'

'*Then* you young people will have to go alone. I draw the line at Dongola.'

I glanced at Philippa.

Then for the first time since her malady I saw Philippa blushing! Her long curved eyelashes hid her eyes, which presumably were also pink, but certainly my mother's broad pleasantry had called a tell-tale blush to the cheek of the young person.

As we drew near Folkestone I remembered the letter, but the sight of the Roding postmark induced me to defer opening it till we should be on board the steamer. When Philippa was battling with the agonies of the voyage, then, undisturbed, I might ascertain what Mrs Thompson (for it was sure to be Mrs Thompson) had to say.

We were now on board. Philippa and my mother fled to the depths of the saloon, and I opened the fateful missive. It began without any conventional formalities, and the very first words blanched a cheek already pale.

'I see yer!'

This strange epistle commenced:

'*I* know why Sir Runan never reached my house. I know the reason (it was only too obvious) for *her* strange, excited state. I know how he met the death he deserved.

'I never had the pluck. None of the rest of us ever had the pluck. We all swore we'd swing for him as, one after another, he wedded and deserted us. The Two-headed Nightingale swore it, and the Missing Link, and the Spotted Girl, and the Strong Woman who used to double up horseshoes. Now she doubles up her perambulator with her children in it, but she never doubled up him.

'As to your sister, tell her from me that she is all right. She has made herself his widow, she is the Dowager Lady Errand.

'The fact is, *the Live Mermaid was never alive at all*! She was a put-up thing of waxwork and a stuffed *salmo ferox*. His pretended marriage with *her* is therefore a mere specious excuse to enable him to avoid your sister's claims.

'Now he is dead, your sister can take the name, title, and estates. I wish she may get them. No reduction is made on taking a quantity.'

CHAPTER VIII

LOCAL COLOUR

I READ the woman's letter again and again, read it with feelings of the most mingled description. First, I reflected with solemn pride that Philippa was *more* than an honest woman; that she really was a baronet's lady! After we were married she should keep her title. Many people do. How well it would sound when we entered a room together—'Dr South and Lady Errand!'

Yet, on second thoughts, would not this conjunction of names rather set people asking questions?

Yes, disagreeable associations might be revived.

My second thought was that, if Mrs Thompson kept her word, we might as well go home at once, without bothering about the Soudan. The White Groom, I felt certain, had long been speechless. There was thus no one to connect Lady Errand with the decease of Sir Runan.

Moreover, Philippa's self-respect was now assured. She had lost it when she learned that she was not Sir Runan's wife; she would regain it when she became aware that she had made herself Sir Runan's widow. Such is the character of feminine morality, as I understand the workings of woman's heart.

I had reached this point in my soliloquy, when I reflected that perhaps I had better *not* tell Philippa anything about it.

You see, things were so very mixed, because Philippa's memory was so curiously constructed that she had entirely forgotten the murder which she had committed; and even if I proved to her by documentary evidence that she had only murdered her own husband, it might not help to relieve her burdened conscience as much as I had hoped. There are times

when I almost give up this story in despair. To introduce a
heroine who is mad in and out, so to speak, and forgets and
remembers things exactly at the right moment, seems a delight-
fully simple artifice.

But, upon my word, I am constantly forgetting what it is that
Philippa should remember, and on the point of making her
remember the very things she forgets!

So puzzled had I become that I consoled myself by cursing
Sir Runan's memory. *De mortuis nil nisi bonum!*

What a lot of trouble a single little murder, of which one
thinks little enough at the time, often gives a fellow.

All this while we were approaching Paris.

The stains of travel washed away, my mother gave a sigh of
satisfaction as she seated herself at the dinner table. As anyone
might guess who looked at her, she was no despiser of the good
things of this life!

That very night we went to the Hippodrome, where we met
many old acquaintances. My own Artillery Twins were there,
and kissed their hands to me as they flew gracefully over our
heads towards the desired trapeze. Here, also, was the Tattooed
Man, and I grasped his variegated and decorative hand with
an emotion I have rarely felt. Without vanity I may say that
Philippa and my mother had a *succès fou*.

From the moment when they entered their box every
lorgnette was fixed upon them.

All Paris was there, the *tout Paris* of *premières*, of *les courses*,
the *tout Paris* of *clubsman*, of *belles petites*, of ladies *à chignon
jaune*. Here were the Booksmen, the *gommeux*, they who *font
courir*, the journalists, and here I observed with peculiar
interest my great masters, M. Fortuné du Boisgobey and M.
Xavier de Montépin.

In the intervals of the performance *tout le monde* crowded
into our *loge*, and I observed that my mother and Lady Errand
made an almost equal impression on many a gallant and enterprising young *impresario*.

We supped at the *Café Bignon*; toasts were carried; I also was carried home.

Next morning I partly understood the mental condition of Philippa. I had absolutely forgotten the events of the later part of the entertainment.

Several bills arrived for windows, which, it seems, I had broken in a moment of effusion.

Gendarmes arrived, and would have arrested me on a charge of having knocked down some thirty-seven of their number.

This little matter was easily arranged.

I apologised separately and severally to each of the thirty-seven *braves hommes*, and collectively to the whole corps, the French army, the President, the Republic, and the statue of Strasbourg in the Place de la Concorde. These duties over, I was at leisure to reflect on the injustice of English law.

Certain actions which I had entirely forgotten I expiated at the cost of a few thousand francs, and some dozen apologies.

For only one action, about which she remembered nothing at all, Philippa had to fly from English justice, and give up her title and place in society! Both ladies now charmed me with a narrative of the compliments that had been paid them; both absolutely declined to leave Paris.

'I want to look at the shops,' said my mother.

'I want the *gommeux* to look at me,' said Philippa.

Neither of them saw the least fun in my proposed expedition to Spain.

Weeks passed and found us still in the capital of pleasure.

My large fortune, except a few insignificant thousands, had passed away in the fleeting exhilaration of baccarat.

We must do something to restore our wealth.

My mother had an idea.

'Basil,' she said, 'you speak of Spain. You long to steep yourself in local colour. You sigh for *hidalgos*, *sombreros*, *carbonados*, and *carboncillos*, why not combine business with pleasure?

'Why not take the Alhambra?'

This *was* an idea!

Where could we be safer than under the old Moorish flag?

Philippa readily fell in with my mother's proposal. When woman has once tasted of public admiration, when once she has stepped on the boards, she retires without enthusiasm, even at the age of forty.

'I had thought,' said Philippa, of exhibiting myself at the Social Science Congress, and lecturing on self-advertisement and the ethical decline of the Moral Show business, with some remarks on waxworks. But the Alhambra sounds ever so much more toney.'

It was decided on.

I threw away the Baedeker and Murray, and Ford's *Spain*, on which I had been relying for three chapters of padding and local colour. I ceased to think of the very old churches of St Croix and St Seurin and a variety of other interesting objects. I did not bother about St Sebastian, and the Valley of the Giralda, and Burgos, the capital of the old Castilian kingdom, and the absorbing glories of the departed Moore. Gladly, gaily, I completed the necessary negotiations, and found myself, with Philippa, my mother, and many of my old *troupe*, in the dear old Alhambra, safe under the shelter of the gay old Moorish flag.

Shake off black gloom, Basil South, and make things skip.

You have conquered Fate!

CHAPTER IX

SAVED! SAVED!

GLORIOUS, wonderful Alhambra!

Magical Cuadrado de Leicestero!

Philippa and I were as happy as children, and the house was full every night.

We called everything by Spanish names, and played perpetually at being Spaniards.

The *foyer* we named a *patio*—a space fragrant with the perfume of oranges, which the public were always sucking, and perilous with peel. Add to this a refreshment-room, *refectorio*, full of the rarest old *cigarros*, and redolent of *aqua de soda* and *aguardiente*. Here the *botellas* of *aqua de soda* were continually popping, and the *corchos* flying with a murmur of merry voices and of mingling waters. Here half through the night you could listen to—

> *The delight of happy laughter,*
> *The delight of low replies.*

With such surroundings, almost those of a sybarite, who can blame me for being lulled into security, and telling myself that my troubles were nearly at an end? Who can wonder at the *châteaux en Espagne* that I built as I lounged in the *patio*, and assisted my customers to consume the *media aqua de soda*, or 'split soda', of the country? Sometimes we roamed as far as the Alcazar; sometimes we wandered to the Oxford, or laughed light-heartedly in the stalls of the *Alegria*.

Such was our life. So in calm and peace (for we had secured

a Tory *chuckerouto* from Birmingham) passed the even tenor of our days.

As to marrying Philippa, it had always been my *intention*.

Whether she was or was not Lady Errand; whether she had or had not precipitated the hour of her own widowhood, made no kind of difference to me.

A moment of ill-judged haste had been all her crime.

That moment had passed.

Philippa was not that moment. I was not marrying that moment, but Philippa.

Picture, then, your Basil naming and insisting on the day, yet somehow the day had not yet arrived. It did, however, arrive at last.

The difficulty now arose under which name was Philippa to be married?

To tell you the truth, I cannot remember under which name Philippa *was* married.

It was a difficult point.

If she wedded me under her maiden name, and if Mrs Thompson's letter contained the truth, then would the wedding be legal and binding?

If she married me under the name of Lady Errand, and if Mrs Thompson's letter was false, then would the wedding be all square?

So far as I know, there is no monograph on the subject, or there was none at the time.

Be it as it may, wedded we were.

Morality was now restored to the show business, the legitimate drama began to look up, and the hopes of the Social Science Congress were fulfilled.

But evil days were at hand.

One day, Philippa and I were lounging in the *patio*, when I heard the young *hidalgos*—or *Macheros*, as they are called—talking as they smoked their princely *cigaritos*.

'Sir Runan Errand,' said one of them; 'where's he gone under? A rare bad lot he was.'

'Murdered,' replied the other. 'Nothing ever found of him but his hat.'

'What a rum go!' replied the other.

I looked at Philippa. She had heard all. I saw her dark brow contract in anguish. She was beating her breast furiously—her habit in moments of agitation.

Then I seem to remember that I and the two *hidalgos* bore Philippa to a couch in the *patio*, while I smiled and smiled and talked of the heat of the weather!

When Philippa came back to herself, she looked at me with her wondrous eyes and said—

'Basil; tell me the square truth, honest Injun! What had I been up to that night?'

CHAPTER X

It was out! She knew!

What was I to say, how evade her impulsive cross-examinations? I fell back upon evasions.

'Why do I want to know?' she echoed. 'Because I choose to! I hated him. He took a walk, I took a walk, and I had taken something before I took a walk. If we met, I was bound to have words with him. Basil, did I dream it, or read it long ago in some old penny dreadful of the past?'

Philippa occasionally broke into blank verse like this, but not often.

'Dearest, it must have been a dream,' I said, catching at this hope of soothing her.

'No, no!' she screamed; 'no—no dream. Not any more, thank you! I can see myself standing now over that crushed white mass! Basil, I could never bear him in that hat, and I must have gone for him!'

I consoled Philippa as well as I could, but she kept screaming.

'*How* did I kill him?'

'Goodness only knows, Philippa,' I replied; 'but you had a key in your hand—a door-key.'

'Ah, that fatal latch-key!' she said, 'the cause of our final quarrel. Where is it? What have you done with it?' she shouted.

'I threw it away,' I replied. This was true, but I could not think of anything better to say.

'You threw it away! Didn't you know it would become a *pièce justificatif*?' said my poor Philippa, who had not read Gaboriau to no purpose.

I passed the night wrestling in argument with Philippa. She reproached me for having returned from Spain, 'which was quite safe, you know—it is the place city men go to when they bust up,' she remarked in her peculiarly idiomatic style. She reproved me for not having told her all about it before, in which case she would never have consented to return to England.

'They will try me—they will hang me!' she repeated.

'Not a bit,' I answered. 'I can prove that you were quite out of your senses when you did for him.'

'*You* prove it!' she sneered; 'a pretty lawyer *you* are. Why, they won't take a husband's evidence for or against a wife in a criminal case. This comes of your insisting on marrying me.'

'But I doubt if we *are* married, Philippa, dear, as we never could remember whether you were wedded under your maiden name or as Philippa Errand. Besides—' I was going to say that William, the White Groom (late the Sphynx), could show to her having been (as he once expressed it) as 'crazy as a loon', but I remembered in time. William had, doubtless, long been speechless.

The sherry must have done its fatal work.

This is the worst of committing crimes.

They do nothing, very often, but complicate matters.

Had I not got rid of William—but it was too late for remorse. As to the evidence of her nurses, I forgot all about *that*. I tried to console Philippa on another line.

I remarked that, if she had 'gone for' Sir Runan, she had only served him right.

Then I tried to restore her self-respect by quoting the bearded woman's letter.

I pointed out that she had been Lady Errand, after all.

This gave Philippa no comfort.

'It makes things worse,' she said. 'I thought I had only got rid of my betrayer; and now you say I have killed my husband. You men have no tact.

'Besides,' Philippa went on, after pausing to reflect, 'I have

not bettered myself one bit. If I had not gone for him I would
be Lady Errand, and no end of a swell, and now I'm only plain
Mrs Basil South.'

Speaking thus, Philippa wept afresh, and refused to be
comforted.

Her remarks were not flattering to my self-esteem.

At this time I felt, with peculiar bitterness, the blanks in
Philippa's memory. Nothing is more difficult than to make your
heroine not too mad, but just mad enough.

Had Philippa been a trifle saner, or less under the influence
of luncheon, at first, she would either never have murdered Sir
Runan at all (which perhaps would have been the best course),
or she would have known *how* she murdered him.

The entire absence of information on this head added much
to my perplexities.

On the other hand, had Philippa been a trifle madder, or
more under the influence of luncheon, nothing could ever have
recalled the event to her memory at all.

As it is, my poor wife (if she *was* my wife, a subject on which
I intend to submit a monograph to a legal contemporary), my
poor wife was almost provoking in what she forgot and what
she remembered.

One day as my dear patient was creeping about the *patio*,
she asked me if I saw *all* the papers?

I said I saw most of them.

'Well, look at them *all*, for who knows how many may be
boycotted by the present Government? In a boycotted print
you don't know but you may miss an account of how some
fellow was hanged for what I did. I believe two people can't be
executed for the same crime. Now, if anyone swings for Sir
Runan, *I* am safe; but it might happen, and you never know it.'

Dear Philippa, ever thoughtful for others! I promised to read
every one of the papers, and I was soon rewarded for the
unparalleled tedium of these studies.

CHAPTER XI

A TERRIBLE TEMPTATION

I HATE looking back and reading words which I have written when the printer's devil was waiting for copy in the hall, but I fancy I have somewhere called this tale a confession; if not, I meant to do so. It has no more claim to be called a work of art than the cheapest penny dreadful. How could it?

It holds but two characters, a man and a woman.

All the rest are the merest supers. Perhaps you may wonder that I thus anticipate criticism; but review-writing is so easy that I may just as well fill up with this as with any other kind of padding.

My publisher insists on so many pages of copy. When he does not get what he wants, the language rich and powerful enough to serve his needs has yet to be invented.

But he struggles on with the help of a dictionary of American expletives.

However, we are coming to the conclusion, and that, I think, will waken the public up! And yet this chapter will be a short one. It will be the review of a struggle against a temptation to commit, not perhaps crime, but an act of the grossest bad taste.

To that temptation I succumbed; we both succumbed.

It is a temptation to which I dare think poor human nature has rarely been subjected.

The temptation to go and see a man, a fellow-creature, tried for a crime which one's wife committed, and to which one is an accessory after the fact.

Oh, that morning!

How well I remember it.

211

Breakfast was just over, the table with its relics of fragrant bloaters and *terrine* of *pâté* still stood in the *patio*.

I was alone. I loafed lazily and at my ease.

Then I lighted a princely *havanna*, blaming myself for profaning the scented air from *el Cuadro de Leicestero*.

You see I have such a sensitive aesthetic conscience.

Then I took from my pocket the *Sporting Times*, and set listlessly to work to skim its lengthy columns.

This was owing to my vow to Philippa, that I would read every journal published in England. As the day went on, I often sat with them up to my shoulders, and littering all the *patio*.

I ran down the topics of the day. This scene is an 'understudy', by the way, of the other scene in which I read of the discovery of Sir Runan's hat. At last I turned my attention to the provincial news column. A name, a familiar name, caught my eye; the name of one who, I had fondly fancied, had long-lain unburied in my cellar at the 'pike. My princely *havanna* fell unheeded on the marble pavement of the *patio*, as with indescribable amazement I read the following 'par'.

'William Evans, the man accused of the murder of Sir Runan Errand, will be tried at the Newnham Assizes on the 20th. The case, which excites considerable interest among the *élite* of Boding and district, will come on the *tapis* the first day of the meeting. The evidence will be of a purely circumstantial kind.'

Every word of that 'par' was a staggerer. I sat as one stunned, dazed, stupid, motionless, with my eye on the sheet.

Was ever man in such a situation before?

Your wife commits a murder.

You become an accessory after the fact.

You take steps to destroy one of the two people who suspect the truth.

And then you find that the man on whom you committed

murder is accused of the murder which you and your wife committed.

The sound of my mother's voice scolding Philippa wakened me from my stupor. They were coming.

I could not face them.

Doubling up the newspaper, I thrust it into my pocket, and sped swiftly out of the *patio*.

Where did I go? I scarcely remember. I think it must have been to one of the public gardens or public-houses, I am not certain which. All sense of locality left me. I found at last some lonely spot, and there I threw myself on the ground, dug my finger-nails into the dry ground, and held on with all the tenacity of despair. In the wild whirl of my brain I feared that I might be thrown off into infinite space. This sensation passed off. At first I thought I had gone mad. Then I felt pretty certain that it must be the other people who had gone mad.

I had killed William Evans.

My wife had killed Runan Errand.

How, then, could Runan Errand have been killed by William Evans?

'Which is absurd,' I found myself saying, in the language of Eukleidês, the grand old Greek.

Human justice! What is justice? See how it can err! Was there ever such a boundless, unlimited blunder in the whole annals of penny fiction? Probably not. I remember nothing like it in all the learned pages of the *London Journal* and the *Family Herald*. Mrs Henry Wood and Miss Braddon never dreamed of aught like this. Philippa *must* be told. It was too good a joke. Would she laugh? Would she be alarmed?

Picture me lying on the ground, with the intelligence fresh in my mind.

I felt confidence, on the whole, in Philippa's sense of humour.

Then rose the temptation.

Trust this man (William Evans, late the Sphynx) to the vaunted array of justice!

Let him have a run for his money.

Nay, more.

Go down and see the fun!

Why hesitate? You cannot possibly be implicated in the deed. You will enjoy a position nearly unique in human history. You will see the man, of whose murder you thought you were guilty, tried for the offence which you know was committed by your wife.

Every sin is not easy. My sense of honour arose against this temptation. I struggled, but I was mastered. I *would* go and see the trial. Home I went and broached the subject to Philippa. The brave girl never blenched. She had no hesitations, no scruples to conquer.

'Oh Basil,' she exclaimed, with sparkling eyes, 'wot larx! When do we start?'

The reader will admit that I did myself no injustice when, at the commencement of this tale, I said I had wallowed in crime.

CHAPTER XII

JUDGE JUGGINS

WE got down to Newnham, where the 'Sizes were held, on the morning of September 20th. There we discovered that we had an hour or two for refreshment, and I may say that both Philippa and I employed that time to the best advantage. While at the hotel I tried to obtain the file of the *Times*. I wanted to look back and see if I could find the account of the magisterial proceedings against the truly unlucky William Evans.

After all, should I call him unlucky? He had escaped the snare I had laid for him, and perhaps (such things have been) even a Newnham jury might find him not guilty.

But the file of the *Times* was not forthcoming.

I asked the sleepy-eyed Teutonic waiter for it. He merely answered, with the fatuous patronising grin of the German *kellner*:

'You vant?'

'I want the file of the *Times*!'

'I have the corkscrew of the good landlord; but the file of the *Times* I have it not. Have you your boots, your fish-sauce, your curry-comb?' he went on. Then, lapsing into irrelevant local gossip, 'the granddaughter of the blacksmith has the landing-net of the bad tailor.'

'I want my bill, my note, my *addition*, my *consommation*,' I answered angrily.

'Very good bed, very good post-horse,' he replied at random, and I left the County Hotel without being able to find out why suspicion had fallen on William Evans.

We hailed one of the cabs which stood outside the hotel

door, when a heavy hand was laid on my shoulder, and a voice, strange but not unfamiliar, exclaimed, 'Dr South, as I am a baronet—'

I turned round suddenly and found myself face to face with

SIR RUNAN ERRAND!

My brain once more began to reel. Here were the real victim and the true perpetrators of a murder come to view the trial of the man who was charged with having committed it!

Though I was trembling like an aspen leaf, I remembered that we lived in an age of 'telepathy' and psychical research.

Sir Runan was doubtless what Messrs. Myers and Gurney call a *visible apparition* as distinguished from the common *invisible apparition*.

If a real judge confesses, like Sir E. Hornby, to having seen a ghost, why should not a mere accessory after the fact?

Regaining my presence of mind, I asked, 'What brings you here?'

'Oh, to see the fun,' he replied. 'Fellow being tried for killing me. The morbid interest excited round here is very great. Doubt you're getting front seats.'

'Can't you manage it for me?' I asked imploringly.

'Daresay I can. Here, take my card, and just mention my name, and they'll let you in. Case for the prosecution, by the way, *most* feeble.'

Here the appearance, handing me a card, nodded, and vanished in the crowd.

I returned to Philippa, where I had left her in the four-wheeler. We drove off, and found ourselves before a double-swinging (aye, ominous as it seemed, *swinging*) plain oak door, over which in old English letters was written—

OLD ENGLISH CRIMINAL COURT

I need not describe the aspect of the court. Probably most of my readers have at some time in their lives found themselves in such a place.

True to the minute, the red-robed Judge appears. It is Sir Joshua Juggins, well known for his severity as 'Gibbeting Juggins'.

Ah, there is little hope for William Evans.

I have learned from a neighbour in court the evidence against Evans is purely circumstantial.

He has been found in possession of a peculiar key, believed to have belonged to Sir Runan.

Well may they call the case for the prosecution weak.

William must have found that fatal key which Philippa took from the slain man.

On that accident the whole presumption of his guilt is founded.

The Grand Jury (country gentlemen—idiots all!) find a 'True Bill'.

The clerk reads the indictment that 'he, William Evans, did feloniously, wilfully, and of malice aforethought, kill and murder Sir Runan Errand, Baronet.'

As the reading goes on Philippa is strangely moved.

'Basil,' she whispered, 'don't you see the splendid, unequalled chance for an advertisement! I'll get up and make a speech, and say *I* did it. Of course they can't prove it, but it will set every one talking, and bring hundreds of pounds into the house every night.'

I now observed that Philippa had half slipped off her mantle and bonnet. Beneath these coverings she was dressed in wig and gown, like Mrs Weldon in the photographs.

'For goodness' sake, Philippa, *don't*!' I whispered.

The clerk turned to William Evans, the prisoner at the bar. 'Are you guilty, or not guilty?'

In the silence a cigarette-ash might have been heard to drop, if anyone had been smoking.

The long silence was broken, but not by the prisoner.

By Philippa!

Rising to all her stately height, with her flowing robes around her, she stood at bay. Then her clear deep voice rang out:

'My lord, I was the party that did it!'

'Order in the court! Order in the court!' cried the ushers.

'I commit you! I commit you!' thundered Lord Justice Juggins. 'Take her away. Five years and hard labour.'

Struggling violently, Philippa was dragged away by the minions of the law.

I notice one visitor turn round, and gaze at the commotion.

It is Mrs Thompson, the Bearded Woman.

Silence has scarcely been restored, when it is again broken.

A manly form rises. A deep voice exclaims:

'My lord, the prisoner is innocent. *I* am the person whom he is said to have murdered.'

The form, the voice—it is Sir Runan Errand!

Again I hear the sharp accents of Mr Justice Juggins.

'Is this court a bear-garden or the House of Commons? Take that man out. Give him five years and two dozen lashes.'

Scarcely had the court resumed its wonted aspect of business, scarcely had the prisoner again been asked to plead, when a shrill voice shattered the stillness.

'My lord, the key found in the prisoner's possession is my cellar-key.'

This time the bold interrupter was Mrs Thompson, the Bearded Woman.

'Five years as usual, and hard labour,' said Sir Joshua Juggins, wearily.

He was tiring of his task.

'Please, my lord, it warn't none of me,' came a hoarse whisper from the prisoner at the bar.

'Who asked *you* to speak? Is that the way to plead?' snapped the judge. 'Give him five years also, for contempt of court.'

William Evans was carried out in hysterics.

The plot, the mystery had thickened.

I now felt that there was only one way of fathoming the secret of the crime. I also must get myself committed! Then I would be able to rejoin the other actors in this strange drama, and learn their motives, and the real facts of the case.

In a moment my resolution was taken.

Springing to my feet, I exclaimed in clarion tones:

'My lord, I am an accessory after the fact.'

Sir Joshua Juggins gave a cry of despair. Then mastering himself, he whispered:

'Take that idiot away, and give him penal servitude for life.'

As I left the court in chains, I heard the next case being called.

CHAPTER XIII

CLEARED UP
(FROM THE 'GREEN PARK GAZETTE')

THE legitimate public interest in the Newnham Mystery suggested to us the propriety of sending one of our young men down to interview all parties. After having visited the Maori King, Mrs Weldon, several Eminent Advertisers, and the crew of the *Mignonette*, he felt that his present task was a light one. He had to see the murderer, William Evans; the murderess, Mrs South, or Lady Errand; the accessory after the fact, Dr South; the victim, Sir Runan Errand; and Mrs Thompson, the owner of the key on which the case for the prosecution hinged.

His adventures in the various Asylums where those unhappy persons are unconfined have little public interest. We print the Confessions just as our young man took them down in shorthand from the lips of the sufferers.

THE CONFESSION OF SIR RUNAN ERRAND
'I need not tell you that I never was even the husband of the woman Philippa at all. She stood in no relation to me, except as one of the persons in the *troupe* which I was foolish enough to manage. Instead of visiting her in January last to settle her pecuniary claims against me, I sent my valet. It appears that the man wore an old hat of mine, which he lost in the storm. That was not the only article of property belonging to me he carried off. I have since had a penitent letter from him. He is doing well in the United States, and has been elected to the Legislature. I have given up dabbling in the freak show business, and

merely keep a private theatre at such a distance from human abodes that no one can complain of it as a nuisance. Since the disappearance of my valet I have been travelling in my own yacht. I reached England the day before the trial.

'No. I never read the newspapers. Thank goodness I am no bookworm.'

THE CONFESSION OF PHILIPPA SOUTH, CALLING HERSELF LADY ERRAND

'I tell you again, as I told you before, I know nothing about what I did that night. Go back to your employers.'

Nothing more of a nature suited to our columns could be extracted from this lady.

THE CONFESSION OF MRS THOMPSON

'I lost my cellar key the night Philippa left my roof. I now recognise it as the key in the possession of William Evans. How he got it I have no idea whatever.'

THE CONFESSION OF BASIL SOUTH, M.D.

'I begin to understand it all at last. The key which I took from Philippa on the night of the storm and supposed murder had not been taken by her from Sir Runan.

'She had brought it with her from the house of Mrs Thompson, with whom she had been residing.

'When I threw away a key, which I believed to be the one I had taken from Philippa, I made a mistake.

'I threw away a key of my own. When I thought I was giving William Evans the key of my cellar (with fatal intentions and designs, hoping that he would never survive the contents of that cellar), I really gave him the key I had taken from Philippa.

'Consequently the key would not fit the cellar lock.

'Consequently William Evans never tasted the fatal fluid, and so escaped his doom.

'I have nothing to add to this confession, except that I am deeply penitent, and will never again offer a thoughtless public a Christmas Annual so absurd, morbid, and incoherent as *Much Darker Days*.'

This last statement made it unnecessary to interview William Evans.

All the other persons in this dismal affair are detained during her Majesty's displeasure.

It is sincerely hoped that, after a year of seclusion, they will return to those places in society which they are so well calculated to adorn, and that their future career may be less chequered by bigamy, murder, original kinds of lunacy, and other real or fancied misfortunes.

THE END

THE DETECTIVE STORY CLUB

FOR DETECTIVE
CONNOISSEURS

recommends

THE BLACKMAILERS

By THE MASTER OF THE FRENCH CRIME STORY—EMILE GABORIAU

EMILE GABORIAU is France's greatest detective writer. *The Blackmailers* is one of his most thrilling novels, and is full of exciting surprises. The story opens with a sensational bank robbery in Paris, suspicion falling immediately upon Prosper Bertomy, the young cashier whose extravagant living has been the subject of talk among his friends. Further investigation, however, reveals a network of blackmail and villainy which seems as if it would inevitably close round Prosper and the beautiful Madeleine, who is deeply in love with him. Can he prove his innocence in the face of such damning evidence?

THE REAL THING *from* SCOTLAND YARD!

THE CRIME CLUB

By FRANK FRÖEST, Ex-Supt. C.I.D., Scotland Yard, and George Dilnot

YOU will seek in vain in any book of reference for the name of The Crime Club. Its watchword is secrecy. Its members wear the mask of mystery, but they form the most powerful organisation against master criminals ever known. The Crime Club is an international club composed of men who spend their lives studying crime and criminals. In its headquarters are to be found experts from Scotland Yard, many foreign detectives and secret service agents. This book tells of their greatest victories over crime, and is written in association with George Dilnot by a former member of the Criminal Investigation Department of Scotland Yard.

LOOK FOR THE MAN WITH THE GUN

THE DETECTIVE STORY CLUB

FOR DETECTIVE CONNOISSEURS

recommends

"The Man with the Gun."

MR. BALDWIN'S FAVOURITE

THE LEAVENWORTH CASE
By ANNA K. GREEN

THIS exciting detective story, published towards the end of last century, enjoyed an enormous success both in England and America. It seems to have been forgotten for nearly fifty years until Mr. Baldwin, speaking at a dinner of the American Society in London, remarked : " An American woman, a successor of Poe, Anna K. Green, gave us *The Leavenworth Case,* which I still think one of the best detective stories ever written." It is a remarkably clever story, a masterpiece of its kind, and in addition to an exciting murder mystery and the subsequent tracking down of the criminal, the writing and characterisation are excellent. *The Leavenworth Case* will not only grip the attention of the reader from beginning to end but will also be read again and again with increasing pleasure.

CALLED BACK
By HUGH CONWAY

BY the purest of accidents a man who is blind accidentally comes on the scene of a murder. He cannot see what is happening, but he can hear. He is seen by the assassin who, on discovering him to be blind, allows him to go without harming him. Soon afterwards he recovers his sight and falls in love with a mysterious woman who is in some way involved in the crime. . . . The mystery deepens, and only after a series of memorable thrills is the tangled skein unravelled.

LOOK FOR THE MAN WITH THE GUN